By KC BURN

TORONTO TALES
Cop Out
Cover Up
Cast Off

Published by DREAMSPINNER PRESS
http://www.dreamspinnerpress.com

CAST OFF

KC Burn

Dreamspinner Press

Published by
Dreamspinner Press
5032 Capital Circle SW
Ste 2, PMB# 279
Tallahassee, FL 32305-7886
USA
http://www.dreamspinnerpress.com/

Cover Art by Reese Dante
http://www.reesedante.com

ISBN: 978-1-62798-129-3
Digital ISBN: 978-1-62798-130-9

Printed in the United States of America
First Edition
September 2013

Acknowledgments

As usual, I have to thank my crew of supporters: Alex, Dottie, and Chudney. I wouldn't be here without you. I'd also like to thank the Mantastic Book Club for lending a sympathetic ear and listening to me whine—ladies, you are awesome! And Dolorianne, thanks for the extra brainstorming.

CHAPTER
One

FROWNING, Rick Haviland smoothed a hand over his abs. Sure, the pink T-shirt was as tight as his clubbing clothes, but it was faded, ratty as anything, and practically falling apart. Then again, he was only going over to his friend Davy's house to help him and Davy's new boyfriend, Kurt, paint their house. Sure as shit, he didn't want to get any of his normal clothes covered in paint, but he also wanted to look good.

Partly because the perennial club boy was what his friends expected, and partly—perhaps stupidly—because of Kurt.

Kurt was a gorgeous cop, who unfortunately belonged—lips, cock, and asshole—to Davy. Despite some rather aggressive flirting before Kurt and Davy got together, Rick wouldn't have actually slept with the sexy detective, no matter how often he appeared in his fantasies. The second he'd laid eyes on Kurt, he'd labeled Kurt as a keeper. Rick didn't have sex with keepers. Keepers couldn't be trusted, nor could a keeper trust him. He'd seen first-hand how badly relationships could fuck people up, and he was already fucked up enough without adding heartbreak or worse.

That didn't mean he wouldn't like an appreciative look or two from Kurt. Maybe a quick grope. Surely Davy wouldn't begrudge him that. Kurt had been recently shot in the line of duty and the whole wounded hero thing worked for him. While Kurt had been in the hospital, though, Rick had been too scared for his friend to even flirt. He didn't quite know how Davy could stand tying his life to a guy with such a dangerous job. Relationships were plenty hazardous all on their own.

The doorbell rang, shaking him out of the contemplation of his outfit. He ran downstairs, even though he was probably just going to get suckered into some theological argument with those cute boys the Mormons insisted on sending out to "spread the word." Rick should never answer the damn door for them, but he relished engaging with young men who didn't quite have the wits to debate properly, and he never seemed to have the strength to shut the door until both sides were thoroughly frustrated. Still, with a shirt so tight his nipples would probably rip the fabric if they hardened up, maybe he'd succeed in enticing one of them into his lair.

Rick swung the door open, hip thrust to the side, the better to display his groin.

"Rick," Oscar breathed, gaze dropping exactly where he'd intended, even if Oscar hadn't been the intended target.

"Oscar. This is a surprise." Rick blinked. They'd had sex last night at Oscar's and Rick had left shortly after midnight. Showing up on his doorstep less than twelve hours later was unusual, to say the least. Then again, as a medical resident, his hours were often weird.

Oscar stepped right into Rick's personal space, then proceeded to get a whole lot more personal with his ass, taking a firm grip on each cheek.

"Didn't I wear you out last night?" Rick asked.

The hard cock pressing into his stomach and the lips on his neck were answer enough, and the answer was a clear and definitive no.

Oscar undulated against him, and Rick's breath came a little short.

"You should have stayed last night." The warm breath from Oscar's whisper made Rick shiver, but the words sent a chill down his spine. He didn't do overnights. He didn't let any of his fuck buddies stay at his place either, no matter how fucked out they were.

Still, with Oscar's talented lips and tongue making hash of his determination not to arrive at the painting party late, he decided to ignore the words. Oscar knew the score. Rick had been very careful to explain that their only relationship would be sexual.

Oscar's hand wormed its way into the front of Rick's jeans, cupping his burgeoning erection, fingers wriggling below his balls.

Clutching Oscar's firm butt, Rick consigned his good intentions to the heated flames of his libido. He was definitely going to be late to Davy and Kurt's painting party. For the best reason: getting laid by a guy who knew what he was doing.

"Or I could have come here last night. Stayed over." Oscar ended his sentence with a firm bite on Rick's earlobe.

Rick froze. Surely this was Oscar's lame attempt at erotic talk and not his only fuck buddy turning into a keeper before his eyes.

Oscar continued to stroke him, keeping his cock interested, which Rick went along with, even though he wasn't sure this was a good idea.

"Uh, Oscar…." Rick pushed halfheartedly at Oscar's shoulder.

Pulling his head back, Oscar looked deeply into Rick's eyes. "I think we should move in together."

The completely unwelcome sentiment gave Rick the strength to push away.

Goddammit! Rick normally had a number of regular fuck buddies, all carefully selected to be good in the sack, careful with their sexual health and have zero interest in a relationship. Oscar was the only one he had in rotation right now after he'd terminated Ivan's fuck buddy status. Ivan, at least, had recognized that Rick wasn't able to provide any emotional connection, but unlike most of Rick's regulars, they'd remained friends. Oscar wasn't going there. Especially not with this full frontal assault.

"Oscar, we're not moving in together. I don't do relationships, remember?"

He had rules to keep this from happening. Most times, he lost guys because they eventually decided they wanted to settle down, but they rarely asked to do so with him. He never met their families and always made sure he had transportation if they met somewhere.

The man reached for him, arms like tentacles as Rick danced to evade them.

"C'mon, Rick. I know you're not seeing anyone else right now. We're already practically in a relationship."

Rick's eyebrows rose into his hairline. He might not know much about relationships, but just because neither of them was seeing anyone else didn't automatically make this a relationship. But that was exactly why he was so pissed. The older he got, the harder it was to find appropriate guys to put into rotation and now he was going to be left in the unfortunate position of… auditioning. He should probably be more enthused, but mostly he was resenting Oscar something fierce for putting him in this position, by turning into not only a keeper but one who wanted to keep Rick.

"Are you crazy? It takes more than a few fucks and a lack of competition to make a relationship. You need to go."

Oscar gave him a wounded look that was presumably meant to be cute, but Rick was done.

"Rick, baby. We could be so good together. And the fucks were epic."

How exactly had a guy who sounded like a stoned surfer managed to make it through medical school, anyway?

"No. Out. Don't call me. No strings, no relationships. You need to go." Rick squared his shoulders and crossed his arms, hoping to look as closed off as possible.

Oscar's eyes widened, and his cheeks reddened. "But I think I love you."

Rick rolled his eyes. "Ridiculous. If you want a boyfriend, go out and get one. You're a catch, you won't be single long, but I'm not that guy."

In love with him? Please. He shoved Oscar out of the doorway and slammed the door shut, locking the deadbolts. Leaning against it, he waited for the inevitable pounding, signifying Oscar hadn't given up. He only had to wait seconds, but it was still enough of a shock to start his own heart pounding.

Oscar called his name, cajoled, begged. Rick's phone rang and rang. He groaned. If Oscar made him change his phone number, he was going to be plenty pissed. First thing he was doing was blocking Oscar's number.

Ten minutes passed like this, and Rick had just started to wonder if he should call the police when Oscar's car finally squealed out of his driveway. Rick was going to need to calm down a bit before he drove over to Davy and Kurt's place. He slid to the floor, waiting for his pulse to return to normal.

He'd have to rush if he didn't want to be too late. Lateness would require explanations. If he'd been late because he was getting laid, that would have been one thing, but he didn't want to explain the Oscar fiasco to his friends. They probably would have told him to give Oscar a chance, but there was no way that was happening.

THE small, neatly kept bungalow wasn't haunted. It wasn't the haven of serial killers or infested with cockroaches. Yet Ian O'Donnell's belly churned and sweat slicked his palms at the thought of ringing the bell. The only scary thing inside was his baby brother, Kurt, who'd fallen in love with a man named Davy, and shocked the family by announcing he was gay at his own fucking birthday party.

No one was upset or angry or hateful. No one except Ian. He'd fled the party, avoiding Kurt and the rest of the family for months. It wasn't the first time Ian had thought the baby of the family had it easier than the rest of them, but it was the first time he'd let those insidious feelings interfere in his relationship with his brother. Then his stupid brother got himself shot in the line of duty, and Ian's bruised feelings ceased to matter. All that mattered was fixing things with Kurt, if only he knew how.

Flicking a glance to the cars in the driveway as he paced on the sidewalk, he wasn't sure if it would be easier or harder to confess to Kurt when other people were around. As tempting as it was to go home and wait for another time, he'd driven by dozens of times since Kurt had been released from the hospital, and this was the first time he'd been able to talk himself out of the car.

Kurt had to forgive him, even though Ian had been a selfish, self-absorbed idiot. If Ian had irreparably damaged his relationship with his brother, it would leave a hole in his life that could never be filled, and he'd have only himself to blame.

With a deep breath, he strode up the driveway and rang the doorbell.

A slender disheveled man led him into the house, led him to Kurt.

There were other men in the room, and the scent of fresh paint was heavy in the air, but it all barely registered.

"What are you doing here?" His baby brother stood, and was immediately flanked by a dark-haired man and a blond. One of them must be Davy.

Ian didn't know how to answer the almost angry question. He wanted to hug Kurt, but he didn't know if the gesture would be welcome or even painful. Ian had gone to the hospital, but only entered the room when Kurt was sleeping, unable to face his brother and his own shame. The faint creases beside Kurt's mouth spoke of hurts still endured, and it killed Ian to see his brother in pain.

Kurt looked… better than he had in the hospital, but considering Kurt had long been taller and more muscular than Ian, the weight he'd lost after being injured had left him appearing almost frail. Ian wanted to turn around and flee, but he couldn't.

"Oh my God, Kurt! He's one of your brothers?" The incredulous tone briefly directed Ian's attention to the small blond man standing next to his brother. Ian sucked in a breath. The guy was fucking adorable. A threadbare pale-pink T-shirt stretched across a well-formed chest and abs. The guy wasn't muscular by any stretch, but he looked strong and compact, like a ballet dancer. The neck of the shirt had a small hole that Ian wanted to wiggle a finger into and yank, ripping the shirt away and baring golden skin. The somewhat looser, paint-splattered jeans might prove more of problem, but there was a rip at the top of one thigh that suggested all kinds of things to Ian.

"Please tell me he's gay too." There was no mistaking the interest in both voice and eyes, and despite the task that had brought Ian here, he couldn't stop himself from holding the blond's gaze. If they were in a club, it would be a matter of minutes before they found themselves in the bathroom, back room, or alley. Unless, of course, this was Davy, the man his brother had moved in with. In which case, he hoped the guy wasn't the type to follow through on the promise in his eyes.

"He's straight," Kurt said with almost no inflection in his voice.

Here it was. Already. The moment of truth. Ian wanted to puke.

But the truth was all he had. The only thing that could mend the breach. The truth he'd never told anyone who knew his full name, much less which superhero he liked to dress up as when he was a kid.

"I'm not."

The blond squealed in a vamped-up expression of enthusiasm that boded well for a good fuck, but his dick had to take a backseat to fixing things with his brother. The brother who stared at him as though he thought Ian was playing a particularly cruel joke. Kurt's lips thinned, his stern cop face in stark evidence, and he grabbed Ian by the arm, steering him to the basement entrance. Kurt released his tight grip and gestured for Ian to precede him down the stairs.

Ian descended into darkness, the creaky stairs almost a soundtrack of him going to his doom.

"Hey, you aren't bringing me down here to kill me or anything, are you?"

Kurt snorted. "I should, you idiot."

"Dirt floors to bury my body in?" Ian couldn't stop from pushing.

"Not fucking hardly. This is our home gym."

His brother clicked on the lights, illuminating a room completely filled with gym equipment. For a moment, the home gym distracted him. Going to the gym wasn't his favorite activity—Kurt was the workout freak in the family—but he could easily see working out on the roomful of high-end equipment he saw.

"Oh my God, Kurt. This is incredible." Was Davy also a workout freak, or was this room all Kurt's?

"Quit stalling. What the fuck is going on?"

God, hadn't he said enough already? Did he have to spell it out and draw diagrams?

"Seriously, Ian, what did you mean up there?" Kurt looked mad enough to hit him. Even the recent bullet wound probably wouldn't prevent Kurt from damaging Ian rather badly if he chose to.

Diagrams and spelling, it was. Ian began to pace, trying to choose the best starting point.

"I… I'm gay too."

Kurt frowned. "What about all those girls? Those strippers?"

His family all thought he was a complete slut. Dogging after anything with a skirt—at least in their presence. On his own, though, he was just as much of a slut, but if they didn't have a dick, he never gave them a second glance.

"I could ask you the same thing. You had girlfriends." But Kurt had had the courage to do what Ian never had, and Ian hadn't been able to stop himself from hating his brother, just a little bit, for that.

"So you're just figuring this out?" The faint hint of skepticism in Kurt's tone told Ian he hadn't fixed things, not yet. Kurt still thought he might be the butt of a joke, like when they were kids. They had five other siblings but only the three youngest—he, Kurt, and Dylan—ever seemed to take endless fascination in tormenting each other. This, though, was not the topic to choose for that sort of joke. Ian knew better than most and he would never do that to Kurt, so it pained him that Kurt didn't trust him not to.

"No, I had it figured out for a while. Years. The women were just a cover."

He'd been hiding his sexuality almost twenty years now, afraid to let anyone, even those closest to him, know that deep dark secret. When Kurt had come out to their family—with no repercussions at all—it had broken

Ian somewhere inside. Aside from a myriad of negative emotions that had welled up as a result of keeping his orientation a completely unnecessary secret, he'd resented the fuck out of Kurt. He'd let his jealousy and anger override all good sense, and now all he was left with was shame and guilt.

"Years? Are you fucking serious? What the hell?"

"I was afraid. I thought I'd lose everyone. So I hid it. When you told me, all… smug… and confident, I thought you'd figured it out and were mocking me. Then, when I realized you were telling the truth, and everyone accepted it without any problems, I was mad at you." Ian's gaze dropped to his feet, unable to face the censure that had to be in Kurt's eyes. His baby brother had been the brave one, paving the way for him, and he'd still been a fucking coward.

"Come here." Kurt dragged him into a hug. Ian didn't deserve Kurt's forgiveness, but he'd take it. He clung to Kurt's strong shoulders, eyes burning. He swallowed a sob and buried his face in Kurt's shirt. Staying away from his family had been lonely, but not talking to Kurt and Dylan regularly had been almost unbearable.

His brother coaxed him down onto a vinyl-covered bench, and they sat in silence for a few moments while Ian composed himself.

"Are you going to tell everyone?"

"Yeah. It was killing me, pretending. I can't believe you had the guts to just say it at your own birthday party." As soon as he'd retrieved his balls from wherever they'd disappeared, Ian had decided it was time to come clean. Kurt was only the first stop. Their mom had a family dinner every Sunday. Not all of the siblings and their kids showed up every week, but Ian didn't care who was there. His parents were next on his list. After that, the other five siblings should be a breeze.

"Well, I had some incentive. Did you see my boyfriend?" Kurt grinned.

Ian smiled in response and wiped at his wet eyes. "The cute little blond in the pink shirt?" The blond had been the hottest guy in a roomful of hot guys, so it only made sense that Kurt had already laid claim to him.

"You got a boyfriend of your own?"

"No, just a lot of one-night stands." A lot. He didn't know a damn thing about boyfriends.

"Well, come on upstairs. Let me introduce you to Rick."

"Rick?" The blond didn't much look like a Rick, but it would be an easy name for him to call out while fucking.

"The cute blond in the pink shirt. My Davy is the tall dark-haired one."

"Let's go. I'm going to stay and help, if that's okay."

RICK slapped a roller, soaked with paint, against the wall, causing a little back spray. God, he was such an idiot. He stroked the roller up and down until he'd used up the paint on the roller, then set it back in the tray before trying to wipe at the lemon-yellow spatters on his arms. He only succeeded in streaking the yellow along his forearms.

He wasn't sure why he'd been so damned flippant about Ian's coming-out statement. He, better than anyone, knew how hard it could be. Of course, the guy had to have some idea about how his revelation would be received, given that the revelation was to an already gay brother who had moved in with his boyfriend. Davy had told him that Kurt and his brother had been estranged for a couple of months, thinking it had something to do with Kurt coming out, but Kurt was a very private person and Rick hadn't heard anything more. For all he knew, the estrangement had been over something entirely different. Family stuff wasn't any of Rick's business, although he might make an exception in Ian's case.

Assuming Ian didn't hate him for acting like a shallow idiot. Rick had played up the oversexed club boy as soon as he'd seen Ian, and reacted before he'd had a chance to realize what import Ian's words held for anyone besides his own cock.

Rick had always had a little crush on Kurt, with that stern cop exterior and those puffed-up muscles. But Ian was like a refined, polished, better-looking version of Kurt, with dark hair instead of auburn and pale-blue eyes instead of dark blue, and in great shape.

"Hey, Rick." Kurt's deep voice had him spinning around, and like his thoughts had conjured him up, there was Ian.

"Uh, hey." No, he wasn't digging himself out of his hole with that stellar oration.

"Rick, this is my brother, Ian. Ian, this is my friend, Rick."

Ian's red-rimmed eyes and the shy vulnerability in his expression tugged at something deep inside Rick. Even if Ian was a keeper like Kurt,

Rick couldn't bring himself to brush Ian off. Not after his thoughtlessness earlier.

He extended his hand. "Nice to meet you, Ian."

Ian gripped his hand. "Nice to meet you too." The heat was back, the heat he'd sworn he'd seen earlier when Ian had raked his gaze from Rick's head to his toes, and especially one particular bit in between. Ian held his hand for longer than customary and rubbed at the inside of Rick's wrist before he let go. Goose bumps flared along Rick's arm at the telling, yet subtle, touch.

Ian turned to his brother. "I think I'll stay in here, help Rick."

Kurt rolled his eyes and left. Rick's heart picked up its pace at the realization they were alone.

"So, I'm pretty sure the paint's supposed to go on the wall." Ian grinned, and the shyness disappeared in a flash as he reached out and swiped a finger along Rick's cheek, down his neck, and to his collarbone.

Blood rose under his skin, heating him and plumping his cock. The combination of embarrassment and sudden, fierce arousal was disorienting but not entirely unpleasant.

"Maybe you need to show me how it's done." Rick's voice had dropped, and the dilation of Ian's pupils, narrowing the ring of gorgeous blue iris, told him that neither of them was too interested in painting. Good thing that Rick's earlier irritation had caused him to work fast and as a result the kitchen was nearly done.

Ian wiggled a finger into a hole in Rick's shirt, and the unexpected contact with the skin on his chest pushed his cock into full, throbbing arousal.

"Maybe I do. Because I think you've ruined this shirt." Ian's words were accompanied by a tearing sound as he dragged his finger down. He didn't go far, and the rip wasn't that much bigger than it had been before, but it was almost like Rick was naked. A glance at Ian's groin confirmed that they were well on their way to some mutual pleasure. Rick wanted to flick open Ian's jeans and suck him down, right here in Davy's kitchen. Only problem was, if Davy didn't kill them for having sex here, Kurt would probably shoot off some of his very important bits. For a gorgeous hunk of a gay cop, Kurt was alarmingly prudish.

Once they were alone, would Ian rip his shirt right off? It wasn't as easy as it looked in porn, but Rick shivered at the thought of having it done.

Ian stepped closer and palmed his cock. Rick groaned and bucked his hips into the warm, welcome pressure.

"Want to get out of here?" Rick copied Ian's grip and was rewarded by a moan.

"Yes, but I did say I'd help." Ian frowned and stepped back, separating them.

No, that would never do. Ian's cock had felt like a work of art and Rick was ready to worship.

"There's only one wall left here in the kitchen. And there are at least four other guys besides Davy working in the rest of the house."

Ian's lips curled up in a feral grin that left Rick breathless. "Then find me a roller and let's get this wall finished."

IN RECORD time, the two of them finished painting the kitchen and cleaned the rollers, despite the number of gropes and grabs that took place between them. Rick was ready to blow, and he suspected as soon as he and Ian were alone, the first orgasm would be fucking quick. Since he intended to have more than one with this man tonight, the speed of the first one didn't matter.

"Looks great." Ian wasn't looking at the walls, and Rick couldn't help but preen, just a little, under the admiring regard.

"Ready to get out of here?"

"Yes." Ian's single word was heartfelt and emphatic. Rick wasn't sure he'd ever been this horny or desperate for a man. Sure, Oscar had revved him up a bit earlier, but he'd never wanted Oscar with this intensity. This lust was all for Ian and Rick wanted to spend hours slaking it.

"Where to?" Rick wasn't about to offer his own place; Ian better not have a roommate.

"My place."

Good.

They slipped out the back door and rounded the house without running into any of the others. Rick stared at his car in dismay. Somehow, he'd gotten boxed in, which defeated the whole purpose of them slipping out without saying good-bye. Neither of them wanted to deal with whatever ribbing would be coming their way because neither his nor Ian's erections had deflated. Any one of his friends would know where they were going.

"You want to text me the address? I'll follow as soon as I get my car out."

Ian pressed him up against the side of… someone's car. Rick was too focused on Ian to pay attention to color, make, or model. "Just come with me. I'll drive you back later."

Then Ian wiggled his hips, and Rick's cock jerked. He never did this. Never left himself without transportation, but this was Kurt's brother. He gazed into Ian's mesmerizing blue eyes, inexplicably tempted to kiss the man. Surely he could make an exception. For the transportation. Kissing was still off the menu. Kissing involved an intimacy that led men to become keepers.

"Okay, fine. Let's go." Strangely, he didn't have a moment of regret for breaking his transportation rule, but they needed to get out of here before he broke any other rules.

USING a firm grip on Rick's ass, Ian guided—or practically shoved—Rick into his condo. He wanted Rick naked and in his bed immediately.

"Nice place you have here." Rick's voice was breathless and he was totally lying because Ian hadn't even turned on the lights.

"Thanks." Ian bit down on the back of Rick's neck and was rewarded by a moan.

"Show me your bedroom."

Yeah, like that was in question. He had a couch that might be really good for fucking over, but while he'd been in the closet, he'd never felt comfortable bringing a guy over, certain that one of his many siblings or even a coworker would find out. The thought of having a naked Rick in his bed, on his sheets, had him so hard he might be able to bust through his fly from the sheer blood pressure alone.

He wrapped both arms around Rick from behind, one hand atop the denim-covered bulge of Rick's erection and the other worming underneath Rick's T-shirt to find the warm, fuzzy skin of Rick's belly. An animalistic sound of want escaped Rick's lips and Ian's already shaky control wavered. Without letting go of Rick, Ian managed to maneuver them into his bedroom.

Once they were in sight of the bed, Rick wiggled out of his embrace and whipped off his shirt.

"Strip, Ian, for God's sake. You've been driving me crazy for hours."

"Me too."

It hadn't been hours, but their painting foreplay had lasted longer than any foreplay Ian was used to. Ian removed his own shirt, certain he'd heard a seam rip from his eagerness, but grabbed Rick by the waistband before he'd done more than pop the top button on his jeans. Ian got both hands in there to get Rick's pants off. Rick's hands at his fly made his own hands unsteady but seconds later, he'd shoved Rick's jeans down to his knees, freeing a healthy-sized cock.

Ian wrapped his fingers around it and stroked. He slid his hand lower and cupped a pair of hairless balls. He wanted his mouth and hands everywhere, but he also wanted to spread Rick's legs and sink deep in his body. He wanted to make Rick howl with pleasure. Shake the walls and burn up the sheets with the intensity of their fucking.

The awkwardness of Rick trying to shimmy out of jeans and shoes while getting Ian's pants down was probably the only thing that kept Ian from blowing his wad at the first touch of Rick's strong fingers against the bare skin of his cock.

"C'mon, c'mon." Rick didn't even bother shoving Ian's jeans and boxers past his ass before grabbing his dick with both hands.

The strangled whimper he let out might have been embarrassing, but all that mattered was getting into Rick and both of them speeding to the finish line. Next time they could be slower, give Ian more time to explore.

"On the bed." If it weren't for the firm grip Rick had on his cock, Ian would have just shoved the guy back like a caveman.

Rick complied without a single protest. He scooted back into the middle of the bed while Ian grabbed lube and condoms out of his dresser. He tossed them at Rick, who snatched up the lube.

"Glove up, sweetie. I'll do the rest."

Ian was confused until Rick coated two fingers with slick and shoved them both up his own ass. Frantic, he squeezed the base of his cock to keep from spurting. Rick writhed and moaned as he stretched himself, and Ian rolled on a condom with shaking hands, afraid he was going to miss the party if he didn't get in there quick.

The touch of his hands on Rick's thighs was like a signal. Rick pulled his fingers out and spread his legs wider in invitation, pulling his knees back toward his chest.

Ian didn't waste any time pressing his cock against Rick's pucker, which gave up against his intrusion without a fight. He slid balls deep and shuddered. Rick was so damn tight and hot.

"Move, damn it, move." Rick's demand was accompanied by a hip thrust, and Ian didn't have it in him to hold back.

Fast and hard, he slammed into Rick, the slap of skin on skin an erotic soundtrack that spurred him on.

"Fuck, fuck, fuck," Rick whimpered in a low voice. He grabbed his dick and stroked twice. The sight of Rick's cum and the clench of Rick's ass sent Ian rocketing into his own orgasm. His muscles locked, his hips jerked, and flashes of color sparked in his vision while he emptied his balls into the condom.

Unable to do anything else, he slumped over Rick, and the tiny part of his brain still capable of thought reveled in the sensation of another man's cum on his stomach. Having body-length skin-on-skin contact was almost enough to get him wired up again. So much naked male flesh and no worries about rushing or hiding. He couldn't wait to do it all over again.

Rick's hands stroked up and down his back, and over the thundering of Ian's heart, Rick's panting breaths spoke of an orgasm that rivaled Ian's.

After a few moments, Ian's muscles finally obeyed some of his brain's commands. He slid, regretfully, out of Rick's body, flicked the condom toward the garbage can, and grabbed his shirt to wipe away the stickiness from them both.

Eyelids drooping, he spooned Rick up against his chest like he'd been doing it all his life, and pressed his lips to Rick's nape. Between his post-orgasm lassitude and an emotionally stressful day, his exhaustion overwhelmed him. He only had time to regret that he couldn't remain awake for a second round before sleep won out.

CHAPTER
Two

RICK clutched his sneakers to his chest and leaned back against the closed door. It was too early for any of Ian's neighbors to be out and about. He didn't do this. He didn't go home with random guys. But somehow, Ian had gotten under his skin. Enough so that when he'd woken up with the man—also something he never did—he thought about waking Ian up for another round. As much of a slut as his friends thought he was, he rarely did the full deed with someone he'd just met. A hand job or blow job at a club was… not much of anything and didn't really count.

Even now, he sort of regretted missing out on morning sex. He'd heard good things about it, but this was the closest he'd ever come to staying the night with anyone. There was something about Ian that tugged at him.

Problem was, he didn't know how to label Ian. Could he add Ian to his fuck-buddy rotation, or was Ian too much like Kurt?

With one last look at Ian's door, Rick slipped on his sneakers and headed for the elevator.

The sky outside was hazy with the newly broken dawn, the humidity already starting to make his clothing cling. Rick cursed his cock. There was no other good explanation for why he'd come to Ian's apartment in Ian's car. Ian's pretty blue peepers had convinced his stupid cock to break one of his damned rules.

For that alone, Ian was dangerous. Rick walked down the street before stopping at a bus stop with a bench. He pulled his slim phone out of a very tight pocket and called a cab. At least this stop had a bus shelter, so the brightening sun wasn't unbearable. He winced slightly as he made contact with chilled aluminum, an uncomfortable reminder that he'd done the full deed with a man he'd just met. Ian was fucking good at fucking, though.

Last night, he hadn't realized at first that Ian was coming out to his brother. Once he did, Ian's shy vulnerability plucked at Rick's heartstrings, as well as another more prominent organ. It hadn't taken long for Ian's shyness to disappear, and the dichotomy left Rick unsure as to whether he was a keeper. Rick hoped not. Because Ian would make a spectacular fuck buddy.

Probably too much to hope for that Ian was also in a uniformed career like Kurt. Rick did love the uniforms, although after the ordeal of Kurt getting shot, Rick didn't know if he'd take another one on, unsure if he could handle one of his men getting hurt on the job. He and Ian hadn't spent a lot of time talking. If he saw Ian again, he'd find out—eventually—what the man did for a living.

The cab pulled up and Rick again cursed his weakness. If he'd only kept to the rules, he'd have had his own car and he'd be home already. He patted his pockets and groaned.

Fuck no.

Rick tapped at the window. "Hold on a minute."

The cabbie obeyed with an indistinct grunt that may or may not have been an actual word. Rick closed his eyes and thought for second. Kurt and Davy hadn't exactly been free with the beer at their painting party last night, and Rick had no alcohol haze over his memories. He'd been able to wedge his phone and wallet in the pocket of his pants, but his keys weren't going to fit. He'd carried them into Davy and Kurt's place and set them on a bookshelf. And never picked them up again when he'd slipped away in Ian's wake.

Fuck.

It was way too early to head over to Davy's and he sure couldn't buzz up to Ian and ask for readmittance. At least he had that broken latch on the basement window at his place. He'd been meaning to get it fixed, but his neighborhood was so safe it hadn't seemed important. Now he was glad he hadn't. The basement window would be a tight squeeze, even for someone as slender as he was, but he could make it, and he wouldn't need to have his walk of shame at an utterly humiliating hour of the day.

"Right, let's go." Rick got into the cab and gave his home address. Thankfully he had his wallet or he'd have ended up at an all-night diner, hanging with a bunch of still-drunk youngsters losing their buzz. He might look like the perennial party boy, but he was looking at the wrong side of thirty-five, had a respectable job and a house. But the party boy was the one his friends were used to, and was the one that got him laid under the conditions he liked. Revealing his "grown up" status might bring more of the keepers sniffing around, and that would never do.

RICK paid the cabbie and got out of the taxi. He was still kicking himself for not having his damn car and for having fallen asleep at Ian's but he couldn't bring himself to regret the evening. Not entirely. Spreading for Ian had been easy, and they'd fit together like nothing he'd experienced. But breaking all those rules? Not wise, not at all. In fact, the warmth that sparked in his belly when he remembered Ian's intense blue eyes and the way he just overwhelmed Rick with lust... those rules weren't only to prevent hookups from becoming keepers. They protected Rick from feeling too much. Feelings led to relationships and a relationship for Rick was utterly impossible.

He glanced up from his sober contemplation of the concrete walkway to his front door and rocked to a stop. Oscar sat slumped there, asleep, with a huge bouquet of mixed white flowers beside him.

Yesterday's weirdness was determined to bleed into today's. Damn. He'd been having a hard enough time reconciling his panic over breaking his rules with the euphoria from some really great—albeit brief—sex. In fact, he could probably blame Oscar for all of it. Rick had been so unsettled prior to going to the painting party, he'd been far too susceptible to Ian's hotness.

Irritation superseded all of his other confusing emotions. Rick stamped up his porch and flicked Oscar on the shoulder. "Wake up. What are you doing here?"

Oscar blinked up at him blearily and smiled. Was that supposed to be cute? Because he really just wanted to crawl into his fucking basement window without the humiliation of an audience and take a shower. Without his keys, he wasn't going to be able to easily escape whatever misguided nonsense had brought Oscar to his doorstep at—well, he didn't know what time it was without checking his phone, but it hadn't even quite been seven when he'd left Ian's place.

Too damned early for visitors of any description.

"Rick, baby."

Rick cringed. "Oh my God, don't call me that. What are you doing here?"

Offering up the bouquet of flowers, which was big enough to double as a duck blind, Oscar smiled, completely ignoring Rick's irritation. Actually, Oscar's pleasant nature had been one of the reasons he'd first brought him into rotation, but right now, it made Oscar seem willfully oblivious or simply stupid. Neither were traits that were endearing him to Rick at the moment.

"I don't know what went wrong last night, but I hate how we left things. I'm sorry."

Manfully, Rick refrained from rolling his eyes. Simply stupid it must be, since Rick had been clear what had gone wrong. But it was a nice gesture.

"Thanks, Oscar." Rick reached out a hand for the flowers, not entirely sure he enjoyed being placated with a bunch of flowers like he was a damned girl, but he couldn't deny the flowers were beautiful.

In an unexpected move, Oscar moved the bouquet to the side and leaned in for a kiss. Rick ducked, but nearly fell backward off his porch steps and irritation bloomed into full-blown anger.

"What the hell, Oscar? We're done. No more nothing. No moving in. No fucking. No phone calls. Over. Understand?"

Oscar's face got a pinched look to it. "I said I was sorry. We don't have to move in together. We can just go back to the way things were. Please."

Just as suddenly as it appeared, Rick's anger fled, leaving only sadness in its wake. "Oscar, I'm sorry. But I can't see you anymore. I told you I don't do relationships, and if you've started to care for me in that way, there's no way we can go back to the way we were before. It's not fair to either of us."

"Please, Rick. Give me another chance. We'll do this however you want."

"No second chances. And I've told you what I want."

Oscar frowned. "Are those the same clothes you had on yesterday? Are you seeing someone else?"

Despite the unwarranted anger that unexpectedly radiated from Oscar, Rick snorted. No one in their right mind would call what he did with Ian last night "seeing." But there was no denying he'd enjoyed himself and even the faint twinge in his backside was enough to make him smile, however conflicted he'd been about breaking his rules.

"That's none of your business." Just thinking about last night's fantastic sex had been enough to soften the edge in his voice, and Oscar's frown morphed into a black scowl. No, thinking about Ian wasn't going to do him any favors. "I think you should go now. Get some sleep."

Huh. He hadn't considered Oscar might have decided on this grand plan while under the influence. For all Rick knew, the guy could still be drunk.

"Did you drive here?" Not that Rick was in a position to offer a lift home. "I could call you a cab."

Oscar snarled and threw the flowers at Rick. "Fuck you."

Without another word, Oscar practically ran to his car, got in, and peeled away.

Rick grimaced. That hadn't gone well, although Oscar seemed to get this message this time. He placed the flowers next to the door, ready to add to his composting, but later. Now, he had a date with his broken basement window and a shower. In that fucking order. If it weren't for the fact he needed to get both his keys and car back, he'd be tempted to turn off his phone and hole up with a book or three for the rest of the weekend. He needed some time to consider if Ian would be a suitable fuck buddy or if Ian unsettled him too much, but he sure as shit didn't need to make a decision right away.

SUNLIGHT streamed against Ian's face, illuminating the insides of his eyelids to translucent red instead of the normal pitch black he preferred at this time of the morning. He twisted away from the heated brilliance and cracked a lid, trying to focus on the alarm clock.

God. He couldn't even see the damned thing due to the nuclear glare pouring in through his windows. How had he possibly forgotten to close his blackout curtains last night? The streetlights outside made it intolerably bright for sleeping and the morning sun was—as he remembered—obnoxious.

Oh, yes. Sex. Awesome sex. He'd been far more intent on getting into that gorgeous, lithe male body than he'd been on shutting his drapes. At least there wasn't an easy way to peer into his bedroom windows, or someone would have gotten a free show. But there was no mistaking that Ian was alone in bed now. He sat up, peering about for the man who should have still been in bed with him. Squinting at the clock, he groaned. There was no good reason to be up at six on a Sunday morning.

Not a sign remained of Ian's one-night stand aside from the crinkled condom half hanging over the edge of the wastebasket like a sloughed-off snakeskin.

Wide awake now, with eyes adjusted to the light, Ian flopped back into his pillows. A faint musky scent hit his nose as he disturbed the bedding, reminding both him and his morning wood of an exceptional night. With athletic activities he would have gladly repeated this morning if only he hadn't woken alone.

He stretched and snuggled back down into the bed. He had nowhere to be until early afternoon. Maybe he could sleep off his disappointment.

Unfortunately, the reminder of the momentous task yet to come at his parents' place later drove away the remnants of sleep. The trepidation was probably unnecessary, but he was drawing unwelcome parallels between the red-shirted dude who accompanied Captain Kirk, or the poor bastard who fought the Minotaur before Theseus tried his hand. The ones who tried and failed and got eaten by monsters for their trouble. No matter how much he reminded himself that his imagination was working overtime, he was getting more and more nervous.

He needed backup, like never before. Ian had always been closest to the brothers that bracketed him in age, Kurt and Dylan. The three of them had been almost inseparable throughout school, and their tight bond hadn't lessened. Except Ian had sold them both short by not trusting them. Dylan deserved to know when their parents found out, and if anyone was going to provide him the moral support he needed, it was his two brothers.

Rolling over, he swiped his phone from the bedside table. He thumbed through his contacts, hoping that maybe Rick had added his phone number, but no such luck. Well, it was a simple matter to rectify that if Ian felt it necessary.

With a sigh, he called Dylan.

"Oh, ho, so your hands aren't broken."

Ian rolled his eyes. "Are you taking guilt trip lessons from Mom?"

"Someone ought to guilt trip you." Dylan's voice was only a little pissed off, and Ian didn't blame him a bit. Even though his brother was all caught up in preparing for his wedding, he'd still made the effort to call Ian, but Ian had either avoided the calls or ditched him as soon as he could. And Ian had almost never taken the initiative to call anyone since Kurt's mind-blowing announcement.

"Look, I'm… sorry. I can explain, but… can you come to dinner at Mom and Dad's tonight?"

"Are you actually going to be there?"

Once again, Ian couldn't blame Dylan for the skepticism in his voice.

"Yes, I promise, Dyl." Ian didn't know what to say to convince Dylan it was important that he show up, without scaring the shit out of his brother or just blurting out his secret. The next time he came out, though, he wanted to do it without just blurting it out. Calm, careful, prepared.

Somehow, though, Dylan could tell. "I'll be there. It'll be good to see you."

"Yeah, you too." Ian's eyes burned and, with his recent practice, he expertly extricated himself from the phone call before he started crying, of all damned things.

He'd thought about calling Kurt too, but clearly his emotional state was a little precarious at the moment. Instead, he fired off a text asking Kurt to show up for dinner as well, then relaxed back into his pillows, a fraction of his tension bleeding off now that he'd taken those few baby steps forward.

Shifting, he caught another whiff of Rick's scent. Smiling up at the ceiling, he scratched at his belly. Meeting the sexy blond had been an unexpected but welcome surprise. Last night had been momentous, and not just because of the spectacular sex. He'd never once brought a guy back to his condo. After spending his entire adulthood in the shadows, he'd looked forward to having a man in his bed, and the fiery, flamboyant blond had been eager to ditch the house painting to follow him home.

Having sex in his bed with the slender, supple Rick had been utterly inspiring. Ian stretched again. He'd well used several muscles that didn't get nearly enough of a workout. Although no stranger to one-night stands, he'd also never let himself explore a man's body in daylight. Starting with

Rick this morning would have been an excellent beginning to his newfound freedom.

Letting his hand drift toward his groin, Ian let those fantasies fill up his mind. He had a few hours left before he needed to see his family and tell them the truth. Rick was missing out on another spectacular orgasm, but it was his own damn fault for sneaking out like a thief in the night.

Bastard. Ian was missing out too. Rick fucked like a dream, and Ian would be searching a long time to find someone who could measure up.

"IAN! It's about time you made it to Sunday dinner."

Ian rolled his eyes at his older sister. "Whatever, Caitlyn. It's not like you're here every week either."

Deirdre and Sean O'Donnell had emigrated from Ireland and opened a family-style pub called Finn's Frolic in the heart of downtown Toronto. All the kids had learned the value of hard work doing chores at Finn's, and still helped out on occasion, although it had never been necessary to keep the business afloat; Deirdre and Sean had made their pub successful early on. It had quickly become a tradition for his parents to ensure hired staff covered Sundays at the pub so that Deirdre could host her large brood—which grew larger every year—for a family meal. It was rare for everyone to show up. Now that most of his siblings had kids and in-laws, the entire family was only ever together at the O'Donnell birthday parties. Not even Christmas was as sacrosanct for his mom and dad. If you were going to miss a birthday celebration, you'd better be half-dead.

"And just how would you know that?" Caitlyn flicked him across the back of the head with a dish towel. "Been weeks since we've seen you."

For the most part, he and his siblings appeared as often as possible, barring the occasional hangover. Not many families with seven kids could boast about how well everyone got along, but they did. Scuffles, arguments, and shouting were common, but underneath it all, they loved each other and no one was ever lonely.

On the other hand, no one was ever alone, either. Someone always knew where you were or what you were doing, even if you wished they didn't. Which had been part and parcel of his need for secrecy. Even after he moved out, he'd lived in fear of any of his family seeing him with a man. Ian had never dated. Never met a man for drinks or a movie. Not romantically or with the expectation of sex, at any rate. There were clubs all over the city where he could go to get off and he did so, almost as often as he told his family he was out scouting for women.

The paranoia had become an all-consuming guiding force in his life, and as much as he looked forward to getting rid of it, he felt an inexplicable sadness. His life was changing—hopefully for the better—but guilt and fear had been his constant companions for almost two decades and he thought he might miss them. For a few minutes, at any rate.

Ian set the table, amazed to see his fingers tremble. This shouldn't be so scary. Kurt had done it—gone and blurted it out like it was nothing. His family hadn't cared. Ian had been the only one to care, and that had been selfishness more than anything. Jealousy that Kurt had found the courage—and the acceptance Ian craved—that Ian had been afraid to look for. Now that he was going to tell the rest of the family, he was afraid. More afraid than he'd ever been. Soul-deep, bone-shaking, stomach-swirling fear filled him.

"So what are you doing here?" Caitlyn waddled into the dining room behind him, her round beach ball of a stomach leading the way, a basket of rolls in her hand.

"Well, it's almost dinnertime and it's Sunday, so obviously I'm here to get Dad's fantasy football picks. What the he… heck do you think I'm doing here?" Ian couldn't hear the shrieks of any of Caitlyn's or his other siblings' kids, but his mom would kill him if he cursed in their presence.

"Dunno. Just haven't seen you in weeks." Caitlyn put the rolls down on the table.

Ian frowned and peered around Caitlyn, looking for her twin, Colleen. He hadn't heard anyone else arrive, but it was a rare day that only one of the twins showed up to a family function.

Before Caitlyn and Colleen had gotten married, the twins were inseparable. After they got married, they still did a lot together, but their husbands took up any gaps. The twins, more than any of the O'Donnells, didn't like to be alone.

Then he shook off his concern. He had other things to think about. Like when would be the best time to break his news. Right before dinner? During dessert? The meals really weren't that formal, but if nothing else his siblings, their spouses, and his parents would dine at the table, with the kids in the kitchen.

"So?"

"So nothing. Just that Mom hates it when you're a sulky little bitch."

"I am not a sulky bitch." Why had Caitlyn chosen those specific words? What did she know?

"Are too."

"Am not." Ian bit the inside of his cheek. Hormones. Had to be hormones. Or simply a sister being a pain in the ass, like they were genetically programmed to be. Getting drawn into one of these pointless squabbles would keep his mind off his upcoming confession, but he wasn't six anymore, and he tried, most days, to act accordingly.

"Whatever." Caitlyn shook her head. "Why did you put the leaves in the table? It's way too big. You're going to have to do this again."

Irritation gripped him, and he almost yelled at his very pregnant sister. Who hadn't been sleeping well, judging by the dark circles under her eyes. "I thought everyone was going to be here."

Caitlyn rolled her eyes. "Where is your brain, idiot? Can't you count?"

Ian gulped and the butterflies in his stomach evolved into pterodactyls. With claws. For some reason, he'd assumed it would be easier if the whole brood were here. He'd only have to do this once and maybe no one would make a scene in front of the kids. Of which, he couldn't hear one. This small, intimate family gathering meant there should be ample opportunity to bring it into the conversation, and now that he was so close to doing it, he wanted to puke. But he couldn't wait any longer. Not only was this secret choking the life out of him, Kurt already knew, and Ian hadn't asked him to keep silent.

Then again, maybe testing the water with a smaller audience would be simpler. If he could only convince his sweaty palms of that.

Instead, he started to redo the table as directed, trying desperately not to think about what he was going to do at dinner.

"Can you help me?"

Caitlyn snorted. "Not likely." She gestured at her belly.

"Then get the hell out. You're in the way."

His sister's glare should have burned him to a cinder, but at least she left, letting him gather his thoughts.

RICK frowned at Davy's door. He should have called ahead—it would be so embarrassing to have to come back. He rang the doorbell and waited.

Davy answered the door with a smile, which relieved Rick's mind on one score. If his friend had been getting laid, it would have taken him a lot longer and he would have been grumpy.

"Rick, what are you doing here?"

Rick took a breath. "Hey, sweet thing. Left my keys here last night." He gave Davy a little kiss on the cheek before pushing inside.

"I thought that was your car parked on the street. Wait, you weren't with Ian all this time, were you?"

Wandering into the living room, he grabbed his keys and pocketed them.

"No, of course not."

"I'm surprised you left your car here at all. I know I've been out of touch for a while, but you were always adamant about having transportation."

He did not want to have this discussion, nor did he want Davy speculating about why he might have broken those rules.

"Your big, hunky cop around?"

Rick bit back a groan. Why had he asked that? Davy was going to think he was obsessed. Hell, Rick still wasn't sure if he'd gone home with Ian because he looked like Kurt.

"Nope. Why, want to ask him about Ian?" Davy's tone was teasing, playful, and Rick cocked his head, contemplating his friend. Davy had had a rough time of it, but Rick was so pleased his friend was happy.

"No, not at all. Why would you think that?"

"Dunno. Ian's pretty hot. And you went home with him."

"Don't read too much into it." Rick kept his voice light, airy, and unconcerned. He wasn't going to get sucked into asking about Ian like some teenaged girl with a crush. "It was nothing more than a one-night stand."

"Okay. Well, if you want to talk about it, I'm here."

Davy didn't know why he had his rules. No one did. But they protected everyone, himself included.

"No worries, hon. Just because you're making happy families with his brother doesn't mean me and Ian are soul mates."

Bitterness darkened his tone, and Davy's brows drew together. Damn. He'd have to do better at keeping things lighthearted.

"Seriously, though. Kurt's at his parents' for dinner. You want to stick around? I've got a nice Chardonnay chilling. We could call for Chinese."

Rick thought about going home. Or going out. Strangely, he wasn't ready to use another man to erase the memories of Ian just yet. It had been a long time since he'd felt so stretched and satiated that he wanted to savor the feeling for a little longer. He also didn't want to brood all night. Given his strange mood and uncharacteristic behavior with Ian, if he was alone, that was all he'd do.

"Sounds good."

Davy made a call to a local Chinese place that delivered. They settled in on the couch with glasses of white wine.

Rick tucked his feet up on the couch and faced Davy.

"So, how come you let the wounded warrior out all by himself?"

Davy grinned. "He's doing much better. And I love his family, I really do, but there's so many of them! Kurt was expecting some drama, so I thought I'd skip it. Besides, his family won't let him overdo things."

"Oooh… drama? What kind?" Gossip could be fun, when it wasn't about him. And family stuff gave him hives, so he understood Davy's need to avoid it.

"Kurt thinks Ian's going to come out to his family."

Rick choked on his mouthful of wine. "You mean last night, when he said he was gay, we—or rather, Kurt—was the first to know?"

"Seems so."

"Oh, well, that's brave of him." There hadn't been a sign last night, aside from tear-reddened eyes and a delicious hint of vulnerability, that Ian had intended something so soul-shaking today. Rick had been a nervous wreck when he'd decided to come out. It had gone badly, so his nerves had certainly been justified and there's no way he'd have been able to fuck someone into a stupor just hours prior. But then, Rick had come out when he was a teenager and his virginal self couldn't have fucked anyone into a pleasant daze on his best day.

"I know. It's a terrifying prospect even when you know it will be okay."

"Yeah." Rick downed the last of his Chardonnay. He already knew Davy's coming out went fine and his own went shit and they didn't need to rehash. It was over and done and as shitty as it had been, it had been marginally better than the rest of his adolescence.

Davy refilled their glasses without comment and Rick took another sip.

"This wine is pretty decent." Rick was usually more of a margarita guy, but lately the tequila had been upsetting his stomach. Wrong side of fucking thirty-five. Wine, though, especially white, didn't have the same effect and he should probably learn a little more about it.

"I know. It's actually a Wayne Gretzky wine."

Rick lifted a brow. "Wayne Gretzky has wines?" He wasn't nearly as into hockey as Davy and Kurt were, but he didn't mind it, and even those with a nodding acquaintance with the sport ought to recognize the Great One's name. "You bought this just for the name, didn't you?"

"Hell yeah!" Davy grinned and clinked their glasses together. "But it's still good. If only he'd played for Toronto."

Rick snorted, more than willing to get sucked into a hockey conversation. Less personal was better, and he wasn't ready to go home and rattle around in his place. His house was home, office, and sanctuary. With a new consult coming in this week, he'd normally spend a pleasant Sunday afternoon preparing for his workweek, but he'd been too unsettled by Ian to concentrate on anything. It hadn't occurred to him to find out if any of his friends had wanted to just hang out, so having Davy at loose ends was serendipitous. As long as he could steer conversation away from his family life or his sex life.

IAN fidgeted in his seat. With only his parents, three of his siblings, and two significant others at the table, he was amazed the conversation never had a lull sufficient for him to broach his announcement. There weren't even any kids eating at the table in the kitchen to create a break in the conversation.

He wasn't even sure what he'd eaten. If it had more flavor than sawdust, he hadn't taken note. He could barely follow the topics of conversation.

Someone mentioned Casa Loma. The scenic castle in the midst of downtown Toronto held some good memories of an office Christmas party a few years back, along with a risky, alcohol-inspired interlude with one of the catering staff.

His brother Dylan had been planning his upcoming wedding to Stephanie, and finally, Ian was able to pretend he was paying attention.

"Casa Loma? Hey, that would make a great place for the reception. They've got this awesome conservatory. Great for pictures too." Ian stopped talking as the entire table stared at him.

"Honey, I'm sure I told you already." His mother's concern deepened as she stared at him. "Dylan and Stephanie decided weeks ago to have the reception there. That's why we're talking about it."

Heat licked at his cheeks. Surely he hadn't been that self-absorbed.

"Sorry, Dylan, Steph."

"S'okay." Dylan waved a fork at him in a gesture Ian had no trouble interpreting as obscene. "I'm sure you've been busy."

Stephanie gave her fiancé a mock glare and a nudge to the shoulder, but Dylan hardly looked abashed. His brother would have been more graphic and crude if he'd been on his own, Ian knew that for a fact.

Ian hadn't been as busy as his family assumed, but last night… yes… he'd been busy. With Rick. And that reminder had his cheeks flaring hotter, even as he recognized this might be the perfect opening.

"You at least remember the date, right? You haven't made plans?" Dylan's teasing was a little gentler than Caitlyn's earlier words, but the truth of them still stung. He'd been completely out of touch for too long.

"Of course I remember the date. I'm supposed to be wearing a tux and everything." He didn't remember the date. At all. Hopefully he'd put it in his calendar but pulling his phone out now to check would only have the whole lot laughing at him. He glared at Kurt. If his brother loved him at all, he'd groan or something, take the attention off Ian's preoccupation. Kurt merely snorted and tried to look invisible. Ian grimaced. After his injury, Kurt had probably got far more familial attention than he wanted.

"Yes, but you did realize they're going to be mustard yellow, right? It's got a special meaning for Steph's family." Dylan smiled adoringly at his fiancée while Ian threw her a horrified look.

He hadn't actually agreed to wear a yellow tux, had he? Where would one even go to find such a travesty? The Tuxedo Junction he'd rented high school formal wear from would be unlikely to carry such nonsense.

Heaven save him, he hadn't agreed to *buy* it, had he? "Er…. Is it going to be specially made?"

Everyone, except for his parents, started laughing, and Ian was pretty sure his father stuffed an extra-large forkful of potatoes in his mouth to prevent himself from doing just that.

His mother's eyes twinkled, just a bit. "Honey, you really should try to get home for dinner more."

"I'm sorry, Mom. But the tuxedo is a joke, right?" Because that needed to be confirmed.

"Of course it is, idiot." Dylan's words were teasing enough that Ian didn't take offense, although his fiancée, Stephanie, gave him a dirty look, and his mother cleared her throat warningly. He'd had two sibs call him an idiot in one day. That was a new record since they'd all graduated university.

His father finally swallowed. "Although we'd prefer our children didn't call each other names…." Dylan had the grace to look chastened. "Boyo, you've met our Stephanie, right? I don't know fashion at all and I can tell she'd not pick something that wasn't classy."

Well, that was certainly true. Dylan had picked a sophisticated, attractive woman who still knew how to have fun.

Ian still needed to check his calendar. For all he knew, he had other wedding obligations that required his presence. The conversation moved on to the wedding dress and bridesmaid dresses, and the interlude for his confession passed. He'd have to pay more attention to the conversation; maybe another decent moment would arise naturally.

The conversation made a turn from seating arrangements to his eldest sister, Erin, and her upcoming birthday party. At least he knew that was in his calendar, since it was practically a hanging offense to miss one of the family's birthday parties. The spouses didn't get a big party thrown at the pub, but Ian was certain once the grandkids turned sixteen, they'd be included in the birthday schedule too.

"Are you bringing a date to Erin's birthday party?" His mother held out such high hopes that her youngest sons would settle down.

Ian swallowed wrong and almost choked. His mother's high hopes would now be pinned solely on him, because Kurt and Dylan, both out of the blue as far as Ian was concerned, had found people to settle down with. He was the only one left.

"A date? No." He squeezed out the words between sputters. Erin's birthday party was ridiculously too soon to consider such a thing. Once this confession was out of the way, he might be able to consider dating, but first he'd have to learn how.

"I told you, Mom. He's such a slut." Caitlyn scraped another helping of vegetables onto her plate as she spoke.

"I'm hardly a slut."

"Well you must be doing something wrong, otherwise those poor women you *date*—and I use the term loosely—might come back for seconds." Caitlyn's teasing, sharper and more pointed than Dylan's, and right on top of the unwelcome realization that his entire family had found something he'd never dared try for, lit the fuse of his anger.

"Are you picking on me because you don't want anyone to notice you're so much fatter than Colleen?" His sisters had both gotten pregnant at the same time—again. Apparently the twins couldn't do anything separately, but the fatter insult was nothing more than a stab in the dark.

He didn't expect Caitlyn to burst into tears as her husband Mark murmured to comfort her, or the rest of the family to glare at him. Fortunately, the tears didn't last long, but the glare Caitlyn directed at him with red-rimmed eyes should have shriveled his balls.

Caitlyn threw a roll at his head, which then dropped on to his empty plate. "If you're not a slut, you're definitely an asshole."

"What did I do?"

Kurt looked rather uncomfortable and wouldn't meet his eyes. Dylan just laughed softly at his predicament, and both his parents turned stern, disapproving looks on him.

Only his dad bothered to answer his question. "I don't know why you've been avoiding us, boyo, but if you hadn't you'd already know this."

There it was, the expected arrow of guilt, right through the heart. But that didn't stop his momentary panic. Was there something wrong with his sister? Why hadn't he paid more attention?

"What? What's wrong?"

"Caitlyn's having twins and Colleen isn't." Again, his dad was the one who answered.

Ian waited, wondering what the terrible follow-up was. After a moment, he realized there wasn't one. "You're kidding, right? That's it?"

"You know your sisters are happiest when they're doing things together," his mother said as though she thought this was normal.

"But they don't have control over this. Why get so upset?"

"You'll learn, boyo, when you've got a pregnant wife of your own." Great. His dad was now on the "let's get Ian settled" bandwagon.

"Please. He's probably impregnated half the city by now and he still can't get a girl to stick around." Caitlyn's tone was more derisive than ever and sparked his wild swirl of emotions.

He stood up and threw the roll back at her. "I haven't gotten anyone pregnant and I don't want a fucking girl to stick around. I'm gay, dammit."

The second the words flew from his mouth, he wished he could claw them back, prevent everyone from hearing them. Kurt smothered a snort of laughter.

Awesome. Kurt found his marvelous confession amusing. Once again, something he hadn't been able to do as well as the baby of the family.

"Ian Seamus O'Donnell." Shit. His mother was truly pissed if she was trotting out his full name.

He spun on his heel and headed for the backyard. He'd like nothing better than to leave, but he was certain his car would be boxed in by at least three others. And they were probably pissed enough to make him stay here all night.

He shouldn't have said it. Why had he said it like that? None of his carefully prepared speeches involved him blurting out his secret while yelling at his aggravating pregnant sister. Ian kicked at a clump of grass before digging the toe of his shoe in the dirt. He stared at the yard, the far end overgrown with trees and bushes that had been a lot sparser when he and his brothers played in it as kids. He was only a year and half older than Kurt, Dylan the same again older than Ian. Being so close in age made the three of them much closer than the other siblings. Mike had been a great older brother but distant, partly by nature, partly by years. Erin as eldest was just too difficult to relate to most of the time. The twins in between Dylan and Mike were more like a single entity growing up than two sisters, and rarely needed the rest of them. Yet, Ian loved them all. He just hadn't trusted them with his innermost secret. Not even the brothers who had been his closest friends growing up.

He hadn't wanted any of them to figure out the truth, and distancing himself when he felt vulnerable had been the easiest solution. He'd done the same thing with his friends, none of whom knew the truth either.

Ian picked up a deadfall branch and tossed it into the foliage at the back of the yard. It made a satisfying *thunk* as it hit a tree trunk well camouflaged with ivy.

Kurt's coming out had been seriously anticlimactic as far as his family was concerned. No one had noticed how much turmoil it had created within Ian, just searching for a way to break free.

The small pinhole he'd made in his protective shield when he'd admitted his orientation to his brother had provided such a break. Instead of calmly outing himself to his family, his anger, fear, and all those years of repression had exploded all over them.

The back door opened and shut behind him. His shoulders slumped. Normally, his parents wouldn't come after him to yell. They were big on admitting your own mistakes. Maybe because in a family with seven kids, *someone* always knew something and hiding things was so impossible you might as well come clean. Did Mike still get in trouble with the parental units? His brother had always seemed so grown-up and perfect, even when he was young, that Ian assumed he'd stopped feeling like a stupid kid long before he'd hit his twenties. Ian was thirty-three and dreading his parents yelling at him.

In many ways, he'd be surprised if his parents hadn't known about him long before this. His parents were intelligent and savvy business people, for all that neither of them had more than a high-school education.

He turned around, ready to face the firing range. Instead of his parents, though, Kurt and Dylan stood there, looking at him with love and concern. Ian's eyes stung and blurred.

"C'mon. Sit down." Dylan gestured to the log bench in the shadow of the enormous maple that marked the southwest corner of his parents' property.

Ian sat first, his back to the house. Dylan sat on his left, Kurt on his right.

They sat there for a few minutes, a warm breeze ruffling the leaves overhead. He sensed both brothers shift as though they were going to speak, but it was like they didn't know what to say. Ian didn't either. He just took comfort from his best friends—brothers—next to him.

Dylan huffed out a breath. No surprise—he was always the most impatient of the three of them.

"Ian, man, you should have said something." There was no censure in Dylan's tone, only regret. "We would have understood. How long have you known?"

It was a legitimate question. Kurt had been oblivious to his orientation until recently. Ian had always assumed his brother was a prude or had a low sex drive. Possibly Kurt had thought the same thing about himself until he'd met Davy.

"Since I was fifteen."

"Fifteen? Ian, why?" Ian knew what Dylan meant. Why had he kept it secret so long? Kurt already knew Ian had been hiding it for years, but he hadn't told him everything.

Ian scrubbed his cheeks with the back of his hand. "You remember that weekend camping trip we took at Wasaga Beach?"

"Yeah, sure." Dylan laughed. "We got into so much trouble."

Kurt grunted. It was one of the few times they'd left Kurt out, only because were sure no one would believe their baby-faced brother was legal, no matter how tall he was or what their fake IDs said. He and Dylan and a couple of Dylan's friends escaped one weekend to drink themselves silly at Wasaga.

"I still hate you guys for leaving me behind." Kurt pouted.

"Whatever." Dylan reached behind Ian's back to punch Kurt in the shoulder. "You got even by squealing on us."

"Ow." Kurt grunted.

"Wuss," Dylan replied.

"I got shot!"

Dylan breathed in sharply. "Sorry. Forgot."

Ian had too, almost. They had so easily slipped into their threesome camaraderie. But he'd had a reason for bringing up the incident that had nothing to do with reminiscing.

"Anyway… your friend from the swim team was there."

"Oh, yeah. God, lost touch with that guy ages ago. What was his name again?" Dylan's question was mostly rhetorical.

"Niels."

"Right, Niels. Oh my God, you had a crush on my friend, didn't you? No wonder you were so damned insistent about coming to all the swim meets, when you could never be bothered to wake up that early before."

"Yes, well, I saw Niels naked in that communal shower at the campground. And it was an epiphany."

"But you chased after cheerleaders all year after that!" Dylan's shock was tinged with disbelief.

Ian let out a bitter laugh. "Because you were. Remember Paul Jenkins? I don't think anyone ever gay bashed him, but he got a lot of shit from the athletes in the school. I don't even know if he was gay, but he was small, clumsy, smart as anything, and pretty as a girl. And I learned I didn't want to be different, not if it brought me attention like Paul got. I didn't want anyone to treat me like that."

"Jeez, Ian." Dylan gave his shoulder a squeeze. "I wouldn't have let you get bashed."

"Nor I," Kurt said. Funny in a way, because even in high school, Kurt was bigger and more muscular than either him or Dylan. He might have been the youngest, but Kurt was far from the runt of the O'Donnell litter.

"It was so fucking easy for you guys." Ian continued to speak over their weak protestations. "I mean it. Dylan was a fucking hound dog, after every breathing object with tits. Everyone seemed to applaud your behavior—except for our sisters. So I mimicked you."

"What about Kurt? He didn't act like that."

Ian shrugged. "I kinda thought he was a bit of a prude. Saving himself for marriage or something. I guess no one gave him shit because he was so big, but it wasn't something I could copy."

"Huh. And I always assumed he just had a low sex drive." Dylan winked across Ian at Kurt, whose face went ruddy in the late evening sunlight.

"Shut up! Ian, you should have talked to me."

"Kurt, you were younger. Not even fourteen when I first saw Niels. How was I supposed to know you'd understand? Would you have?"

His wounded brother patted him on the knee. "Probably not. I didn't understand why I wasn't into girls like you and Dylan seemed to be, and by the time I got to high school I figured I just wasn't that into sex. It never seemed that important. Until Davy, it never even occurred to me to look at guys that way."

"Oblivious little shit," Dylan teased.

Ian hadn't found much about today humorous at all, but this was. "Some detective you are. Is this your way of saying your sex drive *isn't* low?"

He and Dylan both laughed at Kurt's renewed blush. Ian needed to get to know Davy better because he seemed so good for his brother. But Kurt's words confirmed that Ian had been the only one hiding his true self all those years. Instead of focusing on that, he finished his story.

"By the time we left high school, I was known as a player and it seemed like my role in life had been set. At university I fell into a cycle of hitting clubs, finding guys to screw, no strings, no names, no feelings. It was safer and easier to keep pretending."

Kurt sucked in a breath. "You were… careful, weren't you?"

Ian pressed his lips together and nodded. He'd had a scare, just after he'd turned twenty. A scare that he'd not been able to talk to anyone about except the guy at the free clinic. He'd never felt so lonely in his life, especially since he didn't even know the real name of the guy he'd been with. After that, he'd been the king of condoms.

"Well, shit, bro, that sucks. I wish…." Dylan paused. "I wish you'd met someone like Davy earlier."

"You'll find someone." Kurt wrapped an arm around Ian's shoulder. "You're a great catch."

Until that moment, Ian hadn't let himself truly hope there was someone out there for him. But how was he going to break the habit of years? The image of Rick, slim and blond, writhing in his bed, flared hot in his mind. Rick couldn't be the one, but wow. The night had been incredible. But thinking about excellent sex with his brothers seated on either side was just plain weird, and he let the image disperse.

The three of them sat there, letting the wind swirl around, content in their silent companionship.

He wasn't alone. After Kurt came out, he should have realized his own orientation wouldn't be an issue, but knowing something in your head didn't always relieve the anxiety in your heart, and Ian had been playing a part for a long time. A part Kurt apparently hadn't even been playing until he met Davy.

Drawing in a deep breath, he straightened his spine. "How mad are they?" Ian didn't have to specify his parents. They were the ones he'd have to deal with first. Then the sibs.

"Dunno," Dylan replied. "But they were content to wait until you were ready to come back inside."

"Guess I'd better get to it."

"Caitlyn and Mark left already, so it's only Stephanie and the units inside," Kurt offered.

Ian stood. His outburst wasn't any less humiliating, but at least he didn't have to face his sister's sharp tongue. Yet.

SEAN and Deirdre sat at the kitchen table, their soft conversation ceasing as Ian came in the door. The unwelcome sensation of being a kid about to get grounded swamped him.

He slunk into his chair and waited. His parents shared a glance before his mother reached out and placed a gentle hand on his arm.

"Honey. Can we talk about this? Calmly?"

"I'm sorry. I just…." Ian didn't know what to say. Not exactly. No matter how it had come out, he'd really already said the most important bits. Hashing it to death with his parents, when they were mad at him for being an asshole, didn't seem like any fun at all. He was thirty-three years old, not thirteen. When he noticed his lip beginning to pouch out in a pout, he sucked it back in. Because he *wasn't* thirteen anymore. Sulking was pointless.

"Talk to us. It's okay. We love you. No matter what."

Ian's eyes began to burn at his mother's declaration, but hearing it eased something inside.

"I've known for a long time. Since I was a teen. But I never felt I could tell anyone. And then, Kurt just blurted it all out at his party and… and everything was okay. For him. No one cared. And that's as it should be, but…."

His mother smiled. "But you felt cheated, maybe? You'd built it up in your head as this enormous, black secret and suddenly you realized admitting it wasn't as… I don't want to say earth-shattering, because I know it is for you. One day, no one will care whether a person is gay or straight, but until that day comes, you just never know, eh, boyo? But you spent so long wondering about how we'd take it that your baby brother came in and stole your thunder. Not having any negative repercussions just kicked that competitive streak of yours into overdrive."

Ian blinked at his mother. So, he wasn't a sulky bitch, he was a drama llama. Lovely.

His mother wasn't done. "I wish you'd trusted us enough to tell us earlier. I hate that you spent so long worried that our love was conditional. But it's not and never will be."

"C'mere." His father stood and pulled Ian into a crushing bear hug. "What your mother said."

His mother was waiting right after to administer her own brand of hugs. Ian's eyes burned again, but this time he couldn't stop a few tears from trickling down his face.

Pulling back, his mother sniffed and wiped at his cheeks like she'd done every time he'd been hurt.

"You know you owe Caitlyn an apology, right?" His father still had his stern look on, but there was no disapproval or disgust. Nothing was different, and Ian let out a shaky breath.

"I know."

"And Kurt too."

Ian frowned. "I spoke to him last night. I apologized for avoiding him. We're good."

"No, Ian. Not for that. Even though he didn't come to his realization until recently, you are truly mistaken if you believe it was easy for him. It wasn't. Maybe you didn't see it because you were so busy protecting yourself, and that's okay. But talk to him. I think you need to know what he went through. I think you'd be surprised how similar you two are."

"I'll talk to him."

"You're on dish duty." His mother stretched up on her toes to kiss him on the cheek. "But you probably guessed that."

Ian let out a watery laugh. "Yeah, I did."

They left the kitchen and Ian began to run the hot water. His mom had a dishwasher—thank heavens—but she preferred pots, serving dishes, and glasses to be washed by hand.

Dylan and Kurt popped back into the kitchen a few minutes later, Dylan grabbing a beer before continuing on out of the kitchen, but Kurt sat at the table.

Ian gave him a few surreptitious glances. What had his father meant? And was he ready to get into another deep conversation right now?

No. Another time. If he hadn't been laid so well last night, his mood would be worse than flat right now. Hell, it was only eight and he had every intention of calling it a night as soon as he could. Emotional upheaval was more exhausting than he'd imagined. If he had the energy, he'd pop out to one of his usual haunts and get a blow job or something to ease him into a good night's sleep, but more than likely he'd have to ease himself into sleep with the memory of last night.

Or the memory of curling up to a warm male body in his bed. Funny, he thought he might actually prefer the comfort of that to a blow job. That wasn't like him at all. Or at least, it wasn't like the player who hid his sexuality from everyone. Did being out mean he was going to be a cuddler? Rick had felt right in his arms, but maybe any man would do if Ian let them sleep in his bed.

"So, you going to start dating now?" Oh, that wasn't right. Surely his brother couldn't read his thoughts, now, could he?

Ian shrugged as best he could, elbow deep in soapy water. "I guess. I don't… I don't really know how."

Kurt snorted. "Me, neither. I mean, I dated girls, but clearly that wasn't successful. Davy and I never officially dated. What about Rick?"

"Oh, his name was really Rick?" Ian almost never gave his real name when out looking to get laid, and he certainly never presumed he was given his partner's real name. Which was a lonely fucking way to live, now that he thought about it.

Kurt curled his lip. "You met him at my *home*. Helping me *paint* it. While I'm still recovering from being *shot*. It wasn't exactly foam night at Anaconda."

Ian pulled a hand out of the sink and flipped him off, suds flying smack onto Kurt's forehead. Couldn't have done better if he tried. "What would you know about Anaconda? You've been gay for about thirty seconds and let's face it, you're a bit of a prude."

The deflection wouldn't fool his observant cop of a younger brother.

"It's not foam night, here, either." Kurt wiped at the wet on his face. "And compared to a slut, I guess I am a prude." Kurt stood and tossed a wet dish towel at Ian.

Somehow, Kurt's words didn't hurt or make him angry like Caitlyn's had. But Kurt was still his baby brother and deserved a smackdown.

"Hey, I've gotten laid more times than you can count, baby bro." Ian splashed suds at Kurt, soap and water dampening his shirt.

"Quality over quantity." Kurt grabbed a handful of buttered brussels sprouts out of a nearby serving dish and lobbed them at him.

Ian let out a soft curse, and they both began looking for ammunition. Kurt dug into the bowl of sprouts again while Ian plunged his hands into the remains of the potatoes.

"And what exactly are you planning to do with those?" At the sound of their father's voice, they froze, caught with their hands in the cookie jar, so to speak.

"Uh." Kurt's response was singularly unhelpful.

"Right. I think you better call a cease-fire. Your mother doesn't care that you're gay, but if you mess up her kitchen, you'll be cleaning grout with a toothbrush. And Ian, that'll all be on you, because she's not going to let Kurt do anything with that injury."

Kurt got an evil glint in his eyes and feinted another sprout toss.

"No fair." The absurdity of the situation hit Ian as soon as those words left his lips and he started laughing. Kurt and his father did too.

His father clapped him on the back. "For a minute there, I thought we'd dropped through a time warp. But your mother could come in at any minute, so you'd better hurry up and get finished. Don't miss any of those." He raised a grizzled brow at the green sprouts littered over the floor around Ian's feet before he grabbed a beer from the fridge and left.

"I'll pick up the sprouts," Kurt offered.

"No you won't. Sit down. I don't want Mom or Davy to kill me if you overdo it because we had a food fight. I'll get them."

Kurt must have been feeling tender, because he actually obeyed. "Sorry, man. I shouldn't have made a mess."

"Oh, whatever." Ian rinsed potatoes off his hands and dried them before squatting and grabbing each slippery little sprout to toss in the composting bin. Just in time, too, because Ian had no sooner plunged his hands back into the dishwater when their mom wandered in to refill her wine glass. She gave Kurt an assessing look, as if to ensure he was taking it easy, before casting an expert eye over Ian's work.

"Out of practice, my boyo? It's taking a while."

"Just want to make sure it's perfect for you, Mom." Ian gave her his most innocent smile.

"Scamp. Your old mum knows not to trust that snake-oil grin." She grinned back at him and left them on their own.

For a few minutes, there was only the sound of dishes clanking.

"So what are you going to do now?"

Once again, he knew what Kurt meant. "I don't know. This was such a big step, even if I already knew, deep down, that the family wouldn't care. I couldn't think past it. And I wasn't lying. I've never dated. The places I go to get laid are not places to find dates, even if I had any idea what to do. I almost feel like I'm one of those guys who got married young and got tossed out in a divorce after so many years, floundering in the dating pool."

Like that guy at work who'd married his high-school sweetheart, who, twenty years later, "wanted something different." Poor befuddled bastard had to learn how to navigate shark-infested dating waters without a life preserver. And yet, Ian would have to dive right in, heedless of the sharks, if he wanted even a taste of what the rest of his family had found.

"Maybe Davy could help. Offer some advice."

"Yeah, maybe. But let's hold off on that. I need some time to… get used to being out. Being myself." Figuring out who the hell that was.

Kurt smiled at him. "You know I'm here for you, even if I'm so newly out I squeak around the edges."

"I know, baby bro, I know."

Just like that, guilt came welling back up, and he knew he couldn't put it off any longer. Doing so would only benefit him, and he'd already been far too selfish where Kurt was concerned.

He placed the last wet dish in the dish rack, dried his hands, and sat at the table across from Kurt. The kitchen table was only big enough for four people; if the whole family was around to eat together, they ate in the dining room. The kitchen table was more like a cafeteria, catering to the different schedules of a family of nine. Which meant he was too close to Kurt's curious gaze for comfort, and yet, this wasn't going to be a comfortable discussion.

"I know…." Ian's voice cracked, and he swallowed heavily. "I know I wasn't there for you. And I'm sorry."

Kurt shrugged. "We hashed this out last night. We're good."

Tempted to let it go, to take the easy way out, Ian forced himself to soldier on. His parents would know—somehow—if he shirked.

"No, I mean…." What did he mean, exactly? "I wasn't there for you. I was a shit, and I know it. But the thing is, I somehow thought this whole life change had been easy for you. And I'm suddenly realizing it wasn't. It can't have been." In fact, the more he thought about it, Ian knew it had to have been traumatic. Far more so than what he'd gone through. Because Kurt hadn't realized he was gay. He'd probably never paid much attention to how his family or coworkers responded to gay characters on TV or in the movies. He'd never gauged how funny or offensive they found off-color jokes. Never knew if they sneered at, ignored, or even noticed a flamboyant gay man crossing their paths.

Ian had spent years analyzing every tiny reaction. He had made sure to enter a profession that was unlikely to be affected by his sexuality, because deep down, he'd assumed that if he didn't choose to step out of the closet, he might be accidentally outed. Kurt had never had the chance to weigh his choice of profession against his sexual orientation.

Toronto was a pretty tolerant place, both in regards to sexuality and ethnicity. The police force didn't discriminate. But there had to be some deeply seated fear that in a profession like police detective he'd have his work and partnerships suffer. Unlike Ian, who'd had years to consider how to come out, or to imagine every possible response, Kurt would have had all that crowd in on him over a matter of months.

Kurt had always been a pleasant, happy guy whose emotions were never in turmoil like Ian's often were. The memory prompted a pallor in Kurt's skin and a bleakness in his eyes that pained Ian like little else in his life. He may only be a year and a half older, but it was still his job to protect his younger brother, and he'd fucking failed.

"It wasn't. No." His brother's voice was weak. As weak as Ian had ever heard it. Then Kurt broke eye contact to stare at the table, his fingers picking at the corner of a placemat.

"I'm here, now. Tell me." He didn't want to hear how he'd failed his baby brother, but his parents were right. He needed to hear this.

"Ian, I was so confused."

Kurt proceeded to tell Ian everything he hadn't told him last night when they'd made peace with each other.

"I started drinking. My temper was all over the place. If it hadn't been for Simon covering for me at work, I probably would have lost my job. If it had gone on any longer, I might have needed rehab."

Guilt tore at Ian's gut. If only he hadn't had his head up his ass, he could have helped Kurt through this. His parents were right. He owed Kurt an apology. He owed him more than that, but there was nothing else he could do. Not since Kurt had already worked his shit out. Or had he?

"Rehab? Are you okay now? Or are you in AA or something?"

Kurt lifted a shoulder and winced. "I wouldn't be the first cop with alcohol-abuse issues. I think it was probably a one-time aberration, but Davy's insisting I go talk to someone. Just in case."

"And you're going to go?"

"For Davy? Absolutely."

Ian let out a relieved breath. He'd never needed the support of alcohol or drugs to ease the confines of his closet. Probably because deep down he'd known coming out wouldn't mean losing his family. But substance abuse was prevalent in the gay community, and he'd rather rip off his own arm than have Kurt suffer like that.

"I'm glad you found a good man." And he was able to say it with nary a twinge of jealousy that the man had apparently just dropped into Kurt's lap like manna from heaven.

Kurt lifted his head and smiled. "He is a good man. I love him."

Jealousy did spike, momentarily, at the utter peace on Kurt's face. But Ian ignored it, because he wasn't finished.

"I'm so sorry I wasn't there for you. I wish… I wish we'd been at a place in our lives where we could have trusted each other with our secrets, like we used to as kids. Most of that's on me, because if I'd come clean in high school, or even university, this whole thing might have been avoided. But please know, if there's anything you need—even if it's something you don't want to tell anyone else—come to me. Don't let yourself spiral down again, okay? Promise?"

"I promise. But I'm kind of glad this all happened."

Ian must have misheard. "You're glad? You didn't get shot in the head, did you?"

Kurt laughed, his eyes crinkling and color coming back into his face. "Nope. Not a cracked skull, either. But don't you see? If anything had been different, I might never have met Davy. He makes up for everything I went through."

The sweetness of Kurt's statement made Ian tear up just a little, even as his inner drama llama wanted to spit in ire. Even out and proud, he didn't know how to be a boyfriend or a partner. A player was the role he'd built for himself, and it was going to take some time and effort to evolve into something else.

CHAPTER
Three

IAN slid into the seat at the last available table in the café on the main floor of his office building. It had been less than a week since he'd come out to his parents, and he somehow expected a huge change in his life. Expected people to notice he walked taller, with more confidence. Sort of like when he'd lost his virginity, he'd been disappointed there hadn't been a flashing neon sign over his head announcing the momentous occasion. All things considered, his coming out was almost a nonevent, and he really was turning into a drama llama if he couldn't be happy it had gone so smoothly.

Pushing pasta around with his fork, he sighed and picked up his book. It wasn't terribly interesting, but he'd promised his brother Dylan he'd read it.

Trouble was, he wanted to talk with someone and he didn't know who. His friends, while they'd be supportive, couldn't offer any insight into what it meant to be an out gay man. Dylan couldn't either, assuming he'd even have the time with all the wedding preparations. It had been a long time since the rest of his sibs had married, and he'd forgotten how it consumed the attention of the principals, to the exclusion of all else. And Kurt—well, he knew what it was to be a gay man, and he was out, but he plunged straight from penile-y oblivious to out gay man with partner. The whole out gay man looking for… something… had completely bypassed his fucking lucky baby brother. Kurt had offered Davy's help, but Davy's experience at being a single gay man was a decade out-of-date.

Which left him on his own again. Hardly any different from before he'd come out, really, except that should he meet someone special he could bring him home to meet the family. That didn't solve one damned thing right now.

"Hey, there aren't any more seats. Mind if I sit here?"

Ian looked up to find a slim man with shaggy brown hair wearing a black T-shirt and khaki cargo pants, midtwenties perhaps.

"Sure. Have a seat."

At this point, any company was a welcome distraction from his boring book and his unsettling thoughts.

"I'm Leon Barlow." After plopping his tray on the table, Leon extended his hand and Ian offered his.

"Ian O'Donnell." Ian frowned. "Didn't I see you up on the twelfth floor?"

"Oh, yeah, probably. I'm a new graphics designer for *Errant*."

The online celebrity scandal magazine that combined gossip with the weirdness of the now-defunct *Weekly World News* had been Ian's professional home for the past five years.

"No kidding? I'm a senior account manager for *Errant*."

Leon gave him a smile that made Ian revise his initial age estimation down a few years. This guy didn't look much over twenty. But then, graphic designers were cheapest when they were right out of school and Hector Ramos, *Errant*'s owner, always had an eye on the bottom line. Ian's own substantial salary would have made him a candidate for *redundancies* if it weren't for the fact he brought in his salary several times over in ad revenue.

"Oh. Will we be working together, then?"

"Sure, on some projects. Some of our advertisers don't have agencies or in-house talent to create ads, so the account managers will requisition ads from your department."

"Then I'm extra glad I asked to sit here." Leon stuffed a forkful of salad in his mouth and chewed.

Ian set his book down. A complete stranger just asking for use of half his table? In his current mood, he'd probably keep reading, although he didn't mind chatting with strangers. But a new coworker? Continuing to read would be extremely rude.

"Good book?" Leon pointed with his fork.

"Not sure yet." Unlikely, given the topic, but he hadn't been able to read enough to be sure.

Their conversation returned to *Errant* mostly, but Ian was surprised, even discussing work, how quickly the time passed.

"We should be getting back upstairs."

Leon didn't argue, just began gathering his lunch detritus. "Ian, you're from around here, aren't you?"

"Uh." That was a rather ambiguous question. His condo—not far from the office—was within spitting distance of Boystown, so it rather amazed him no one had figured out he'd made that choice deliberately. Was Leon asking if he was gay? Because Ian was rather sure Leon was.

In a fraction of a second, Ian's shoulders tensed up. He'd outed himself to people he cared about, and obviously every one of his random fucks knew he was gay, but it had never occurred to him that he could very easily experience a twinge of anxiety every time he considered admitting it.

"I mean, from Toronto. I just moved here from Winnipeg a couple of months ago and I don't know many people in the city. Maybe we could hang out sometime."

Ian let out a breath as his muscles relaxed, and he realized the majority of his anxiety had resulted from fear Leon was asking him out. The guy was way too young for him to date, and he wasn't about to have a one-nighter with someone he worked with. That was trouble waiting to happen. But if Leon just wanted to be friends, Ian could do that. He could use a friend without too much personal baggage.

"Yeah, I'd like that."

THE pulsating beat settled deep in Rick's stomach as he swiveled his hips to the vaguely familiar song. All around him, bodies writhed, the tang of musk and beer strong in his nose. Many of the men around him had already removed sweaty shirts and the humidity in the air was laced with sexual tension.

Rick breathed deeply, nostalgia sweeping him. At thirty-five, he'd done a lot of clubbing in his life, and while the venues, clothes, and booze du jour might have changed, the scent of dancing, horny men never did.

Closing his eyes, he let his other senses guide him, partly because he wasn't keen on comparing his slowly aging body with the strong young forms around him. Not that he'd gone completely to seed, but it took more effort to keep himself tight and toned than it did ten years ago. Hell, even two years ago his metabolism made his friends jealous.

Then he let his eyelids flip open, because he was also partly here for the scenery. If he had to be here, dancing and sightseeing were part of the agenda. Getting laid wouldn't hurt either, but he wished he had one of his fuck buddies with him for guaranteed sex. He'd already seen one too many pitying looks by Anaconda's clientele, which definitely skewed much younger than he was.

It didn't make any sense, but older twinks weren't as acceptable as older bears. It wasn't like he had a choice in the matter. He was five-nine, slim, and blond. At twenty, he'd been mobbed at clubs. At thirty-five, he still enjoyed the sensual mood of a club, but he usually frequented venues that catered to his age group. Probably be a million times worse if he was looking for a partner or husband, instead of a quick hand job in the bathroom or a blow job in the parking lot.

Then again, if he'd wanted something serious, Oscar would undoubtedly be waiting. Rick pursed his lips. It sucked when he had to break up with one of his fuck buddies. Most times, Rick was the one "dumped" when one of his guys decided they wanted something more and found it with someone else. Oscar's decision that they should move in together had taken Rick by surprise, but it wasn't the first time someone had suddenly transformed into a keeper without any warning, wanting strings and emotions and full disclosure. Not in a million years was he signing up for that.

Nevertheless, the attrition of serious relationships had his rotation down to none, and he had a strong suspicion that Ivan, his police detective and possible backup, had found a guy he was getting serious about.

Rick certainly didn't expect to find anything tonight. He wasn't here for sex, but if some found him in this sea of hard male flesh, he sure as shit wouldn't say no.

The song changed to one with a slower beat. If he'd had any serious prospects, he'd have taken the opportunity to grind up against a groin or ass. Touch palms to pecs or the sweaty curve of a lower back. Perhaps even slide a finger under a waistband, seeking haven between taut, muscular buttocks.

Instead, he chose to indulge another craving and headed to the bar.

The bartender appeared in front of him in a gratifyingly short time.

"What'll you have?" The man smiled appreciatively, but Rick had learned long ago not to trust the interest of either bartenders or strippers. Not when they were on the clock.

What would he have? Beer, beer or beer? Rick waved at the amber bottle his neighbor was drinking from.

"That will be fine."

"He certainly is fine." The bartender winked. "Oooh. The beer. Got it."

A comedian. A bad one. Rick barely suppressed an eye roll and placed some cash on the bar. He picked up the beer and moved away to stand by the wall.

He grimaced after a sip. Beer wasn't his drink at all, but given the average age of the young men dancing, he didn't imagine the wine cellar at Anaconda would be worth trying to expand his wine palate.

Probably should have gotten water.

"Rick!"

Turning, he saw Jon walking toward him, all fetished up in his leather harness and skintight leather pants. Pants he suspected most of the clientele would have to subsist on ramen for a month to be able to afford. A far cry from the tailored suits Jon wore to work every day, and Rick couldn't decide which one made his friend look hotter.

"Yummy." Rick ran a finger across Jon's abs. "You look amazing. Just as good as when we met."

Jon preened and Rick didn't blame him. Jon was a year older than he was, but when Rick had first met him, he'd been stripping at the same club where Rick had been bartending. Neither of them was a waifish skinny twink; both were built more like competitive swimmers. With similar height, build, haircut and color, they looked enough alike that the owner had tried to convince them to do a regular show together to capitalize on the whole twincest thing, but Rick had never wanted to strip. Even without stripping, he and Jon had played up the resemblance enough to entertain the clients. The tips had been… healthy.

Strangely enough, it was their resemblance that had cemented their friendship, because Jon hadn't wanted to fuck his "twin" and neither had Rick. Without any real lust for each other to complicate matters, Jon had become the first real friend Rick had had when he moved away from home.

"What are you doing drinking beer? I made sure they ordered in the supplies for your mangoritas."

He pouted. Mangos were awesome, especially when they were used in margaritas. "I'm sort of off tequila right now. But that was very sweet of you, honey." He kissed Jon's cheek and got an armful of half-naked Jon hugging him.

They both pretended the sudden stir of interest in the area had nothing to do with them. Rick grinned at Jon before licking a broad, slow stripe from the rounded curve of Jon's shoulder to his earlobe. Jon shivered and several guys groaned. As the air thickened with pheromones, a couple of the onlookers pressed hands to their groins as other things thickened too. Men. All the same.

"Naughty, naughty," Jon whispered in his ear, looking for all the world like he was nibbling at Rick's ear. Warm breath coasting over the sensitive skin just under his ear gave Rick a little shiver of his own, and even in the moist humidity of the club, his nipples peaked.

"This isn't why you invited me?" Contrary to appearances, Jon wasn't at Anaconda to troll for guys. He'd recently invested in the club and had asked him and a few other friends to stop by and check the place out. Well, he'd also asked the rest of their group of friends, when they'd been painting Davy's place last weekend, but Davy and Kurt were still recovering from a lot of shit. Rick didn't think Kurt had ever been to a gay club, and he so wanted to be able to observe Kurt's first time.

"Well, it doesn't hurt." Jon winked.

Yeah, if someone started a rumor that one of the new owners was…. Rick laughed. He didn't mind Jon indulging in a little harmless promo.

"You here alone? What about Davy and Kurt?" Jon peered around as he asked, like more people would suddenly materialize behind Rick.

"You didn't think I'd bring a date, did you, darling? You know I don't do that. And the lovebirds are engrossed in the new release of some game."

Kurt probably wasn't much of a clubber anyway, and Davy was more than happy to stay home and suck his dick while Kurt played *Call of Duty* or whatever was the current geek special. Not that Rick wasn't geeky, but his own brand of geek didn't often involve video games.

"Of course. Doesn't matter. You're the most important one."

He was? "I am?"

"Yeah, idiot. You've been in more clubs than anyone I know. You're the one I trust to assess this place, see if I need to change anything."

Rick laughed. It was rare anyone wanted him in clubs for anything besides his hand job proficiency. "What kind of remuneration can I expect?"

"What? I can't hear you over the music." Jon cupped his ear.

"Bullshit." But Rick laughed anyway. He'd only been teasing about recompense.

One of the bartenders made a beeline for them, and from the pinched look on his face, Rick didn't think they'd just run out of maraschino cherries. "Looks like you gotta work. I'll look around, catch up with you later."

He smacked Jon on the ass, a satisfying thwack with leather-amplified sound. Jon squeaked, glaring at him before putting on his "I'm respectable and in charge" face and slipping through the ring of observers that had surrounded them.

"Show's over, kids. Come back at midnight." Rick shooed them away, even the few that took a step toward him, lustful promises on their faces. As beautiful as they were, he'd spent the last week thinking far too often about Ian. The man knew his way around a dick. Several times he considered asking Davy for Ian's number, but even if Ian wasn't a keeper, he didn't think getting involved with Kurt's brother would do wonders for the group dynamic. Kurt fit in with their friends, despite his jockish tendencies, but if something went wrong between him and Ian, Rick didn't want to fuck up his friendships. He had no family and never intended to have a relationship. His friends were it.

Rick slipped away from the group who'd been hoping he and Jon were going to strip and go at it right there on Anaconda's floor. If he were going to screw someone tonight, he'd rather not *know* they were picturing him and Jon together.

On the other side of the dance floor, he leaned against the wall to finish his beer. There was a time when he'd head out onto the dance floor with a drink, but he wasn't going to add a potential safety liability to Jon's new investment. The view from this side was just as good, but irritatingly he found himself searching for dark hair and light eyes. There was no call for that sort of emotional nonsense.

He made room for a couple seeking the shadows beside him. In his peripheral vision, he noticed one of them drop to his knees and in moments, even over the deafening din of music and shouted conversation, the guy's moans were audible. In fact, Rick could easily pretend he heard a wet sucking, and his pants constricted. Enough of this wallowing. He'd never had a problem finding someone to get him off and tonight he'd prove that to himself.

After downing the last of his beer, he set it on a nearby ledge, whipped off his shirt, and dove back into the undulating throng.

RICK smiled up at a large red-haired guy. Muscular, sexy, and judging by the hard length pushing against his stomach, hung. Some guys didn't like the gingers, but Rick was an equal opportunity player. He rubbed up against the guy, but wasn't quite tempted to leave the dance floor to find a secluded area.

He let the music take him and soon ended up dancing with another sexy guy, this one a slim Asian guy with bleached blond hair. Again, he enjoyed dancing, teasing, touching, but despite the obvious invitation, he didn't allow himself to be led off. This time, the guy shrugged and danced away, leaving Rick on his own. He really must be getting old, because neither of those guys, as cute as they were, looked nearly old enough to be drinking. Orgasm with a side of dirty old man? No, thank you. Definitely not what he wanted out of the evening. Hell, he might have to booty call one of his ex–fuck buddies in the hopes they wanted a simple, no-strings night.

Closing his eyes, he danced, trying to decide if he should give in and call Oscar. No, that would be a mistake. Worse than calling Davy to get Ian's number. He ought to just consider the evening a favor for a friend and leave it at that. Go home, let his right hand provide satisfaction, and get some sleep.

The song changed and he paused for a moment. Before he could turn to head toward the door, a pair of strong hands slid around his waist, pulling him flush against warm, shirtless skin. The man behind him, though taller, was closer to Rick's height than most of the other guys who'd demonstrated interest tonight. His shoulders were broad enough to make Rick feel oddly safe and comforted while he ground his bum against a nice hard cock. This guy fit just about perfectly with Rick.

He brought his hands up to caress a pair of lightly furred, veined forearms, and he wrapped his own arms around them, tucking them closer to his belly.

They swayed together, the chin of his faceless suitor tucked into the curve of his neck. Like Jon had done, this guy nuzzled the soft skin under Rick's ear. Unlike with Jon, his cock filled and pushed against the fly of his pants. Faceless guy extricated one of his hands and slid it down Rick's sweat-slicked belly, fingers teasing at a treasure trail that Rick knew could be felt more than seen with his blond fuzz.

An index finger slid under Rick's waistband, fingernail barely grazing the sensitive slit at the tip of his penis. Rick groaned and let his head fall back against that strong shoulder. This was what he'd been searching for all night.

"I'm Steve, and I love your ass," the guy whispered in Rick's ear before his lips moved to Rick's neck and sucked. Rick's pulse sped up and he wiggled, trying to get his erection more contact with a hand that wasn't his own.

"Hello, Steve." Rick tried to put some of his normal flirty flounce into his words, but this guy had gotten him too hot, too fast. His tone was nothing more than a throaty invitation to take him. He was almost ready to offer his ass up in the bathroom, and it had been years since he'd wanted that from a club bunny.

Rick turned in Steve's arms, hoping for some face-to-face action before they took this into a shadowy corner. He enjoyed a strong grip on his ass almost as much as a firm hand on his cock.

He slid his hands up into Steve's dark hair, tugging a little to pull his head back.

Slumberous blue eyes widened in sudden recognition as Rick tugged sharply at the hair still caught in his fist. That tiny flare of eyelids was Rick's only indication that Ian truly hadn't realized he'd been doing his best to fuck someone he already knew. The shock of seeing Ian hadn't diminished Rick's erection any; he was primed to blow. How the fuck had his body recognized Ian's touch, Ian's smell?

Nevertheless, the unexpected but not entirely unwelcome sight of Ian allowed him to put a playful, teasing note in his words, hand still twisted in Ian's dark hair, holding him exactly where Rick wanted him.

"Steve, darling. My name is… Kurt." Rick didn't give him any time to react to the fake name before he tilted Ian's head and gave him the same lick from shoulder to ear he'd given Jon earlier. Again, the move was far more explosive than any teasing he'd done with Jon, and when Ian moaned, he shivered with power.

"You little shit," Ian hissed. Rick couldn't contain a cackle.

"I take it you don't intend to call out my name when you come?" They hadn't stepped apart, and Rick thrust his hips into Ian's. Shock hadn't deflated him, nor had Rick's calculated choice of fake name.

Ian pressed him up against one of the posts that lined the dance floor. There was heated, sweaty skin on either side of him, but Rick couldn't take his eyes off Ian. He did, however, pull his hand out of Ian's hair, in favor of sliding it across Ian's hard nipple.

"Why ever not, Steve?" Rick gave special emphasis to the name Steve. "It's a short, easy name."

"Hell no."

Ian might not call him Kurt, even in the interest of role-playing, but he wasn't truly upset. Not if the hardness pressing into Rick's belly was any indication. Rick wasn't upset either. Keepers rarely went looking for a nameless fuck in bars. Which meant it should be okay if Rick added Ian to his roster. Exactly as Rick had wanted.

"No? Please, Steve, oh please…," Rick begged like he was almost ready to beg for some relief, amused at the disgruntled expression on Ian's face.

"Fucking hell, Rick," Ian muttered before he grabbed Rick's face and swooped in for a bruising kiss.

All of Rick's muscles froze into stunned immobility. He didn't do this. Didn't kiss. Not even during his frantic fuck with Ian last weekend.

Ian used tongue and lips to gain entrance to Rick's mouth, tongue sweeping in to plunder. Rick fed Ian a little moan and his muscles moved, but they didn't obey his brain. Instead, he kissed Ian back, the last thing he intended but almost the only thing he wanted at the moment.

Until Ian's perfectly timed hip thrusts, matched in rhythm with the thorough tongue fucking he delivered to Rick, sensitized Rick's dick almost to the point of no return.

Panicked, he pulled his lips away and pushed at Ian's shoulders. "Wait, wait."

"What?" Ian's lips, puffy from their assault on Rick's face, looked even more delicious than they had mere moments ago.

"I'm not coming in my pants like…." Rick was going to use the teenager analogy, but given they were surrounded by guys who were at least a decade younger than either of them, dirty old man was more apropos than ever. "Like... I'm just not." Although if Ian didn't stop looking so sexy, Rick might have to whip it out right here and spill on the dance floor.

"Then come home with me." Ian's blue eyes implored him in a way that made Rick nervous, but that didn't change how much he wanted to say yes.

He'd only had one beer, so it must be the lust fizzling through his veins, clouding his judgment.

"Okay."

Ian kissed him again quickly before grabbing his hand and leading him out of the club.

RICK didn't even have time to regret getting in the car with Ian again. Ian's place was surprisingly close to Anaconda; being near Boystown had to make it easy for Ian to get laid without worrying overmuch about being outed. On the flip side, he also didn't have time to find out how coming out to his family had gone. Or anything else about him, which was worrisome that he even wanted to know.

The need for words became secondary to pleasure as Ian pushed him against the wall in his condo. Like last week, their time out in public had fed the lust, magnifying it. Dancing made it even more intense for Rick because there were so many pheromones in the air at the club. He was ready to pop, and from all signs, Ian was ready to repeat the previous week's sexual frenzy.

Then Ian did the most unexpected thing. He stepped back from Rick, just an inch or two, and stared into Rick's eyes. Weren't they going to fuck?

Ian grinned, as though he could hear Rick's question, and swooped down, taking his mouth with all the skill and aggression he'd shown in the club. A moan vibrated his chest, but Ian's lips and tongue muffled the sound.

Rick was unsure how to proceed, because he really didn't kiss guys. Not on the mouth. Not like Ian was dying of thirst in a desert and Rick's mouth the only source of water. He wiggled his hips, hoping for some cock-on-cock contact before he expired of terminal hard-on.

Pulse racing, he pulled his head away. "Are you getting some sick sort of pleasure from torturing me? Touch me already. Or fuck me. That'll do too."

This time, Ian's grin was positively feral as he splayed his hands on either side of Rick's face. "I am touching you. Just enjoy."

Having been prepared to answer some flippant comment about bossy bottoms, he stood there stunned, again, while Ian sealed their mouths together. Having Ian's fingers moving over his cheeks made the experience even more intimate and erotic, in a way Rick had never known. He sensed—and how, he wasn't sure—that Ian had no intention of repeating their quick sex, no matter how much Rick cajoled or demanded. Under normal circumstances, he'd assume the guy was playing games with him and he'd just leave, but this wasn't game playing. This was something different.

Hard and aching, he wanted nothing more than to strip their pants away and hump until he spurted, but he let Ian's mood infect him and he dug his fingers into Ian's shoulder instead of his waistband.

Rick had sucked a number of cocks in his lifetime and the skills he learned on cocks had to be transferable to mouths; he wasn't content to remain passive in this unusual encounter. Ian's quick breaths heated the skin of his cheek, and the moans he wrung from Ian gave him more pleasure than just about any blow job he'd ever given.

With glacial speed, they made their way to the bedroom, fused together at the mouth. When Ian pulled his mouth free to guide Rick to the bed, a bereft whimper welled up in his throat, but he managed to swallow it before it escaped. He didn't know how long they'd kissed, but it had been a long fucking time and his lips tingled at the sudden lack of pressure. Ian's lips were puffed and pink and when he licked them, Rick couldn't stand the distance any more.

Grabbing Ian's head, Rick pulled him back and starting kissing him. Ian didn't resist one bit, but instead of touching his face, Ian moved his hands down to Rick's waistband. This time, there was no disguising the whimper. God, he needed to come so bad.

By the time Ian flicked open his fly, the front of Rick's skimpy briefs were already soaked with precum. Ian yanked his pants and briefs off, leaving Rick naked, since he'd lost his shirt somewhere between the club and Ian's car.

"Naked." This time, Ian obeyed Rick's demand and stripped himself quickly and ruthlessly. Rick scooted back on the bed, but before he could ask if they should get out the lube, Ian sealed his kiss-swollen lips around one of Rick's nipples and sucked. Strongly. Rick arched and groaned, trying desperately to get some friction on his cock. Without even trying, he knew wrapping his own hand around his cock wasn't on Ian's agenda.

Ian moved to the other nipple, first kissing it before closing his teeth gently around it. This was it. Rick was going to die of torture by mouth.

His heart thundered and he was just about ready to beg again when Ian moved swiftly and opened his mouth around the crown of Rick's cock, completely stealing his breath.

Ian slid down his length, swallowing him down in one small movement, and undulated his tongue against the vein on the underside of Rick's cock. His breath returned and he yelled as he exploded on Ian's tongue. He wanted to reciprocate, but his vision had grayed from the force of his orgasm, and he could only lie there, paralyzed, while Ian laid himself full length against Rick's body and rutted. A final kiss, flavored with Rick's cum, was enough to send Ian spurting between them.

Rick must have dozed for a few moments, because the next thing he knew, he was cum-free and tucked up beside Ian, who'd turned on the television. Maybe if he'd been aware when Ian shifted them into such a cozy position he could have found the energy to grab his pants and leave, but he was oddly content to lie naked next to Ian, watching reruns.

RICK slid down the wall in the hallway outside Ian's condo and sat on the carpet to put his shoes on. This was getting to be a habit and not a good one.

He'd made those rules for a reason. A damn fine one. Now he'd broken both the sleeping one and the transportation one twice in as many weekends, as well as thoroughly ignoring the no-kissing rule. *Thoroughly.*

Once again, he'd managed to awaken early enough to sneak out of Ian's before most anyone was up and about to witness his stealthy departure, but in the face of Ian-induced orgasms he was so fucking weak.

Stepping out into the early morning dawn, he shivered and walked to the same bus station bench he'd called a cab from last weekend. At least he had his keys and could take a taxi right to his car, since wandering around shirtless in skintight pants screamed "walk of shame," if it didn't scream "sexual predator." Neither of which was a goal for a respected speech-language pathologist with a thriving practice. Be worse if he had to break into his house—again—looking like he'd been ravished.

He ran a gentle finger over his lips. Although he hadn't taken the time to check them out in the mirror, they felt like Ian's had looked after their marathon make-out session. Kissing for hours was like some particularly sadistic edging game, and when Ian had finally sucked him, he'd come so hard he'd almost blacked out.

Which only meant kissing was as dangerous and intimate as he'd believed when he'd made his rules, but at the same time, he thought he might not object if Ian was keen on doing that again.

Then, surprisingly, they'd lain on the bed and watched reruns of *Friends* and *Robot Chicken*. He'd been amazed that their sense of humor had been in sync. Ian had wrapped an arm around Rick, and they'd fallen asleep like that. Rick had woken up in the exact same position, and it hadn't been easy to extricate himself without waking Ian.

Shit.

He scrubbed his face with a hand. During a commercial, Ian had mentioned exchanging phone numbers, but they'd fallen asleep before Rick had had to decide if he wanted to do that. Even now, as much as he wanted to have another night like this one, the thought of exchanging numbers with Ian made his breath come short as his throat closed in panic.

Not like he was going to go back and ask for a number now. Nor was he going to ask Davy. He'd chalk it up to his subconscious protecting him from a guy with keeper tendencies. Awesome night, but not seeing Ian again was safer. Rick could get used to Ian's brand of fucking all too easily, but he wasn't going to get caught by a keeper in a player's thong. No way.

The cab pulled up, and unbelievably, it was the same cabbie as the previous weekend. Fuck. There was no mistaking that look. That pitying look.

This couldn't happen again. Ian couldn't happen again.

THE line at the café was longer than normal, but Ian didn't care if he was late to work. Getting spectacularly laid did wonders for his mood. Rick may have run out on him—again—but there was no denying it was the hottest sex he'd ever had. Ever. Some of that Ian could attribute to the newness factor of having a guy in his bed, but Rick just did it for him. They fit together so well, but he hadn't even gotten the man's number yet. He would. Of course he would. He'd just have to be patient.

His phone buzzed and he glanced at the line. Probably enough time to grab a call without being rude to the barista at the counter, especially since it was the cute twink today. Pulling it out, he saw Kurt's name flash on the screen. He frowned and answered.

"Hey, Kurt. Is everything okay?"

"Yeah, why?" There was no mistaking Kurt's confusion.

"It's just early for you to be calling me, is all." Ian injected a bit of levity into his tone. "I didn't think slackers like you got up before noon."

"Ha, ha. Years from now, people are probably going remember the time I got shot as those weeks I was *slacking*. Besides, I'm hoping to go back to work soon, so I'm trying to get back into a regular sleep schedule."

"Okay, but it's still early for you to be calling, whether there's something wrong or not."

"Davy gave me shit about forgetting to call you this weekend, so I wanted to catch you before work."

"Whoa. Davy gave you shit. Never thought I'd see the day when…."

"Oh shut up." But there was no heat or ire in Kurt's voice, as he'd known there wouldn't be. It was such a relief to fall back into the comfortable friendship with his brother, stronger now than ever, thanks to their secrets being bared to each other. "Are you coming or not?"

If it weren't for how publicly he was having this conversation, he might have said something dirty to the opening Kurt had given him. "Coming to what?"

"My housewarming. Saturday."

"You're having a housewarming on Saturday?"

"Yes, we invited everyone at the painting party… oh, wait, that's right. You snuck out with Rick before we could invite you too. You work fast, bro."

Damn. Kurt wasn't going to let him forget that, was he? But he wasn't ready to admit how much he'd thought about Rick since then. That was a secret Kurt didn't need to know. Not yet, anyway. Instead, he tried to divert his attention.

"Lots of practice, bro, lots of practice. I could give you some details."

His brother fake-retched into the phone. "Don't you fucking dare. Just show up on Saturday, okay?"

"Sure thing." Ian paused for a moment, but there was no way he could ask Kurt now if Rick was also going to be there. He'd just have to go and hope. Even if Rick didn't go, now that he and Kurt were talking again, there would be other events to find Rick.

"Good." Kurt disconnected the call, and with two people still in line in front of Ian, he let himself think about how he might ease Rick's skittishness. It would be a challenge, since he'd never faced such a problem before.

Someone sidled up beside him and nudged his elbow, disrupting a very explicit vignette, and he scowled at the newcomer.

"Hey, Ian."

"Oh, hey, Leon." Ian tamped down his irritation. He shouldn't be thinking about Rick naked anyway. Last thing he needed was to go into work with a boner. Or to give the cute barista the wrong idea. "How are you?"

"Good, good. You mind if I get in here with you? The line is…." Leon waved a hand at the line of people behind Ian.

Ian shuffled a bit and smiled at his new friend. "Did you have a good weekend?"

"Not as good as you did, I bet." A raised brow accompanied Leon's suggestive tone.

What the hell was that supposed to mean? "Um…."

"I saw you at Anaconda. I wouldn't have thought that was your type of place, but you seemed to find a guy just fine."

Oh holy hell. Despite the fact he knew other gay guys worked at *Errant*, he'd dreaded the day someone saw him at a club. At least he'd actually come out before it happened, although he hadn't much been intending to make it common knowledge at work.

"Yes, well." The person in front of them departed and Leon stepped up to order. Ian hadn't quite tamed his blush by the time the barista took his order, and this time, there seemed to be a little extra heat in the guy's smile, which only made Ian's blush worse.

"Sorry, man, we don't have to talk about it, but if you ever want company, give me a call, eh?"

Ian had no idea how to respond. He'd never gone to clubs with anyone before. How would that work, exactly? Besides, it wasn't really his scene anymore. He didn't know for sure, but he suspected finding dates at Anaconda would have been harder than picking up a straight man there. And he was starting to think he might have outgrown the anonymous fuck stage of his life. Before he could formulate a response for Leon, the guy had already barreled on.

"I'm supposed to work with one of the senior editors this week. Avery. Do you know her? Got any tips?"

Ian let out a small sigh of relief as they headed to the office. This was far more comfortable territory for a guy who'd spent most of his life in hiding. He wanted a gay friend, but letting himself open up to one would have to be a work in progress.

"Avery's great. She's a real hard-ass when it comes to work, and always has an eye for which stories will generate the most attention, but if you listen to her, you'll learn a lot."

Leon grimaced faintly and Ian laughed. "Don't worry. She can also be a lot of fun. But trust me, you do your best work for her and she'll treat you right."

The elevator opened, depositing them on their floor.

"Thanks, I'll keep that in mind." Leon saluted with his coffee cup and darted in the opposite direction of Ian's office.

Ian smiled. He wasn't sure if this would end up being a friendship or a mentorship, but he felt good about it, nonetheless.

CHAPTER
Four

RICK toweled off and stared at himself in the mirror. He didn't look too bad. Still pretty hot. But what was he going to wear tonight? It had to be good.

God. He had to shake off this freakish insecurity. And the butterflies in his belly had to give it a rest. Yes, he was hoping Ian would be at the housewarming, as much as he was hoping Ian wouldn't be there. This wasn't the first time he'd arranged a fuck buddy before; there was no reason for all this anxiety. Most of which seemed centered around Rick's fear that Ian would turn him down. Stupid, really. It was just sex. Great, awesome, possibly stupendous sex, but nothing more. If Ian said no, there'd be other guys, even if Rick was having difficulty finding them lately.

Maybe he hadn't been fair to Oscar. After all, Rick hadn't had an actual rotation in a few months. It had only been Oscar, sporadically, for the past few months.

Perhaps, to Oscar, it had resembled a relationship. Still, after the guy got some much-needed sleep, he'd realize he'd been misconstruing things. Rick didn't know how people became doctors when their trial by fire included months or years of sleep deprivation almost to the point of torture.

Not that Oscar's schedule mattered to him anymore. Shit. He still hadn't found out what Ian did for a living. Too much to hope for that he'd be in a uniformed career; the uniforms did turn his crank. Rick snorted. Ian hardly needed any help in that department. But Ian's schedule would be of interest. He seemed to have weekends off, which was much easier to deal with than shift work. He had to make sure he looked as hot as he could tonight, all the better to tip the scales in his favor. If Ian was drooling, there wasn't a chance he'd say no to Rick's proposition.

A faint banging sound snagged his attention from contemplating all things Ian. Was that the basement? He shivered a bit. Maybe he should get a cat, so he could blame any weird noises on it. Still, his basement window didn't latch properly and as he well knew, a person could wiggle into it.

After tying the towel securely around his waist, he detoured to his closet and grabbed a baseball bat. He spared a second to consider flip flops. The basement floor was concrete and fucking cold, but if he was trying to sneak, he wasn't going to do it while sounding like a guy getting spanked at fetish night.

Ears alert for anything out of the ordinary, Rick crept downstairs. It wasn't even dark out, so he wasn't particularly scared, but more like… cautious. Because the last thing he wanted to do was come home after Kurt's housewarming, buzzed and possibly with Ian in tow, to find his house had been robbed.

He also really hoped he wasn't going to have to report a break-in like this.

There were no sounds out of the ordinary for an average Saturday evening, but that didn't stop the tiny chill of apprehension from raising goose bumps on his nape when he stepped into the basement.

After checking a few places where someone could hide, of which there weren't many in his basement, he headed right for the broken window. There was something on the floor below it.

He leaned over and pushed it with the end of the bat before he shrieked and jumped back. A squirrel. A dead squirrel. This time, the shiver became a full-blown shudder. At least it was stiff, so it had probably been some roadkill that one of the neighborhood kids thought would make a good joke. At least he hoped so. Surely Oscar hadn't been that mad about their "breakup."

Nevertheless, the squirrel had to go. Now.

Grabbing a broom and dustpan, he considered if he should throw it in the garbage, but his garbage pickup wasn't until Tuesday. There was no help for it. He was going to have to get dressed, take the squirrel out… somewhere. The public trash can two streets over or the patch of shrubbery at the back of the house. Then he was going to have to disinfect that patch of floor and shower—again.

Next week, he was fixing that window.

RICK'S finger hesitated over the doorbell. Then he shook himself. Ian shouldn't have any power over him. He was already here earlier than he'd planned, but he wasn't sure if that was because he was hoping to avoid Ian or to make sure he didn't miss him. Or if the squirrel intrusion had just plain freaked him out.

Fuck. This was a party and if nothing else, he was good at parties.

Grabbing the handle, he swung open the door and waltzed right into Davy's house.

There were a few people milling about in the living room, but he didn't know any of them. An odd disconcerting sensation bloomed in his stomach. Relief. It had to be relief.

He strode directly for the kitchen, because that's where Davy would be. Hell, Davy might even spend most of the party in the kitchen, futzing with appetizers and drink mixers. Slaving at their painting party two weeks ago had definitely made a difference. The kitchen, with its brand-new lemon tones, was sunny and welcoming, even though it was getting dark outside.

"Darling, you look awesome."

Davy turned at his words and smiled. "Hey, Rick. I wasn't expecting you this early. Guess you've got a hot prospect tonight, eh?"

A frown wanted to form on Rick's face, but he kept his pleasant smile pasted on. Did his friends really think of him that way? Davy had spent ten years in a hyper-isolated relationship with a closeted cop so terrified of coming out that he'd practically kept Davy under lock and key, the last few years of which included never seeing his friends. When the guy died, Davy had found them again, and they'd come together almost like they'd never been on hiatus. Rick had been so pleased Davy had not only found someone new but laid down the law about hiding—as in, he wasn't going to do it. This housewarming was more a celebration of that than simply Kurt moving in. Did they think he was too shallow to understand that?

"No, hon. Not at all. I simply didn't want to miss a single crab puff." Rick grabbed one off the carefully arranged plate Davy held and popped it in his mouth.

Then again, if he kept saying things like that, no wonder everyone thought he was nothing more than a two-dimensional club boy.

He took the plate from Davy and set it on the counter. "Listen, hon, I know I'm rarely serious. And I know I've never said this to you, but I'm so damn proud of you. As far as I'm concerned, this isn't a housewarming, this is about strength. Your strength to stand up for yourself and get the relationship you want and deserve. Kurt's strength in doing the right thing in coming out, even though he was scared. Even though he thought he'd already lost you."

Davy blinked at him, eyes suddenly shiny. Rick found he needed a few extra blinks himself to see past the unexpected blurring of his vision.

"You're right." Davy threw his arms around Rick and they hugged. He didn't have many friends and losing touch with Davy had left a pretty gaping hole in his life.

Rick graciously ignored Davy's sniff and quickly wiped his eyes with the back of his hand before he let Davy go. "Probably I should have become a psychologist. Be easier to say stuff like this."

He'd certainly thought about it. But at the time he'd needed help, a speech-language pathologist—or more correctly, a student—had been the only one willing and able to help him. As a gesture of gratitude, he'd gone into the same line of work, although he was mature enough now to realize psychology might have been more useful. He did like helping people, though. Made the career choice worthwhile.

Davy cocked his head and opened his mouth, but footsteps interrupted. Actually, Rick had been surprised it had been just the two of them in the kitchen for this long, but it was still early. Once people got their initial introductions out of the way, they'd spread out.

"Hey, Rick."

Rick turned to Kurt, intending to say something outrageous. The man didn't fluster—much—but he did love seeing Davy come to his aid.

Instead, though, he looked at Kurt, and couldn't speak. It wasn't hard to imagine Ian's dark hair and light-blue eyes taking the place of Kurt's auburn hair and dark-blue eyes. Which sent his mind leaping all over the place, imagining Kurt doing the intimate, exciting things to him that Ian had. He wasn't nearly as attracted to Kurt as he'd thought at first, and their bodies were shaped differently, but he couldn't help but feel almost like he'd fucked Kurt, and the sensation was so disconcerting it had stolen his voice.

How in the hell did people actually fuck brothers, either at the same time or serially? Rick was weirded out in a way he never expected.

The looks of concern he got from both Kurt and Davy were impetus enough to push a few words out. "Uh, hi, Kurt."

Judging by the frown drawing Kurt's brows together, Rick hadn't managed to display even a modicum of his usual flair.

A hot, fiery flush lit up his cheeks as he suddenly wondered if Kurt's dick was built along the same lines as Ian's. Then he flushed even hotter, because Rick never got embarrassed about sex. Never. He'd mentally undressed Kurt and imagined them fucking every time they'd hung out, although he would never, ever do such a thing in real life. Not to Davy. Not even if Kurt and Davy broke up. His friendships were more important than sex with anyone. But not once, not until he'd gone home with Ian after meeting him at Anaconda, had he ever felt awkward.

Davy nudged his shoulder. "You okay?"

No, he didn't think so. "I just need a drink. Long day." Not a lie. This was the one Saturday a month he saw clients and it was always packed from start to finish, with barely time to breathe in between, never mind necessities like eating or pissing. If it had been anyone besides Davy—or perhaps Jon—he would have declined the invitation, because a Saturday client day drained him like few things could. The dead squirrel hadn't helped either.

Kurt nodded. "Sure thing. We've got more of that wine you and Davy polished off a couple of weeks ago. Davy said you were off tequila."

The blush had started to recede, but Kurt's words made it return. There was no recrimination in Kurt's tone, only amusement. But he'd been here drinking that day because of Ian.

"Super. Is it in the fridge? I can get it." But Kurt blocked him and bent into the fridge to get the bottle. Like a train wreck, Rick couldn't help but stare at Kurt's ass, and speculate and compare and….

"Got a glass?"

Rick jumped at the unexpected question. He hadn't even noticed Kurt standing up and turning around. Nor had he noticed Davy leaving the kitchen.

Kurt stepped closer and leaned into him. Rick pressed back into the counter and peered frantically over Kurt's shoulder, both praying for and dreading a rescue, but entirely unable to force his muscles to obey a command to escape. Surely Kurt wasn't…. Davy would never forgive him, never speak to him again.

Rick stared up at Kurt, confused, afraid, and flustered as all hell, when suddenly Kurt smirked and pulled back, presenting Rick with the wine glass he'd retrieved from the shelf above Rick's head.

Relief flooded him so strongly his knees weakened. Grabbing the glass with his right hand, he used his left to clutch at the counter, keeping himself upright.

He congratulated himself on exhibiting nothing more than a faint tremor that didn't affect Kurt's pour one bit.

Like he knew Rick was going to drain the glass dry the second his back was turned, Kurt smiled and set the open wine bottle on the counter next to Rick's white-knuckled left hand.

Kurt gestured at a dish of hummus and chips on the kitchen table. "Bring that out with you, will you? I've got a bunch of beers to get."

Back in the fridge for almost no time at all, Kurt pulled out several beer bottles and left Rick alone in the kitchen.

He tossed back the entire glass of wine like he was at a fraternity beer-chugging competition and breathed deeply, letting the booze settle his shakiness. This was all Ian's fault. When the hell had good sex fucked with his head as much or more than any other body part? Rick knew Ian and Kurt's two other brothers weren't gay, but he was hoping to meet them tonight. See if he had a similar reaction to them. Maybe it was nothing more than having a tiny crush on Kurt, followed up by having amazing sex with a brother that closely resembled him. That had to be it. There wasn't anything special about Ian O'Donnell.

That determination didn't stop him from pouring the rest of the wine into his glass, leaving the liquid a mere millimeter or two away from the lip.

He'd just picked up the glass, bringing it near enough to his mouth that the fruity scent of the Chardonnay tickled his nose, when an older woman walked in. She was a little plump, but she had a cheery, serene face, almost like Mrs. Claus. She bore enough of a resemblance to both Ian and Kurt that there wasn't much doubt as to her identity.

"Well, hello, honey." She inspected him from head to toe, and Rick considered the possibility of playing dead. This was shaping up to be the worst night ever. "You must be Rick."

How had she known that? Rick opened his mouth, but nothing came out. It was high school all over again. His heart hammered as sweat popped out on his upper lip.

"I'm Deirdre O'Donnell." She smiled her sweet smile, but Rick knew how easy it was for those motherly types to show fake smiles and speak poisoned words to a world that only saw sugar and honey.

He managed a nod, his larynx paralyzed.

"My son described you perfectly. A hot, outrageous blond." Her grin got wicked. "I very much like your shirt."

Rick glanced down, relieved he wasn't totally naked, although he was wearing a tailored burgundy dress shirt made out of sheer, transparent fabric, tucked into pants tight enough to read the veins on his cock like a phrenologist. He'd even put on some eye makeup this evening, smudgy black and sparkly burgundy to accentuate his clothing. But in the crosshairs of the O'Donnell matriarch, he was lucky to remember his own name, he was so fucking freaked out. Sweat continued to form on his face and under his armpits.

"Oh, there's the hummus." The wily Mrs. O'Donnell grabbed the dish Rick had been told to bring to the living room. "My Sean's been asking. Loves the stuff, he does."

She pinched his cheek before she left. "We'll chat later."

Rick stood and trembled in the wake of Kurt's... Ian's mother. This time his hand shook so bad, wine sloshed out and onto the floor.

Damn, damn, double damn. Instead of grabbing a paper towel, he took a deep breath. Several deep breaths. Dealing with doting mothers—real or fake—through his work was one thing. He was able to mentally prepare for each one. Stupidly, he should have expected Kurt's parents to show up at the housewarming, but he hadn't prepared, not at all, and he'd been thrown back to that awful time in high school where he'd been incapable of speaking to anyone at all.

He raised the glass and took a swallow before setting it carefully on the counter. He sang a few bars of a simple nursery rhyme, an exercise he'd been given when his voice had started to return. Hearing himself vocalize put his emotions on a more even keel, and he finally grabbed some paper towels to wipe up the spill.

It wasn't until he was squatting down, wiping at the floor, that he remembered what Mrs. O'Donnell said about him.

Which son had told his mother Rick was hot?

RICK smoothed his hands over his shirt and took a deep breath. In, out. Again. He couldn't hide out in the kitchen all goddamn night.

He'd be able to avoid Kurt's parents. They were older. Surely they wouldn't stay too long.

Picking up his glass of wine, he pasted on a smile and strode into the living room as though he was the choicest piece of prime man candy.

No one stopped and stared when he stepped into the room. No one pointed and laughed. Everything was so painfully normal, the tight tension around his chest eased. He quickly scoped out the room, making careful note of where Mrs. O'Donnell laughed with a younger woman who bore enough resemblance to Kurt that she must be one of the sisters.

Wearing a cloak of insouciance, Rick moved to the exact opposite corner of the room as though that were exactly where he'd wanted to be. Then he blinked. A familiar and unexpected man stood just meters away, his arm wrapped around a pretty young thing that called to mind the sea of newly legal man flesh at Anaconda.

Rick squealed in pure pleasure. "Ivan, I didn't know you'd be here!"

Ivan lifted his eyes from the rapt contemplation of the twinkie in his arms, and his eyes lit with recognition.

"Rick? How are you?"

He hugged the man who could have had a star position in his roster if it weren't for the fact he'd been a keeper through and through. Rick eyed Ivan's boyfriend, although he couldn't quite remember the guy's name. Parker, he thought, but it wasn't as though they'd actually been introduced. Rick didn't want a relationship for himself, but if that's what Ivan wanted, he deserved the best. Was this kid mature enough to give his friend what he needed to be happy?

"I guess you know Kurt, right?"

Ivan was gorgeous, muscular, and warm, and Rick was enjoying the comfort of being held by someone who cared for him but didn't expect anything at all in return. Parker's darkly jealous looks gave him a guilty pleasure too. Nice to know a cutie like Parker could feel threatened by his almost-over-the-hill ass.

"Yes, I know Kurt. We're going to be in the same department when I go back to work. How do you know Kurt?"

Made sense that Ivan knew Kurt. After all, there couldn't be that many gay police detectives in Toronto, could there? And if there were more, how did Rick find out who they were? There was something about a cop—or firefighter or EMT or soldier—that got under Rick's skin.

"Davy's one of my best friends. So, my big strong cop, are you feeling better?"

The last time he'd seen Ivan, he'd been buried under the weight of some crazy clusterfuck at work. Rick hadn't pressed, but he'd gotten the impression it had involved Parker. Given Ivan's relaxed, happy attitude, and Parker's presence, he must have been mistaken. But he hadn't been mistaken about the cornered look of a wounded animal he'd seen in Ivan's eyes.

Parker's eyes flashed and he stepped closer. "He's my big strong cop."

"Oh, ho, the boy has teeth." And a possessive nature, but any idiot could see how much that pleased Ivan, and so Rick was also pleased.

"Rick, enough." It was cute that they were protective of each other. Rick just hoped they'd last.

"I'm not a boy and he's mine."

Rick pressed his teeth together, trying not to laugh. Parker was so adorable; there was no doubt as to why Ivan had fallen. Probably he should let go of Ivan's neck, but he was interested in just how far he could provoke Parker.

"Really, Rick? Aren't you a little old to be getting in a catfight with a twink?"

Everyone swiveled their heads to check out the newcomer. Rick had recognized the voice immediately, but the bite of anger and bitterness in Ian's words had shocked him.

"Ian?"

"Ivan?"

Oh, fuck no. He tightened his arms around Ivan's neck, but he wasn't sure if he was trying to make Ian jealous or if he wanted to wring Ian's—or Ivan's—neck.

This time, though, there was no mistaking Parker's upset. "Ivan. Have you slept with both of these guys?"

Rick had been trying to push Parker's buttons, but it had been Ian who'd committed Parker to true anger.

Squaring his shoulders, Ivan pulled himself free of Rick's embrace. Rick edged away, his nerves twanging from the tension. Between two opposing forces on the field of battle was the last place he wanted to be.

Ian, though, didn't give a damn about the drama brewing between Ivan and Parker. He fixed an angry blue gaze on Rick.

"Doesn't look like he'll be taking you home tonight. Whatever will you do?" Ian sneered, surprising Rick with his vehemence.

So many retorts came to mind, but every one of them would make Rick sound like a petulant teenaged girl.

"What will I do? What about you?" That wasn't any better, but at least he and Ian had moved out of earshot of everyone else.

"Well, I certainly wouldn't slip out of his bed like a thieving whore."

An inarticulate sound of rage escaped his lips. Ian's sarcasm stung like a thousand paper cuts, and all of Rick's confusion and fear surrounding Ian coalesced into a fiery ball of fury.

"I'm not the one going around looking for anonymous hookups at bars filled with chickens, too scared to use his own name, darling."

He let the last word trail out like a diva drag queen, knowing it would piss Ian off. Rick hadn't missed that Ivan knew Ian's real name and the knowledge rubbed like lemon juice in the wounds Ian opened up with his vicious words. He hoped he could return the favor.

"You little prick. Where the hell do you get off?"

If Rick hadn't been so damned mad, he'd have had made a joke about getting off at the end of Ian's dick, but there was nothing funny about this.

A lighthearted laugh cut through the heavy, angry tension between them. Rick glanced at the rest of the room and remembered he was at a party.

"I'm not doing this here." Or ever, actually. He took a moment to assess that he did in fact have keys and wallet before he pushed past Ian and out of the house. He'd apologize to Davy and Kurt later for his precipitous departure, but he wasn't going to embarrass them or himself by having some weird screaming match with Kurt's brother. Ian may have given him some spectacular orgasms in the past two weeks, but there was no reason for all this... emotion.

He slowed as soon as he exited, the déjà vu surprisingly strong, considering how dissimilar the circumstances of him leaving Ian behind this evening were, compared to two memorable mornings. Despair, black and sticky, wound tendrils through his chest, making it hard to breathe. Could this be a side effect of the wine? Maybe he drank it too fast? Surely he wasn't upset because this meant he could never sleep with Ian again.

"What the fuck?"

Rick flinched. He shouldn't have slowed once he'd left, but he truly hadn't expected Ian to follow him. The sudden spurt of relief that Ian had followed him was more terrifying than the despair. Because he didn't get like this about guys he was fucking. It wasn't smart, it wasn't possible, and it wasn't safe for him to get involved. It wasn't going to happen.

"Rick." Some of the anger had bled out of Ian's tone, but it was too late. Rick walked down the driveway and across the street, toward his car, without even glancing over his shoulder. Ian might be one sexy bastard, but Rick didn't need this. His fingers twitched, seeking a cigarette he hadn't smoked in over a decade.

Standing beside the driver's side door, he fumbled trying to get the keys out of his pocket.

Ian's footsteps alerted him to his presence. Why wasn't he going to let this go? They didn't mean anything to each other; they weren't even friends. There was no reason for this doggedness, even if he grudgingly admired Ian's determination.

Whirling around, he backed up against his car.

"Who'd you wear this for? Him?" Ian's voice was low, with an almost menacing undertone.

"What?"

Ian hadn't appeared drunk, but no other explanation came to mind.

"This." Ian stepped close and ran his hands up Rick's chest from waist to pecs before pinching his nipples through the sheer shirt. "Did you wear it for Ivan?"

"No." The apparent jealousy surprised the denial out of him. "Not that it's any of your business."

Ian's lip curled up in a semisnarl. "Who, then? Kurt? Davy? All of them?"

Rick's brows rose. Where the hell had that come from? Maybe it didn't matter. Ian might be too volatile and emotional to add to his roster. He'd learned his lesson with Oscar, but that didn't change his stupid hope that he and Ian could maintain a sexual relationship on his terms. Even the fact he was waffling over this should have him running away at top speed. Instead he glared at Ian.

"Maybe you could take your hands off my tits." He put as much venom in his voice as he could, since Ian had already discovered how much he enjoyed nipple play and he didn't want to give Ian the chance to dissolve his anger in a haze of lust.

Under other circumstances, the harder pinch Ian responded with would have sent Rick to his knees, mouth open for a cock. Tonight, though, had been an emotional roller coaster, with Ian at its vortex. Ian's attitude killed any possibility of an erection.

"What the fuck is the matter with you?" Rick shoved Ian back, heedless of the fingers still groping him.

Ian stumbled back, his eyes draped in a shadow cast by a nearby streetlight. The deep gloom prevented Rick from determining if Ian was more or less pissed off than before, but Rick had learned long ago to defend himself when necessary.

Rick waited while Ian chewed at his lip. "I just… I thought…."

"Thought what? Acting like a jealous asshole would make me… suck your dick in front of your family? Attacking me on the street would get me to spread my ass on the hood of my car? Or was it Ivan finding someone else that's got a burr up your butt?"

"No, no…." Ian had trouble coming up with a response, but Rick hadn't really intended for there to be a good response to his questions. "I didn't realize you and Ivan had slept together."

"Oh, so being a douchebag is the correct response to that information? Good to know, darling. I'll remember that next time you meet a fuck buddy of mine."

Ian pressed his lips together.

Good. Every word out of Ian's mouth tonight only dug him deeper in shit. The amazing thing was that Rick was sticking around long enough to watch him sink.

"Honey, neither of us were virgins. But neither were we in a relationship. We had sex. Twice. And after this… nonsense, we'll have to be content with that. Clearly we want different things."

Ian grunted like Rick had punched him in the stomach. Strangely, Rick was also having trouble breathing, like he'd taken an unexpected blow to the solar plexus.

"See you around." Rick turned back to his car and fished the keys out of his pocket.

The restraining grip on his shoulder was firm but not painful. "Please, I'm sorry."

Rick let his head fall forward for a moment, contemplating breaking another rule. He took a deep breath and gave in to Ian's wordless request to turn around.

This time, he didn't say anything. He just waited. And told himself he was giving Ian a second chance only because the man was Kurt's brother and he didn't want to cause discord in his friendship with Davy.

Ian's hand drew slowly away and moved to rub the back of his neck, the move indicative of some internal distress.

"I'm sorry, Rick. You're right. I was an asshole. And I know I have no reason to be. We're not boyfriends, we're not friends, we're nothing. I've never gotten jealous like that. Not ever."

Which scared Rick, but there wasn't any denying how gratifying it was to hear. Not that he could let anything come of it.

"I've been going through some stuff. You know I just came out, right? Well, when I took you home, that was the first time I'd taken anyone home."

Rick snorted. He wasn't actually going to take Rick's joke about being a virgin and claim it was the truth, was he? No one, not even Casanova himself was that naturally talented. Playing a man's body like a finely tuned instrument came of years of practice. "Don't lie to me. There's no way you were a virgin."

A surprised laugh escaped Ian's lips. "Uh. No. I haven't been a virgin for a long time." Ian sighed. "Can we go somewhere? I know I need to apologize and explain and maybe we could do that somewhere more comfortable than standing in the street."

He wasn't falling for that. Again. "Coffee? Not at your place." He'd have to get decaf, this late.

"Sure. Of course." Ian looked around as though a Starbucks was going to materialize right there. Then again, maybe Ian wasn't familiar with the area. Davy's house wasn't especially close to Boystown, and Ian's condo was kissing distance from Charles Street.

"There's a coffee shop two blocks north of here on Jane. Follow me." Rick sighed as Ian stopped his forward momentum abruptly. Without Ian's touch mesmerizing him, he wasn't going to break his no-transportation rule again.

"Right. Yes. My car's around the corner. I'll just be a minute." Ian stared at him a moment as if assessing whether Rick was going to take off the minute he turned his back. Which was no less than Ian deserved, and was the wisest course for all concerned, but Rick knew he wouldn't do that to Ian. Age was making him soft. He'd better not be this lenient with everyone he slept with from now on.

IAN followed Rick into the coffee shop, remorse and regret killing any urge to indulge. He paid for their decaf lattes and let Rick lead them to a corner with plush chairs. It was surprisingly secluded.

Over the rim of his cup, he let his gaze wander while Rick added four packets of sweetener and stirred. Under the fluorescent lights, Rick's sexy gay nod to Goth couture should have looked harsh or overdone. But he looked just as sexy here as he had at Kurt's and outside in the dark summer night.

The sheer burgundy fabric looked stunning with Rick's golden-blond coloring. Even though it left nothing to the imagination, Ian still wanted to rip it from his shoulders. Then there were the skintight pants. Stripping Rick down to nothing would be a challenge but a welcome one.

Ian lifted his eyes to take in Rick's eye makeup. It was outrageous enough that even the late-night coffee shop cashier had blinked, but Ian had been hard the second he'd seen it. Ian had fucked a number of guys who wore makeup. He'd always liked it well enough, but something about the dramatic contrast to Rick's light coloring made it seem so much more deliberately sensual.

Lack of blood to his brain wasn't much of an excuse for his shitty behavior, but it certainly was a factor. He hoped Rick would understand.

Focusing his gaze on his own cup, he realized he hadn't doctored his latte. He quickly stirred in a sugar and lifted his gaze to find Rick staring at him as though he was an alien species.

He sighed and took a sip and manfully held back a wince. Too fucking hot. He set his cup down on the table and settled back into the chair.

"So." *Great start, Ian.* Rick would be unable to resist him after that stellar beginning.

"So," Rick mimicked him, but with a tiny lilt like he was amused at Ian's turmoil.

"I wasn't lying. You were the first man I'd taken home. You were the first man I had sex with in a bed."

Rick's eyes rounded comically before narrowing, suspicion glinting in those blue eyes.

"But not a virgin." Ian forestalled the question.

"No. Impossible. There's no way. How could it possibly be that good?" Even though Rick didn't sound pleased, his words still brought an embarrassed blush to Ian's cheeks. Guys he'd fucked had never complained, but knowing he'd made it good for Rick was deeply satisfying. And the knowledge didn't do a damn thing to deflate his erection.

"Look. I'm not a virgin. You saw me at Anaconda."

Rick's eyes narrowed again. "Yes, I did. Steve."

God. He rarely went to Anaconda, preferring to find a like-minded man at a club that catered more to his age group, but he'd been trying to put Rick out of his mind, and he'd thought Anaconda would be the last place he'd find Rick.

No one had caught his eye until he noticed a slender blond dancing on the dance floor, his back muscles glistening from the sweat of exertion.

Ian hadn't ever had a type, but sleeping with Rick had apparently triggered one, and he'd gone in for the kill. Only to find he'd zeroed in on the very man he'd been trying to purge from his mind.

Once he'd had Rick in his arms, though, he'd lost all of his upset over Rick's stealthy departure from his bed. He'd been determined to fuck Rick into oblivion, or failing that, sleep lightly enough to distract Rick from leaving his bed in the morning. He'd failed on both counts, and he'd still done nothing but brood about the loss.

"I'm no monk. I've fucked lots of guys." More than he should probably admit. "But I've been in the closet until recently. I've never dared to go home with anyone, nor have I trusted anyone to come home with me. I've fucked guys behind clubs and in bathrooms, but I've never had the luxury of time. I've never been able to explore, or let them explore me. I know we're not boyfriends or husbands or committed in any way. I know it was just sex." He wasn't entirely convinced it was just sex for him, though, but Rick was already skittish enough. Ian wasn't going to admit he was interested in more if it was only going to make Rick bolt. But there was something about Rick's obvious fear of commitment that attracted Ian. Stupidly perhaps, but he sensed it wasn't due to lack of interest or an overwhelming desire to fuck anything that moved. There was a reason behind that fear, and Ian wanted to know what.

"Then why the jealous freak-out?"

"It wasn't jealousy, not exactly." Yes, exactly, but even Ian knew jealousy was too crazy and presumptuous for such a short acquaintance. "It was more that I was... hurt. The way you snuck out of my bed made me feel inadequate. Like you were embarrassed that you'd sunk so low as to sleep with a loser like me."

"Honey, I'm sorry I made you feel that way. I don't regret sleeping with you, at all." Unexpectedly, Rick's mocking remoteness disappeared and he reached over to pat Ian's arm. Even that tiny contact made his skin tingle. He had no idea if his attraction to Rick had anything to do with him being the first after coming out, but he had to keep Rick in his life.

"I'm glad, because it was the best I've ever had."

Perhaps it wasn't cool to admit that, especially when Rick had been so determined to ditch him, but Ian wouldn't call back those words. Not when they caused a blush to rise in Rick's cheeks and caused the man to lose his normal insouciance.

"Oh, uh, honey, that's...." Flustered, Rick's gaze darted around the coffee shop as though the other patrons might be able to tell him what to say next.

Charmed beyond belief, Ian could only stare.

Rick sipped at his latte, trying to recover his composure. It wasn't hard to tell when he'd gathered his shield around him, because he set his cup down and looked at Ian with a saucy little grin.

"We need some ground rules. If we're going to keep doing this."

"Shoot." He wasn't quite sure he was ready to agree to anything Rick laid out as rules, but he was definitely okay erring on the side of what made Rick more comfortable. He might be open to exploring a relationship, but he suspected neither of them had any idea how to conduct one. Which meant that right now, all that mattered was keeping Rick talking to him. Talking was usually something he was good at. He spent forty hours a week trying to negotiate the most reasonable and beneficial compromises for all parties involved. There was no reason he couldn't do that in his personal life.

"I don't do relationships. No strings. No expectations."

Ian considered that for a moment. Because for once in his life, he *wanted* expectations. The desire for such might be unexpected and might be sudden, but now that he'd allowed himself to consider he could be a man *with* expectations, he wasn't willing to let it go. And maybe he didn't have to.

"I understand that, but I think we also need to take into account that our connection has some unusual elements. Because we've already got strings."

"What are you talking about?" That fear flared to life in Rick's eyes, and Ian spoke immediately to calm him. Ian had never ridden a horse in his life, but he'd read about lathered horses that needed to be gentled to the saddle, and Rick forcibly reminded him of a wild horse who'd never felt a saddle on his back.

"You're friends with Davy. And Kurt's my brother and my best friend. Even if you and I end up hating each other, we're going to be thrown together periodically. Strings."

Rick's breathing evened out a bit. "Yes, that's true. And I'd rather not be worrying about... our drama. In those situations."

So close. Ian just had to bring it home. "Me neither. I think the answer here is to become friends."

"Friends?" Rick clearly hadn't expected that option.

"Friends. With benefits. No strings, no exclusivity." Ian had to work hard not to strangle on those words, but it was too soon. Hell, Ian wasn't ready for strings or permanence. Not yet. Unlike Rick, though, he was willing to entertain the idea as a future state. Willing, hell, he was more than just willing, but he needed to dial back his enthusiasm. "But we'd have the ability to hang out comfortably, and when the occasion arises, we end up in bed."

The fear in Rick's eyes disappeared as he thought about Ian's words. "Friends with benefits. Isn't that the same as a fuck buddy?"

"You ever hang out with a fuck buddy when you weren't fucking?"

"Well, no, not really. Except for Ivan."

Ian's nostrils flared. He wasn't going to have a jealous outburst. He wasn't. "Okay, so what made him an exception?"

He deserved a fucking medal for keeping his voice evenly modulated.

"Not sure, exactly. I'd met him not long after he'd gotten out of a long-term relationship, and he was gorging himself on men. We'd had sex a few times, but it soon became clear that he was going to want a relationship one day. Most times, when a guy decides he wants something permanent, he's ready to stop seeing me altogether. Ivan, though, wasn't ready for permanent but we both knew it would happen and not with me. Somehow, we ended up just hanging out periodically without sex. It was nice."

God, he hated thinking and talking about Ivan, because that green-tinted anger still existed, no matter how hard he tried to hide it.

Ian had a sudden thought. "What about your other friends? Davy and Jon? You ever have sex with them?" He'd been introduced to a couple of other guys at Kurt's house-painting party but he didn't recall their names.

Rick's eyes narrowed. "Why do you want to know?"

Ian raised his hands palms out, as though to ward off a blow. "Just want to make sure we're going about this the right way."

Rick frowned but replied, "No, never. Came close a couple of times, but it never happened."

If Ian's cock were capable of speech, it would have let out a wail of distress. It was exactly as Ian feared. Sex wasn't going to help his cause any and would probably hurt it. If he wanted to get closer to Rick, he'd have to do it without the benefit of… benefits.

"Okay, then. Let's work on becoming friends. There's a midnight showing of *Raiders of the Lost Ark* at an indie theater near my place. Want to go catch that?"

"Harrison Ford in his heyday? Yeah, I could so do that."

Ian did not miss Rick's lascivious tone, and Ian agreed. It was one of his favorite movies, for several reasons.

"But how shall we occupy ourselves until then?" Rick stared at him as though expecting him to say "sex."

Ian forced himself to shrug. "Dunno. Did you eat? We could grab a late dinner. Get to know each other better."

"This sounds suspiciously like a date, darling."

One day, Rick was going to call him by an endearment that he didn't use with every random person he came across. One day.

"Don't you eat with Davy? Have drinks with Ivan? See a movie with Jon?"

A reluctant shrug answered his question.

"What about the benefits?"

"Let's focus on the friends thing first. We can figure out the benefits later, play it by ear." Much to his cock's dismay. But the look of pleased determination on Rick's face told Ian he was doing the right thing. He needed to gentle this horse to his way of thinking.

"Sounds good, darling." Rick stood and extended his arm. "Let's go be friends."

THE Tuesday after the housewarming party-turned-movie night, Rick followed Ian into a small bar filled with people. They bypassed the hostess and several tables to ascend a narrow staircase. After walking past a few more tables, Ian pushed back a curtain and led him out onto a wood plank patio. The area was enclosed by wooden fencing that Rick associated with backyard swimming pools or barking dogs that were likely to bite. Oddly, the patio appeared to have been built around a few trees, and both fencing and trees were festooned with tiny white Christmas lights.

They took a seat at a table in the corner and Ian ordered them beers.

"This is a great place," Rick said as soon as the waiter departed.

"Yeah. They actually film part of some TV show out here. Supposed to be set in Washington DC, but a bar's a bar, right? I like this outdoor bit back here."

Rick could see why. The atmosphere was very backyard barbecue, even though the specials marked on a nearby chalkboard were gourmet burgers and fusion cuisine. He sipped at his beer and checked out the clientele. Seemed like normal, everyday people.

For several minutes, they sat and drank.

The silence between them began to make Rick antsy. After all, wasn't the whole point of this… appointment… to get to know each other? He resolutely refused to call it a date, even though it was probably more like a date than getting a simple beer with a friend or colleague. Because underneath it all was Ian's request that they work on being friends. He didn't recall ever having to work to make any other friendship develop, but then, as Ian had pointed out, he rarely slept with his friends. He still suspected ulterior motives.

Ulterior motives or not, drinks on a Tuesday night was so low pressure Rick hadn't even hesitated in accepting when Ian had called wanting to get together after a late meeting. Three days ago, they'd had a great night seeing *Raiders*, and if Rick had started getting agitated in the intervening days, wondering if Ian had been serious about his offer of friendship, no one needed to know.

Ian ordered them a second round and when it arrived, Rick couldn't contain himself any longer. "Aren't you going to ask me anything?"

"There's no real rush, is there? You haven't double booked yourself tonight, have you?"

Well, put it that way…. "No. I just thought you had questions."

"Sure I do. But this isn't an interrogation. We can sit here and just enjoy each other's company."

With a supreme force of will, Rick managed to not roll his eyes. "Oh, well, of course, darling. I can do that." For another ten minutes, maybe. The suspense was killing him.

Ian laughed. "If you're so eager, why don't you ask me something."

Tilting his head to the side, Rick assessed Ian. What, if anything, did he want to know about this man? Not that there was any reason to suspect

Ian and his big, hunky brother were anything alike beyond their looks, but Rick already knew a fair amount about their family just from the time he'd spent with Kurt and Davy. Truth be told, he probably knew more family stuff than he wanted, and he couldn't quite believe they were as good as Kurt made them sound.

Jon never seemed to mind hearing the stories, but then, Jon still missed the stupid family that tossed him out when they found out he was gay. There was absolutely nothing Rick missed about his own family. The only nostalgia he had around his childhood involved pop culture, not family.

"Where do you work? What do you do?" Rick thought Kurt might have mentioned what all of his siblings and their spouses did for a living, but if he had, Rick wouldn't have bothered trying to retain that information.

"I work for *Errant*."

"Shut up. Honey, you don't really, do you? I thought only Gothy vampire children and backstabbing old fags worked there!" *Errant* took a different spin on the celebrity scandal site, adding in the weirdest stories, like how to tell if your neighbor was a space alien or a vampire or a chupacabra. The best ones were when they managed to combine celebrity scandals with a whiff of ridiculous paranormal, like cursed jewelry or movie sets. The entire thing was like a mashed-up version of the paper that regularly reported sightings of Bat Boy with the celebrity scandal rags. Along with a decidedly Canadian spin, of course. Rick secretly read it all the time.

Ian laughed. "Well, there are probably a couple of both. And I've certainly heard the owner call himself an old fag. But I recognize that look. You're a fan, aren't you?"

"No, darling, the site is absurd. Surely there can't be that many cursed movie sets in the world."

"Uh-huh. Why don't I believe you?"

"Okay, okay. I read it. It's a total guilty pleasure."

"Exactly what the owner intended."

"It's weird. The combination shouldn't work at all, and yet it does. And implying the last big blackout was due to an alien incursion—simply genius!"

Ian took a moment to order a plate of fries with an assortment of flavored mayos and aiolis. Evil man must have the same fast metabolism as his brother; Rick had never seen Kurt consider the fat grams of anything he put in his mouth.

"I know. But the owner loved both concepts and couldn't decide which way to go. So he went with both. Between all the TV and movies filmed here, and the Toronto Film Festival, there are tons of celebrities and the fantasmical paranormal nonsense gave *Errant* a unique spin, which I can attest, works."

"So, darling, are you responsible for taking photos up celebrity skirts or researching the mating habits of the Canadian werewolf?"

"Ha, ha. I'm not one of the writers or editors. No, I'm a senior account manager. I'm the one who brings in the advertising money. Well, not the only one, but I did increase the incoming revenue by two hundred percent over the past three years."

"Oh, well, then, I guess tonight's on you, honey."

"Actually, my job is how I heard about this place. A lot of local bars and restaurants advertise with us, and I'll often check out the ones that look interesting."

"Smart boy."

Ian grinned at him and raised his beer bottle in a halfhearted toasting gesture.

The fries arrived, hot and greasy and salty. Saliva pooled in Rick's mouth and he had a regrettable moment where he actually hated how unconcerned Ian looked when he popped four fries in his mouth at once.

"Have some."

Rick shook his head, but with each inhalation, his resolve weakened. He braced himself for a return question about his career. He certainly wasn't ashamed of what he did for a living, but inevitably people wanted to know why he'd chosen the path he had, and that was something he didn't share with anyone.

"What about you? How do you support yourself?"

There it was.

"I'm a speech-language pathologist."

"Huh. What is that, exactly? I mean, I can probably come up with the gist of it, based on the words, but it might be wrong."

He dug a fingernail into a gouge on the table. "I help adults mostly. Dyslexia, speech disorders, various language issues relating to strokes or diseases. Sometime I help kids, but most times, there are SLPs attached to the schools. Sometimes a kid will require more attention than he or she can get at school and the parents will seek me out."

"That's amazing. Much more noble than what I do. How'd you decide on that?"

This was where it all fell apart. "I don't want to talk about it."

Ian swallowed and licked salt from his lips. However functional the movement may have been, it still made Rick squirm. Ian was a sexy, sexy man, and Rick had up-close-and-personal knowledge of how Ian's lips and tongue felt against his body. In silence, Ian assessed him, one eyebrow levered slightly up as though trying to categorize the results of an experiment. In an attempt to alleviate his discomfort at the inspection, Rick gulped down the last of his beer and slammed the empty bottle on the table. Glancing around, he signaled for the waiter, all the while pretending to be unconcerned about Ian's intent perusal.

"Okay. How did you end up hanging out with Davy and the others?"

Relief flooded him at the divergence from discussion of his career. That question he could answer—mostly.

"Jon and I met while we were in university. We both worked in the same club and became friends." No need to mention that they initially became close because the owner wanted them to strip together, nor that the club in question was in fact a strip club. "He and Davy were friends from high school, and they sort of adopted me into the group."

He'd been unbelievably grateful that he'd found them. They ended up having a lot in common, but the simple act of finding friends had made his life tolerable. Good, even, though it was hard working so many hours while going to school. None of them knew the details around why he'd left home and moved to Toronto, but that hadn't changed their acceptance one bit.

"We had a lot in common, and when we weren't hanging out in someone's dorm room, we were out in the clubs. Then, Davy moved in with his boyfriend, the one before Kurt, and over time we saw less and less of him until he died and Davy met Kurt."

Did Ian want to be part of them? If so, was that because he wanted to hang out with Rick, wanted to find some gay friends, or wanted to spend more time with his brother? Rick had no idea if brothers spent a lot of time socializing with each other, but even Rick, who tried to avoid emotional situations, had been able to tell Ian's rift with Kurt, before Ian came out, had hurt his brother.

Then something changed, clicked into place. It might have been the cumulative effect of the alcohol, it might have been the lack of pressure from Ian, or it might have been exhaustion from keeping up his walls, but the conversation relaxed and flowed naturally. Rick even allowed himself to have some fries.

RICK stared up at the flashing lights of the marquee. He'd been a little surprised, but not displeased, that Ian had called him so soon after their Tuesday outing. He did love watching movies.

"Aside from last Saturday, it's been a while since I bothered to go to a movie. What did you want to see?"

There was something too depressing about going to the movies alone. Clubs weren't a problem, especially if he was looking to get laid. But movies and dinner out—those were things that always made him feel like he was on display with a big neon sign hanging over his head telling everyone he was alone. The older he and his friends got, the more everyone became homebodies. By default, Rick had become more of a homebody too. Most times he didn't mind—he'd always enjoyed his own company—but sometimes his house seemed too big for just him.

"Doesn't matter. We can just grab the next showing." Ian pulled out his wallet and stepped into line.

Rick followed—physically, at any rate, because he certainly hadn't followed Ian's statement. "The next showing of what?"

Flipping his wrist over, Ian checked the time. "It's eight now. Are you hungry?"

Rick shrugged. "Not hungry, but I do like to get popcorn at the movies."

"Okay, then. We'll just grab whatever movie's next. Unless it starts in the next ten minutes. Then we'll take the one after that."

Had he missed something? "Don't you want to go to a specific movie?"

"Nah, not really. My parents couldn't afford to take the whole family out to the movies very often and on the few times they did… with seven kids there was absolutely no possibility for consensus. So my parents started the 'next showing' policy. Whatever time we arrived at the theater, we'd go see the next showing. Back then, there were sometimes exceptions made based on rating, but most of us just got into the habit of taking the next showing of whatever was at the theater."

"But, but…." Rick couldn't come up with a coherent argument. He'd never heard of anything so Zen. Not when it came to anything to do with schedules. "What if the next movie's awful? Or not a genre you like?"

Ian spread his hands out, the ultimate gesture of "whatever." "I've seen a lot of good movies that I might never have otherwise seen."

"Uh-huh. And the shit ones?"

The boyish grin he got was just adorable. "The shit ones give you plenty to talk about."

"So how come you knew about that midnight showing of *Raiders* on Saturday?"

"Mmm. It's a classic. I've seen it tons of times and had heard it was having a small revival at the indie theater. It doesn't have to all be forging into the unknown, you know."

"Okay, then." Rick gestured him forward. Unsurprisingly, it took Ian a few moments to convince the girl behind the glass that he really did want two tickets to the next movie, whatever it might be, but it didn't take nearly as long as Rick expected. Then again, Ian had already convinced him to break or bend several rules.

He'd never met one of the proverbial silver-tongued devils before, but he suspected Ian might be one of them. Convincing cats to become vegetarian and selling sand to Egyptians. At this point, Rick was beginning to believe Ian could charm the blue from the sky.

Ian returned from the box office waving two tickets. "Better hurry. We've got fifteen minutes to get munchies."

Rick grabbed the tickets. "*European Death Knot*? What the hell is that?"

Ian shrugged. "Dunno. We'll find out, won't we? C'mon."

The man was nuts and if this movie was utter shit, he'd make sure Ian made it up to him forever.

RICK sagged against Ian, still giggling as they walked out of the theater. Ian badly wanted to put an arm around Rick, show everyone they were on a date, but he didn't dare. Rick had relaxed around him, but if he moved too fast or took too many liberties outside of the "becoming friends" bucket, he suspected Rick would pull back into his shell.

Ian snorted. To the average onlooker, Rick was never in a shell. He was out there and proud. But Ian had seen glimpses of the inner Rick, the real person beneath the mask he showed the world, and that was the Rick Ian wanted to know.

"That was hilarious. Fucking awful, but also hilarious," Rick wheezed.

"Yeah, I have to admit with a title like *European Death Knot*, I was expected a kidnapping or maybe something exploding."

Rick loosed another chuckle. "Me too. I can only assume the success of that movie where the guy gnawed off his own arm made the makers of this assume any rock-climbing movie would have equal success."

When they exited the building, the night was dark and clear with an unexpected bite in the air. Rick stayed close, their body heat increasing the temperature in the few millimeters between them.

"Didn't he cut his arm off?"

"Gnaw, cut… to-*may*-to, to-*mah*-to."

Ian laughed. He really enjoyed Rick when the man wasn't worried about what he said or how he presented himself. Sarcastic, happy Rick was a man he wanted to spend all his time with.

"Still, when they started throwing out terms like Alpine Cock Ring, edging, daisy chain, and tea bagging, I thought someone had accidentally loaded up a gay porn," Ian said.

"I know, right? If there was any such thing as a gay agenda, that's an example of it right there."

"Really?"

"Darling, of course some diabolical gay man came up with those terms. Nothing like having a bunch of unsuspecting straights talking about tea bagging and cock rings in everyday conversation. Whoever invented those terms probably literally died laughing."

"Maybe we should take up rock climbing." Ian had thought about doing so even before he knew half the terms sounded like being in the middle of a gay porn flick, but never bothered looking into it. If the whole thing was so amusing to Rick, it might be fun. With that trim little body, there was no doubt Rick was fit enough.

Rick jabbed him in the arm. "Really? You want me to go out and risk life and limb while I'm trying not to wet myself laughing? That's just mean, darling."

If Ian thought for one minute Rick had reserved the name darling for him alone, he might have liked it. As it was, he wondered if it was yet another way for Rick to keep people from getting too close by not individualizing them. But it was early days yet. He didn't think he believed in love at first sight, but the first sight of Rick had changed him in some fundamental way and anything he could do to get closer to Rick, he'd do, even if it meant being one of a million of Rick's darlings. For now.

"I'd never want to be mean to you." The temptation to add the word darling on to the end of his sentence was strong, but Ian knew he couldn't say it with the same flair as Rick. It would come out either mocking or bitter, neither of which would endear him to Rick. "So rock climbing is out. How about coffee in the meantime? We can discuss another hobby to take up."

Rick yanked his phone out of a pocket and checked the time. "It's a little late, isn't it? I mean, we both have work in the morning."

Like a kid pleading for five more minutes, Ian wasn't ready for the night to end. "If you were at a club, would it be too late? You wouldn't be heading home yet, would you?"

There was no mistaking the leer on Rick's face. If Rick were at a club right now, he'd probably be getting blown in the bathroom. Ian twisted his hips away from Rick as he unlocked the car door so his immediate reaction wasn't visible. He'd promised friends first, and that meant no relieving his hard-on. Not with Rick, not yet.

"That's what I thought. We've got plenty of time for coffee."

"I suppose. Although I don't go clubbing midweek so much anymore."

Ian sighed. "Me neither." All too often, even getting laid wasn't enough to energize him to get dressed up and go out during the week, especially if he had early meetings the next day. Rick, though, energized him like he was a teenager again.

Rick echoed his sigh. "And caffeine this late keeps me from falling asleep."

"Me too." It hadn't always, but as the years passed, things changed. "But I bet we can get something decaf."

"Okay, we can do that."

He had to try. "Or we could go back to my place. Have a drink there."

Shit, shit, shit. Big mistake. In a heartbeat, Rick's relaxed attitude dissipated, and he frowned at Ian like he was a sexual predator.

"Hey, it was only a suggestion. Nothing more, I swear." Right. He'd already figured out that Rick's place was off-limits. Clearly, Ian's was as well. Good to know. He put his most innocent expression on, hoping Rick would accept the truth. Because the suggestion really had been nothing more than convenience. He was committed to laying a foundation first, because that was the only way they were going to be able to go forward and trust each other.

Rick relented and Ian let out a relieved breath. "We'll go out for a coffee only, or whatever the late-night equivalent is."

"Good."

A head of dark shaggy hair caught his eye, and Ian craned to take a look.

"What?" Rick looked in the same direction too, but the guy Ian had seen slipped away.

"Nothing. Just thought I saw a friend from work, that guy Leon I told you about. I was going to say hi, but maybe I was imagining it."

"Seeing things, are you? Maybe you need sleep more than coffee." Rick winked at him, but he wasn't taking that suggestion. No way.

"Let's go. There's a decent café the next block over. We can keep our parking spaces here and walk over."

The whole way to the café, Ian's fingers twitched from the desire to grab Rick's hand and walk down the street as though they were a couple.

CHAPTER
Five

RICK wasn't sure how it happened, but over the past few weeks, he and Ian had fallen into almost a pattern. Tuesday nights were drinks at some funky bar or dinner at some trendy place Ian had read or heard about. For some of the more popular places, it could be weeks before a reservation was available on the weekends, but Tuesdays were much easier. Thursday had become movie night. Saturday afternoon and evening had become a wild-card day.

In addition, he'd also had some terrible luck. Aside from the dead squirrel, he'd had three flat tires, his car keyed, a minor garbage fire, some unpleasant surprises in his mailbox, and a bag of burning shit that scorched the outside of the basement window he'd fortunately fixed, otherwise he had no doubt it would have ended up on his basement floor. He hoped ignoring it was the right tactic to take. Ian wanted him to go to the police or even tell Kurt about it, but Rick was convinced the kid or kids would get bored eventually. Unless, of course, he caught the little fucker at it. That would be a different story. Right now it was mostly harmless stuff, and none of it able to deflate his good mood. Spending time with Ian was the most fun he'd had in a long time.

They'd visited places in and around Toronto that Rick had never been to or had only been to on school trips. Fort York, Casa Loma, the CN Tower, Toronto Island. The Festival of Beer hadn't been edifying, but they'd had a lot of fun. It wasn't only sightseeing places either. They'd gone mini golfing and glow-in-the-dark bowling. Not once had they run out of things to talk about. Rick had even shared a few stories of his childhood. Simple ones, with no real baggage attached, but he generally didn't speak of his childhood at all.

He still saw Jon and the others on Friday nights, but he hadn't mentioned—not even to Kurt—that he'd been seeing Ian. All of them had assumed he and Ian burned out their attraction after two nights in the sack. Thing was, every "friendship date" they had only fanned Rick's flames, and he'd started dreaming about sex. Sex with Ian. Lots and lots of sex with Ian.

Under normal circumstances, he'd already have been trying to find someone to add to his fuck-buddy roster. But he had no desire to go looking because he was waiting for Ian to realize they were good enough friends to move on to the "benefits" stage of their… friendship.

But it had been a long time since he'd been celibate for seven weeks. Nevertheless, he was enjoying his time with Ian too much. Every "friendship" night gave Rick a raging hard-on despite the fact that they didn't do more than brush arms, hands, or hips "accidentally," but he couldn't quite bring himself to ask Ian when they were going to have sex again. There was a deep-seated fear that sleeping with Ian would turn him into a keeper, and the thought of never seeing Ian again gave Rick a sick feeling in the pit of his stomach.

However, he had realized that each of their "dates" thus far had been planned—very well—by Ian. It was about time Rick stepped up, and the pleasure in Ian's voice when he'd called to invite him out for a Wednesday night let him know he'd done the right thing. Especially since Ian would be unavailable on Saturday because of his sister's birthday party.

Ian was meeting him at one of the places he'd only shared with close friends. Most of his roster never knew what a geek he was, and tonight, he was going to let Ian in on that secret. Ian likely already had suspicions, but tonight, Rick was going to confirm them. He, Jon, and Davy had long ago decided that geeks didn't get laid enough, so they'd gone to great pains to hide their geekiness from anyone but each other.

"Hey there." At the sound of Ian's greeting, Rick whirled around.

The huge smile on Ian's gorgeous face was becoming more and more necessary for Rick's happiness.

Ian leaned in, almost as though he was going to kiss Rick, but he stopped himself at the last moment. But his smile didn't falter a bit.

"I've never heard of this place."

"I'm sure you haven't. Advertising with *Errant* is likely way out of their budget, but their clientele keeps them busy enough."

"Lead the way. I'm ready for anything."

After opening the door, Rick searched for a free table, all the while trying to imagine Ian's thoughts seeing it for the first time.

Off to the left, a couple rose, leaving a booth free. "There. Let's take that one."

Ian followed him and waited for him to select which side of the table he wanted, before sliding onto the bench across from him.

"Hmmm." Ian glanced around. "I deduce, based on the number of game boards and game pieces on all the tables, you've brought me to your favorite strip club."

An odd, snorted laugh escaped through his nose. Spending time with Ian was never boring. He very nearly offered to wager on the outcome of their game, that the loser would strip for the winner, but he was trying to be good. He was trying to give this as much effort as Ian was.

"It's a good thing you're pretty, darling," he cooed at Ian, dragging a fingernail along Ian's forearm. Seeing Ian's shiver and the gooseflesh that appeared on Ian's skin made Rick want to raise his fist and cheer. He definitely wasn't the only one feeling the effects of the attraction between them.

Ian wiggled his brows. "Okay, so tell me about this place."

"Games. We grab a game from the wall and play. That's it. The menu's a little sketchy, but the beer is cold."

Holding his breath, Rick waited for Ian's response. But Ian didn't run or sneer. He just smiled the fond little smile he had, the one Rick was never sure what he'd done to prompt it.

"Mmm. I knew you were a closet geek."

There wasn't much he could say to refute the statement. It was true. "I am, a bit." Although he didn't think he'd been that obvious about it.

"I can already see that I don't recognize any of these games, so I'll let you pick. Are there servers here or is it bar service only?"

"Bar service only, I'm afraid."

"Go pick a game." Ian glanced at a few nearby tables. "These are a little more complicated than Clue, so you can set it up while I get us drinks."

Huh. That had been amazingly easy. Rick got up, making sure to put an extra little swish in his step. Just in case Ian was watching.

Twisting to look at the available games, he positioned himself so he could take an unobtrusive look back at the table. Sure enough, Ian had his eyes directed at Rick's ass. He knew they weren't going to do anything about it yet, but it was nice to know Ian still liked his ass as much as he claimed when they'd fucked each other into sweaty, boneless heaps.

Then he turned his focus away from the sexy man waiting for him and toward the game selection. He loved *Settlers of Catan*, and it wasn't bad for a first timer, but it was a minimum of three players. Same with *Betrayal at House on the Hill*. *Arkham Horror* had too many fiddly bits and rules for a first timer. Oh, wait, *Pandemic*. Perfect. Not too many rules, and instead of working against each other, they'd be able to cooperate to try to defeat the oncoming pandemic.

He didn't know how well Ian took to losing, but he himself had a tendency to gloat when winning. He wasn't entirely sure they were good enough friends to survive that, at least not when there would be just one winner and one loser. In a group it was easier to gloat without incurring any hard feelings. With *Pandemic*, they'd either both win or both lose, and Rick liked those odds much better.

By the time Ian returned from the bar, Rick had all the game pieces set up. Ian was smart and he paid attention. It took almost no time at all to explain the rules.

"So, is this one of the games you play with Davy and the guys?" Ian moved his wooden marker across the board.

"Oh, yeah. We do. How did you know?" He may have mentioned his Friday nights with the guys, and possibly that they played board games in passing, but he didn't think so. After all these years, the whole hiding-the-geek thing came almost as naturally as avoiding talking about his childhood.

"Kurt's invited me along a couple of times."

The mouthful of beer went down the wrong way and he coughed and sputtered. "He has?" Rick had no idea what to do with that information. Did that mean Ian had no interest in games at all and was faking it for his benefit tonight?

"You okay?" Ian was halfway out of his seat, poised to do the Heimlich or something, but Rick waved at him.

"Fine, fine. Just swallowed wrong." Not something he said very often, that was for sure.

"Did you want a glass of water?"

"I'm good." That, on the other hand, was something he said frequently. He drank another sip of beer to prove his point.

"So, Kurt's invited you to game night? How come you've never accepted?" Dammit. They'd only had a couple of rounds and already had outbreaks in Miami and Sydney. Rick had a bad feeling they were going to fail to prevent the pandemic.

Ian shrugged and added more infection markers to the board. "I know you don't want anyone to think we're a couple or anything, and I didn't want to make you uncomfortable with your friends, so I've put him off. Of course, he's starting to think I hate geeks, but you know… I don't hate geeks at all."

The heat in Ian's eyes produced an immediate reaction in his groin. Damn him. At least they hadn't lost the game yet. No reason for him to get up and show everyone how Ian affected him. Which didn't do anything to mitigate how guilty he felt that Ian hadn't come to game night. The man didn't really have any gay friends that Rick knew about, and Rick's hang-ups were preventing him from not only socializing with the brother he was very close to, but also from getting to know Kurt's life partner and making a new group of friends who had more in common with his new out-of-the-closet life.

"I'm sorry."

"That I don't hate geeks?"

"No, darling. That I'm preventing you from…." There was no good way to finish that sentence. Anything he could say would make him sound like a selfish asshole.

Ian placed a warm palm atop his hand, stopping him from making his next move in the game. "Hey. It's okay. The most important thing right now is that we're good. Solidifying our friendship is what I'm interested in right now. I promise."

Rick nodded.

"But this is a lot of fun. When you're ready, you let me know and I'll come along to game night."

This was too good to be true, and yet, he'd thought that more than once since he'd met Ian. Not once had Ian truly disappointed him.

"READY to grab something to eat?" Rick needed something to soak up the beer or he just might take Ian home with him. They'd lost two games of *Pandemic*, but they'd enjoyed every minute. He'd been amazed how much Ian had enjoyed it. Which made him feel even worse that Ian was refusing to attend game night because of him, but the thought of telling his friends about Ian made his breath come fast and his palms sweat.

"The food here really isn't worth it?"

"No, darling. Really, no." When they were in university, splurging on supersalty and borderline-stale snacks while they played had been a real treat, but as soon as he'd got a real job, he'd never eaten there again.

"Where to?" Ian followed him as he put the game back on the shelf.

"Lettie's?"

"Lettie's? I haven't been there in years. We always went when we were drunk. The food's good sober?"

Rick wasn't quite willing to attest he was one hundred percent sober, but Lettie's was a regular for him and his friends. The diner was open twenty-four hours, making it one of the more popular spots for the drunks who got kicked out after last call and those with incipient hangovers. Since it wasn't even ten thirty yet, the crowd would be mostly sedate.

"Come on. Let's go."

"I'm trusting you."

"Darling, you're going to love it. Home cooking like…." Rick tilted his head. "Okay, well, you've had an invested mother who's been around your whole life. It's probably home cooking like you get at home, but maybe not quite as good. But I like it."

"That's good enough for me."

Forty-five minutes later, they were comfortably ensconced in another booth at a brightly lit fifties-style diner polishing off the remains of meatloaf and chicken potpie. Ian was so fucking bad for both his diet and workout schedule. They'd have to have sex before Rick ate his weight in sexual frustration.

"I admit it. That was damn good."

"But not better than your mother makes, right?"

"You should come to family dinner night and find out."

Adrenaline spiked at the thought of running across Mrs. O'Donnell again. "Uh, no. You know I don't do family stuff."

It wasn't the first time Ian had suggested he come along to a family function, but Ian always backed off. Like hanging out with the guys, though, he wasn't sure how long he could keep refusing. Even if he wasn't introduced as anything more than a friend, the secrecy was going to speak volumes all on its own. He'd always refused to add married men to his roster because he didn't want to deal with the dirty secrets. And yet he was becoming a dirty secret all of his own making, because he'd insisted Ian not tell anyone about them.

"I know, I know. One day I'll wear you down."

Not fucking likely.

Ian smiled at him and stroked the back of his hand. "No family stuff. You don't need to say it again. You ready to go?"

"In a minute. I just have to hit the bathroom."

Rick made his way through the maze of tables to the bathroom. Before he got there, a hand grabbed his arm and spun him around.

"You fucking liar!" Beer splattered on his arm as a drunk, angry Oscar waved a glass around, his other hand fisted and cocked like he was going to take a swing.

"What the—"

"You told me you weren't interested in anything more than fucking. But here you are on a date."

Oh, this was not happening. Not at all. He had to fucking pee. "What the hell is the matter with you? What I do now has nothing to do with you."

Oscar stabbed his finger in Rick's face. "He needs to leave you the fuck alone. I saw you first. I get dibs."

Dibs? "Oscar, how fucking much have you had to drink?"

Oscar wobbled back on his feet.

"For God's sake, you can't call dibs on me."

"That asshole can't have you." Oscar threw his glass to the floor where it shattered in a shower of shards and lager.

Rick bared his teeth. "Don't fucking do this. You don't have anything to say about it." Oscar couldn't ruin what he had with Ian; he just couldn't.

"Shut up, Rick. You don't know what you want. You don't know what's good for you. It's not that guy."

"Oscar, you need to sober the fuck up. Get out of here before someone calls the cops." They'd only go unnoticed for so long. He wasn't worried about getting hurt—he'd taken more than his fair share of self-defense and martial arts courses, but that didn't mean some well-meaning customer or waiter wouldn't call the cops.

"Shut up, Rick. All I can do is think about you. Drinking is the only thing that lets me sleep at night." The words were slurred, but there was no mistaking Oscar's words. He didn't want to be responsible for this, but he should have noticed earlier that Oscar was a keeper. Not only that, but a clingy keeper. And one who became a complete asshole with the addition of booze.

"You need to leave, Oscar. Or you're going to get arrested." Rick tried to remain calm and collected, but it only seemed to aggravate Oscar.

Rick glanced around the restaurant. No one was looking at them… yet.

Oscar grabbed him, fingers biting into his shoulders, and pushed him against the wall. Fuck, he had to take a leak so bad.

Faster than the drunken Oscar could deal with, he brought his arms up and broke Oscar's hold.

The sirens that sounded outside could have been headed their way. They probably weren't, but he was going to use it.

"Holy shit, Oscar, the cops are coming. You'd better get out of here, or they're going to arrest you."

Something must have soaked into Oscar's alcohol-addled brain because his eyes flared in panic. He turned and stumbled away.

Ian showed up while he was rubbing his shoulders.

"You okay? You were gone kind of a long time."

Rick continued to rub his shoulders. "Yeah, I just saw Oscar. I haven't seen him since he brought me flowers after I told him I couldn't see him anymore. He was a little drunk and… belligerent."

"Are you okay? Do you want to call the cops or something? Or should I just go beat him up for you?"

The last question made him laugh. "Not to impugn your manhood, darling, but Oscar's a big guy."

"I don't know. I've got three brothers, one of whom is a cop. You pick stuff up."

Ian puffed up a bit and Rick would never admit to having a tiny little fantasy of Ian and Kurt tussling with each other. For the first time, he understood why guys always wanted him and Jon to make out.

Good thing he wasn't ready to accompany Ian to any family functions. Bright red wasn't a good color for him, and he was very much afraid the next time he saw Ian and Kurt together, he'd blush like crazy.

"I'm fine." Rick rubbed his shoulder.

"Are you sure?" Ian reached out and touched the spot he'd just been rubbing.

"He grabbed me a bit. It's nothing."

"He grabbed you?" This time, Ian appeared dark and menacing and so fucking hot.

"Hey. It was nothing. He was upset that I stopped seeing him. But he was drunk. I promise it won't happen again." He hoped.

"Well, if you're sure. Let's get out of here."

A sharp cramp knifed through his bladder and he realized he'd forgotten why he'd come back here in the first place. "Uh, yeah. Just give me a minute." Rick whirled around and dashed into the bathroom.

"I CAN'T go. Stop pestering me about it." Rick stole a fry from Jon's plate. He never ordered them, but sneaking a few here and there shouldn't adversely affect his waistline. "And how much do you work out, anyway, to be able to eat BLTs and fries whenever you want?"

Jon pulled his plate farther away from Rick. "No more fries if you don't stop deflecting. You're going to Erin's birthday party."

Rick turned his attention back to his grilled salmon. "No, I'm not. You know I don't do family things."

He'd had enough of a taste of family functions at Kurt's housewarming, and he wasn't willing to put himself in that situation again.

"Kurt's our friend, and he wants us at his sister's birthday party. It's a big event. More importantly, Davy wants us there. Don't you want to make sure Kurt's family is treating him right?"

"Wow, honey. Guilt was exactly the right note. Now I really want to go!" Rick rolled his eyes and stole another fry.

"Family things aren't my style either; you know that."

Rick did. Being disowned by their families for being gay had been one of their initial reasons for bonding when they'd met at the strip club, so many years ago. Jon was the closest friend he'd ever had, but he'd never admitted the full extent of his family issues to him. There hadn't been a need. Jon didn't have any family hovering, and Rick had already decided he wasn't going to gain any through a boyfriend. When Jon had introduced him to Davy, none of them had a lot of family to speak of. Rick had settled into a very comfortable existence surrounded by friends and a few fuck buddies. He'd fought his way into a career that gave him a sense of pride and accomplishment. He'd always assumed life would just sort of continue the way it had for the past few years. There had been no indications of any bumps in the road. No potholes, no cracks, and no deviations from the path he'd been on.

Then Davy had to go and find himself a partner with parents and six siblings, all of whom seemed unnaturally involved in their son's and brother's life. That family kept spilling into Rick's life. And he didn't like it.

"So why are you going? I mean, I haven't even met Erin. Why would anyone want me at her birthday party? In my opinion, it's just weird." Another fry found its way into Rick's mouth.

"Okay, one, do I need to order more fries?"

"Only if you want to, darling." That was as close as he'd come to saying yes, because he shouldn't have fries and wasn't going to admit he wanted any.

Jon shook his head and signaled for the waiter. Jon knew him a little too well, it seemed.

After the waiter left, Jon picked up exactly where he'd left off. "Two, didn't you listen to Kurt? It's not like we're intruding on a small, intimate family dinner. It's more like a big party at the O'Donnells' bar. There's always lots of people there and Kurt wants us to go. So we should. Besides, it might even be fun."

Fun. Rick would rather get a root canal without anesthetic, but if he didn't have a good excuse like a funeral or an unexpected hospital stay, he'd probably have everyone on his case, not just Jon.

"Your reluctance wouldn't have anything to do with one particular O'Donnell brother, would it?"

Rick stared into Jon's eyes. Jon knew he'd left Kurt's place twice in Ian's company but he hadn't told Jon anything about the "friendship" he and Ian were developing. Nor had he mentioned the Oscar incident. Normally Jon would have been the first one he called about a thing like that. He wasn't sure why, but he still wasn't ready to mention he'd been spending time with Ian.

"No. Not at all."

Jon lifted a blond brow. "Are you sure?"

"Of course I'm sure." After falling into a regular dinner and movie night schedule, he wasn't worried about running into Ian at this party, other than appearing too friendly with the guy. He was rapidly developing a case of blue balls, though, along with a friendship. None of the benefits had kicked in, and for some reason, Rick hadn't bothered interviewing for a new roster to help him relieve them.

He just wasn't interested, and even found himself looking for additional activities to do with Ian, knowing full well they weren't going to dive back into bed until Ian was sure they were friends. Ian had been considerate enough to do his best to stay away from group events until they could be sure there wouldn't be any weirdness, and he assumed that was why Ian hadn't been the one to invite him to Erin's party. But weirdness with his friends wasn't the reason he didn't want to go to this party. Not at all.

"I don't know. What happened with you guys? Ian seemed like a nice guy. Totally hot."

Well, he wasn't going to discuss Ian's hotness with Jon. Not when Rick hadn't been able to familiarize himself with it in far too long.

"Fine. I'll go."

"To the party?"

"Yes, of course, the party. You know, what we've been discussing? You've got a birthday coming up too, old man." Rick switched their plates. "You obviously need to eat my salmon, honey. I hear Omega-3 oils do wonders for your memory."

"Jerk," Jon muttered, but started eating Rick's salmon anyway. Rick popped another fry in his mouth. The universe would be unjust, indeed, if a plateful of fries stolen so deftly had the same number of calories as if he'd ordered them for himself.

RICK hung back a little, letting his friends lead the way across the parking lot of Finn's Frolic. It was much bigger than he expected, but if Kurt was to be believed, the back room was big enough to hold fifty or sixty people at least, plus there was the public front room. Based on the number of cars out in the lot, the place was packed.

He'd agonized over what to wear. Intellectually, he knew the O'Donnells were accepting of Ian and Kurt's sexuality. But he couldn't bring himself to trust that the goodwill would extend to him as well, so he didn't want to dress like he was going to a club. No one ever had trouble determining his orientation when he dressed up. Just to make himself extra crazy, he *wanted* Ian's family to like him. He wanted to make a good impression on them. He wanted to know if they would treat him differently if they thought he was more than a friend to Ian. As if that wasn't enough, he'd begun taking some delight in enticing Ian. Nothing openly provocative, but enough to make Ian regret his temporary sex moratorium.

Jon held the door open for him, and he couldn't put it off any longer.

Finn's was loud and filled with people. Looked like a normal bar, as far as he could tell. Pretty much as he expected an Irish bar and restaurant to look. The crowd consisted of a variety of ages and styles, but there didn't seem to be any reason to assume any of them would suddenly become crazy homophobes and leap off their chairs to lynch him. As instructed, they headed for the back room. Jon gave their names and they were ushered right in.

The back room was just as busy as the front. Along the right-hand side were several pool tables and dart boards. A dance floor covered with several occupied tables existed between the entrance and a small raised platform, too small to call a stage. Some room had been left clear for dancing, but no one was taking advantage. The left-hand side of the room was where all the action was. An old-fashioned wooden bar extended almost the entire length of the room and nearly half of the people were gathered in clumps within touching distance of the bar.

Kurt and Davy left the game of pool they were playing and headed over, big smiles on their faces.

"I'm so glad you guys could make it. Come, let me introduce you to everyone."

"Everyone? Didn't we meet everyone at your housewarming?" Jon sounded as freaked out as Rick felt. Kurt just laughed.

"No, not everyone. Other events aren't required attendance for the family, but birthday parties are. C'mon."

Rick let them go and made a beeline for the bar. He managed to squeeze into a spot behind two pregnant women who looked very much alike. Presumably these were the pregnant twin sisters Ian had mentioned, but he had no burning desire to introduce himself. Maybe after a glass or two of wine.

Rick ordered a white wine and waited.

"Did you see that guy Ian brought?"

Those words were enough to have Rick leaning away from the bar to listen in on the twins' conversation.

"So cute. Think there's another romance in the air?"

"I don't know. He may be cute, but he's also pretty young. Ian said he was just a friend."

"A friend. Yeah, right. Ian can call it whatever he wants, but that Leon kid wants to eat him up."

Leon? Ian brought Leon? Rick remembered Ian mentioning some friend of his from work named Leon. Who was also gay, if he recalled.

A dagger built of agony and despair gave him an unaccustomed painful taste of jealousy, and he didn't enjoy it one bit.

The glass of wine arrived and Rick snatched it up, not sure if he was going to walk out this minute or go and find Ian to throw it in his face. The logical part of his brain clamored for reason because he was the one who'd insisted on no strings. No commitment. Even if he'd wanted them, Ian surely wasn't the type of man to want them. This was how it should be. It was best this way.

Glass in hand, he searched the room for his friends and headed their way. The dark head he saw in the corner of his eye more than likely belonged to Ian but Rick was fairly short. Maybe Ian wouldn't see him in this crowd.

The hand on his shoulder—warm and familiar—told him otherwise. "Rick! You made it."

He could do this. Pasting on his cheerful yet vacant smile, he turned to Ian. "Hello, darling."

A tiny frown skittered across Ian's face for a moment before his smile returned.

"How are you?"

Confused. Angry. Horny. Rick inspected Ian's crisply pressed pale-blue shirt that made his eyes electric, matching dark-blue tie and black pants. Add a tailored suit jacket and Rick might cream on the spot. None of which he was going to admit. "Fine. You?"

Ian grinned. "You look great, although I have to admit I was hoping for the sheer burgundy shirt."

Rick gave a halfhearted laugh and put his hand on his hip, striking a pose like a model. "Well, now, kind of like a wedding, it wouldn't be fair to have all the attention on me, would it?"

Laughing, Ian grabbed his hand. "Come with me."

"I've already met most of your family." Rick couldn't stop the panicked words from spilling out.

"I know. Come meet Leon. He's my friend from work. I think I mentioned him."

Leon. Okay, yeah, Rick wanted to meet this guy. He followed Ian over to a small cluster of guys by a dart board.

The second they inserted themselves into the knot of men, Ian dropped his hand and a shaggy-haired young guy sidled up to Ian like he belonged.

"Leon." Ian wrapped an arm around shoulders broader than Rick's. Taller too. "This is my friend, Rick."

"Pleased to meet you, darling." Rick extended a hand, hoping he didn't look as uncomfortable as he felt.

"Rick. Nice to meet you too." Was that a sneer that accompanied Leon's words? The faint curl of his lip could have been a smile, but Rick had been playing the social game for a long time, and he was certain Leon felt nothing but disdain for him.

Fuck a duck. He was adorable too. Whip his shirt off and he'd have fit right into the young, toned crowd at Anaconda the other night.

"Ian, did you want another beer?"

Ian nodded at Leon. "Sure thing." He tried to hand Leon a twenty, but Leon just shook his head. For a moment, it appeared as though Leon was going to lean in and kiss Ian before he left, but thought better of it and departed for the bar.

The conversation grew to include the three other men who'd just finished a darts game, but Rick could do nothing aside from sip his wine and smile as white noise filled his brain. Anaconda. Ian had been at Anaconda. Which meant that despite finding Rick, he must have been looking for a younger man much like Leon. In fact, Rick was probably staring at the embodiment of Ian's type.

Everything Rick wasn't and could never be. And he'd never felt the lack more keenly. It was more painful than he'd ever want to admit that Ian might have lied to him. That he may have been nothing more than a convenient fuck. That Ian might want to be friends but might never intend to seek benefits again—at least while Leon was in the picture too. This was a mistake. A complete and utter mistake. All the things he'd told Ian, believing the friendship line. Some, he'd never told anyone, not even Jon. He was an idiot.

He scanned the bar. The back exit was closer than the front. If he used the back, he'd be outside and in cab that much faster.

"Excuse me a moment." No one heard him, and no one cared.

Rick placed his wine glass on a nearby table and headed for the back. Maybe everyone would think he was heading for the restroom.

IAN hadn't been able to keep his eyes off Rick. It was killing him not to touch him or kiss him or take him home and fuck him. Until tonight, he was certain he'd been taking the right tactic. Already they'd fallen into regular weekly outings that Ian privately called date nights, no matter what "friendship" spin he put on them to make Rick feel at ease.

Every minute he spent with Rick made him care more and more for the mysterious blond, and he had every confidence about where this relationship was going.

Until tonight.

Rick had thrown up another wall, one that included Ian in that vacant-headed expression. He smiled and laughed and Ian doubted anyone but himself could see there was no real emotion behind any of it. Not even when he looked at Ian. This couldn't just be a family thing. Sure, Erin's birthday party was bigger than Kurt's housewarming, by a long shot. But only a few sibs had missed out on Kurt's housewarming and as overwhelmed as Rick had been, Ian had still been able to see real emotion.

"Hey, man." Dylan clapped him on the shoulder from behind, and Ian stepped out of the circle he was standing in to speak to him. "They're bringing out the cake. It's picture time."

Oh, cake picture time. Just as the birthdays were sacrosanct, the cake picture was an inviolable rite of the birthday party. It had morphed slightly over time. Always was the picture with his parents and all the sibs standing behind the cake. Then spouse and kids of the birthday target, then the whole extended family. If the birthday target didn't have a spouse or kids, the family just took two pictures. Ian smiled.

"Be there in a minute." Maybe when his birthday rolled around, he'd get three pictures. He turned back to excuse himself and noticed Rick missing.

"Where'd Rick go?"

Leon glanced behind them and waved a hand. "Dunno. Back there. Bathroom, maybe?"

Ian pressed his lips together and scanned the back of the room. No familiar blond head appeared. The restrooms weren't the only thing back there. There was also an emergency exit, and Rick's first response to stress was flight.

"I'll be back in a minute."

Ducking into the hallway, he bypassed the restrooms. Rick might be taking a leak, but if he'd left the building, Ian wouldn't have much time to catch him at all. The man was sneaky and quick.

From habit borne from years of practice, Ian opened the door and stuck a quarter in the door jamb to prevent himself from getting locked out and stepped out into the back.

"Rick!"

The man had just about broken free of the area sheltered by trees and out into the parking lot. But he still paused and turned.

"What?"

"Where are you going?"

Rick closed his eyes for a moment, and when he opened them, they were filled with mocking contempt of the sort Ian hadn't had directed his way since their fight at Kurt's housewarming.

"Darling, I'm leaving, obviously. Not much of a scene here and it's Saturday night. The clubs are waiting."

Ian gritted his teeth. Rick hadn't been to a club on a Saturday night in weeks, as he had good cause to know. Saturday night had become one of their regular nights to hang out. "What happened?"

Like two opposite charges, he and Rick approached each other.

"Nothing happened." A faint sneer twisted Rick's words, hiding the hurt that lay beneath. Hurt that Ian wouldn't have been able to see six weeks ago.

"Hey. Whatever it is, we can fix it." Ian stepped into Rick's space, unable to stand how carefully Rick held himself, like he wanted to run or hug himself, but didn't dare do either. He cupped Rick's chin, tilted his face up, and did what he'd been longing to do for weeks.

The first press of lips was light, tender, and sweet. Ian had a moment to revel in the fact that Rick wasn't pulling away, wasn't taking him to task for breaking a rule, wasn't acting like a cornered cat. Then he stopped thinking about anything but Rick's mouth, lips, and tongue, and where kissing could lead. Kissing had never seemed as vital to his existence as it was this very moment.

Rick's mouth opened under his and Ian took advantage, letting his tongue dive in to twine and play with Rick's. The tartness of the wine Rick had been drinking disappeared after a moment, leaving nothing but Rick behind. Was tonight the night he moved things on to benefits? Had he kept them on edge long enough to convince Rick they could be good together on a more permanent basis? Rick's compliance—no, his active participation—convinced him he'd managed to allay Rick's fears of commitment.

Relaxing into the kiss, he slid his hands away from Rick's face to pull him close. With no conscious direction from his brain, his hips ground against Rick like that last time they danced in a club. Rick felt so good in his arms. Better than anything else.

Rick pushed him away, and Ian stumbled from the unexpected force.

He stepped forward again. His unevolved lizard brain wanted nothing more than to continue the pleasure, and hadn't quite caught up to current events. Rick was angry. Angry like Ian had never seen.

"No. No more."

"Why?" The lizard brain still held too much control, because Ian was a hell of lot more eloquent than that.

"Shouldn't you be doing that with your *date*?" This time the sneer wasn't faint, at all.

"My date? I don't have a date."

"Oh, really? And what about Leon?"

"Leon? You're not jealous of Leon, are you?" Ian hadn't meant to say it aloud, but the possibility had warmed him inside. Sure, Leon was cute, but he was a baby. Even if Leon had been his own age, he just wasn't Rick. But the question made Rick angrier.

"Of course I'm not jealous," he snapped. "Why would I be?"

Ian wasn't sure where to go from here. After watching his sibs reel in their chosen mates, he'd thought he had this all under control, but he'd never been in a relationship before, and he was one hundred percent certain he wasn't going to be able to jolly Rick out of his anger like he would one of his brothers.

"Leon's just a friend."

"Right. And that's why you invited him here."

"He is." Rick's antagonism was pricking Ian's anger, but he did his best to control it. "I knew Kurt was going to invite you, so I didn't. I thought it would help take the pressure off, since it was a family thing."

"Oh, really? And what difference should that make to me?"

Ian threw out his arms in exasperation. "After all the time we've spent together? I thought you'd be happy about it."

"Please. If you wanted to date Leon, you could have just told me."

"I don't want to date him. Leon's a friend."

"Like I'm a *friend*? Bullshit. That's why you were at Anaconda that night. You were looking for Leon, or someone like him."

True, sort of. He'd gone because he'd figured he'd find someone who wasn't Rick and wouldn't even remind him of Rick, but fate had had other ideas. "I went home with you, though."

"Oh, don't make any sacrifices on my account. You're free to seek out whatever companionship you want. If the scent of Clearasil turns you on, you go for it. No strings, no entanglements, remember?"

This time, the sarcasm about Leon's youth and contemptuous sneer on the face of the man Ian was fucking falling for was too damned much.

"No strings…. Who the fuck are you kidding? Haven't you figured it out yet? Friends are strings. Friends are entanglements. And you need to get it through your head—we're already more than friends, even without the sex."

Rick's eyes flared wide at Ian's anger, and he wanted to call back his ill-thought-out words as soon as he'd said them.

"Well, I'm cutting this string now. We're done, Ian. Whatever you thought this was, it's over. Don't call me again."

Eyes glittering, Rick squared his shoulders.

"Wait, what? Rick, don't—"

The door behind him burst open and hit the side of the building with a metallic bang, making Ian whirl.

His dad leaned out of the opening. "There you are, boyo. We've been looking all over. Inside, now. I'm starting to think Erin might be pregnant too, the way she's carrying on about waiting for you and that cake. It's picture time."

Ian nodded and turned to beg Rick to come inside, give him a chance to… do whatever he had to do to reverse that final-sounding pronouncement, but he was already gone.

"Come on, now. What are you doing out here, anyway?" His dad eyed the area. "Hmm. It's getting pretty overgrown out here. We'll have to fix that, maybe add a few more lights. Don't want anyone thinking they can get up to any funny business out here."

Ian wasn't sure if his dad thought he'd been up to "funny business" but it didn't matter. Rick was gone and his father would kill him if he took off now. Resigned, he followed his dad inside. His dad continued to talk, but all Ian could hear were Rick's words on repeat. Done. They couldn't be done. Minutes ago they'd been kissing, kissing like Ian had never kissed anyone else. He'd been so sure of Rick. They *couldn't* be done.

His eyes burned, and he swallowed heavily. The last thing he wanted was to explain to everyone what had happened. He could put a good face on this until after the cake cutting and somehow manage to smile on command, although he'd never felt less like smiling in his life.

LAUGHTER grated on Ian's ears. Even when he was scoping out hot guys and pretending he was checking out women, he'd always liked the bustle and noise of the bar. It energized him in a way. Hell, the party room wasn't even as full as it could be, but the noise and number of people buffeted him like body blows. Nothing compared to the near mortal wound Rick had delivered just moments ago, and he was still absorbing the shock of it all.

This was his first stab at a relationship of any sort, and there was no way his heart should be involved this soon, but it must be. This hollowed-out feeling in his chest was more than simply a bruised ego. With six sibs who never pulled a metaphorical punch, he was more than familiar with the sensations of bruised ego and hurt feelings. This was so far beyond he had no idea why people kept trying to find this. His failure was nearly enough to send him back into the closet.

"Come on, Ian, you're the last one." Erin beckoned him over with a huge smile. A woman shouldn't be so happy to be turning forty-five, but his eldest sister, just like their mom, never seemed to mind the advancing years. Then again, neither of them was making the march alone. Although Ian had his family, he'd met the man who he'd be able to share his life with, in a way he couldn't with sibs and parents.

Ian approached the table that held an enormous birthday cake. Without question or complaint, Ian let his sisters position him for the photos, tucking him into the family between Kurt and Dylan.

"You okay, man?" Kurt whispered while they jostled together for the photo.

Ian couldn't look him in the eye. Nodding seemed less of a lie, so that's what he did before plastering a big, fake smile on his face when the bartender, called over to take the pics, yelled "Cheese!"

Two blinding flashes of white later, his mother clapped her hands. "The rest of the family, now."

Spouses and kids, all used to the routine by now, pushed their way into the huddle to stand with their own "sib." A hand brushed Ian's side and he turned his head to look at Kurt.

Grief gripped him by the throat. The hand he'd felt had been Davy's as he pushed his way into the group and wrapped his arm around Kurt's waist.

Ian had known. He'd known that day he'd come out to his family that he was the only one who wouldn't have someone in this photo, but he hadn't known how much it would ache.

If he hadn't started falling for Rick, hadn't imagined Rick standing next to him, part of the O'Donnell clan, maybe he'd only have a lingering sense of remorse and a renewed urge to get out there and date. Problem was, he didn't want to find anyone else. He didn't even want to head out to any of his usual haunts to get laid. He was hung up on a guy who never wanted to see him again, and he didn't know what to do about it.

Glancing across the room, he noted Leon standing next to Parker and Ivan. Leon was becoming a good friend and might keep him company at a club, but he wasn't sure how Rick could even think there was anything between them.

Finally the interminable picture was done, although each couple seemed to have the uncontrollable need to kiss. He stared out at the cheering crowd and more flashes went off as additional pictures were snapped.

Surrounded by family and friends, Ian had never felt more alone in his life. Wasn't coming out supposed to have fixed that? Wasn't telling the truth about himself supposed to make him feel whole? It was a relief, sure, that he didn't have to pretend, but this yearning for Rick ruined what should have been a watershed moment in his life.

His sister handed him a piece of cake on a paper plate, and Ian picked up a fork and cut off a bite out of habit. When he got it to his nose, the sugary sweet scent of the icing made his stomach turn. He set the plate down, the churning in his stomach matching the whirl of his dizzying thoughts.

The noise and laughter in the bar got steadily louder and louder. He had to get the fuck out of here.

He turned, intending to sneak out the back—the same way Rick escaped—in order to avoid any extended conversations. Leon wasn't a problem. He'd just have to text Leon from the car or home to tell him where he'd gone.

"Honey, what's wrong?"

Damn it. On the days when it was most inconvenient, his mother's psychic skills peaked.

Ian drew in a deep breath. His eyes burned and his lip trembled, but he managed a credibly strong, "Nothing."

"Bullshit."

Ian blinked, surprise pushing back his upset to an almost manageable level. His mother almost never cussed and usually only did so to make a point. He just didn't know what point she was making now.

"You think I don't know when something's wrong with one of my kids?" Her blue-eyed gaze moved to Kurt before landing on Ian again. "Even when he was avoiding us, I knew in my heart. With you right here, under my eyes? I can see how brittle you are right now. I'm your mum and I love you."

Ian's ears got hot, a jumble of memories from childhood where his mother's open love for all her family had embarrassed them all at one point or another. But the birthday girl had started opening presents and no one's attention was on him and his mom.

He was afraid to speak. Afraid he'd let all that unexpected emotion come tumbling out. But his mother wasn't going anywhere until she got an answer.

"I think I just got dumped." He couldn't manage to speak in anything more than a harsh whisper.

His mom gave him a soft, sad smile and stared into his eyes. "Oh, honey. That boy is as new to this as you are. And he's scared."

"I'm scared too."

She let out a little bleat of laughter. "Not nearly as much as he is. Trust me. He's adorable, but when I spoke to him at Kurt's, I thought he was going to bolt like a frightened rabbit."

Ian frowned and glanced at Leon, who'd never been to Kurt's, never mind had a chance to talk to his mother. If his mom was going to assume he was falling for anyone, wouldn't she assume it was Leon? He certainly hadn't mentioned anything about Rick to his family, although Kurt had to know they'd slept together a couple of times.

His mother responded with a light slap to his shoulder. "I'm not daft, you know. That boy is young enough to be my grandson. No, I knew the minute I saw that sweet Rick, and the way the two of you looked at each other."

He should never doubt his mother's powers.

"He said he didn't want to see me anymore. I… I…." Ian shut his mouth, afraid tears were going to fall along with his words.

"Did you do anything stupid? Like inviting that boy here?" His mother raised a brow.

"Leon's just a friend. And I knew Rick was nervous about… anyone thinking we're anything to each other." God, he felt fifteen again, awkward and unsure. It fucking sucked.

Shaking her head, his mom grabbed his hand and held it, transferring a little more comfort. "I think you care a lot for that Rick, my boyo. Which means you're going to need to show him you care, even if it's not what he thinks he wants. And that includes showing him you're not going to find an attractive substitute just because it's easier. You need to go get him. Fight for him. Straighten this out. Make sure he knows Leon has no chance, because as sure as I've got eyes in my face, that Leon would scoop you up in a hot second."

Okay, his mother wasn't infallible. Leon didn't like him like that. Ian would be able to tell. But the rest of her advice… he'd have no chance with Rick if he allowed Rick to cut off contact entirely. He needed to fix this. Now.

"Go on, honey. It's early still. I'll make your excuses."

Ian smiled and his mom wiped away a stray tear that escaped. "Thanks, Mom."

"You know I want to see you happy. All of you. Rick's going to lead you a merry chase, but if he's the one, he's the one."

Ian hugged his mom and ran for the door he'd been intending to escape through just moments ago.

He slammed through and was about to head for his car, but he stopped short and pulled out his phone. After sending a short text, he paced, waiting for a response. His mom had said she was going to make his excuses—showing up back in the bar would ruin her good work.

A few minutes later, Kurt opened the back door.

"What the hell is going on?"

"I need Rick's address."

"What? Why?"

"I need to talk to him. Tonight. It's important."

"He's here at the bar. Talk to him inside."

Ian almost let loose a tirade about how unobservant his police detective brother was, but when he thought about it, his whole fight with Rick and Rick's departure had probably taken place twenty or thirty minutes ago. Forty-five minutes, tops. There was no reason for Kurt to know Rick had already left, not considering how many people were still in the bar.

"He's gone. We had a fight."

"Ian, what the hell is going on? Rick doesn't fight with people. Nor do you, not really."

This time, he made himself look Kurt in the eye. Let all his wounded fear out for his brother to see. "I screwed up and I need to fix this. Please."

The tightness around Kurt's eyes softened. "I wouldn't do this if you weren't my brother, you know? Rick's not big on letting people know where he lives."

That was weird, wasn't it? "Is there something wrong—"

Kurt sliced a hand through the air to cut off Ian's words. "No, man, but he's one private little guy. I mean, he's far more likely to get up on a table and rip off his pants than he is to let just anyone into his house."

"I'm not just anyone. I promise." God. He had to be something more than "just anyone." Had to.

"Then you need to promise me that if you can't fix this—whatever it is—that you'll lose this address. Rick doesn't need any of your shit. Got it?" Kurt suddenly became all benevolent but stern police officer, and if it weren't for the fact he was desperate to get to Rick's place, he would have rolled his eyes.

"I swear, I swear."

Kurt pursed his lips, then texted Ian an address. As soon as his phone vibrated with the message, Ian hugged his brother and ran for his car.

CHAPTER
Six

RICK locked the door behind him and fell against it, panting. He barely remembered the drive home, but he drove like the devil himself had been chasing him. Sinking down to the floor, he drew his knees up to his chest and wrapped his arms around them. In the safety of his home, he let the tears fall, the same tears that had been blurring his vision and burning his eyes since the bar.

How could Ian have done this to him? Ian had told him that he couldn't spend their usual Saturday night together because of his sister's birthday party. Kurt had already begged him to attend with Jon and the others, so it wasn't an issue. He'd stupidly thought Ian had avoided asking him to attend because he'd figured out his family made Rick nervous.

And they did. But they were a big part of Ian's life, so he'd given in and gone, hoping it wouldn't be so nerve-wracking if he was there as Kurt's friend, rather than some sort of pseudodate of Ian's. He didn't want anyone speculating about their… relationship.

But Leon had changed everything. Turned everything he thought he knew upside down. Made him wonder how many "friends" Ian had. Which of them were getting the benefits he should be getting. How many more lies Ian had told him.

In a matter of minutes, he'd become a jealous idiot.

Goddammit. He'd been happy, spending time with Ian, able to pretend they were friends. About to be friends with benefits. He'd even been thinking of other things they could do together, ways he could spend even more evenings with Ian. All under the comfortable fiction of friendship.

Then, Ian had to rip off his blindfold.

Like poking an open sore, trying to make it bleed more, he let himself remember Ian's words.

We're already more than friends, even without the sex.

They were. Which made Ian's decision to invite Leon all that more inexplicable. Damn him. Ian had made him care, more than he should. More than was safe. Cutting things off between him and Ian was the wisest thing he'd ever done, but why did it have to hurt so much?

A sob caught in his throat. Had he really told Ian he didn't want to see him again? The number of Ian-less hours in a week stretched endlessly before him. If only Ian had left things alone, they could have still had their friendship. Rick could have pretended he didn't care so much about Ian, and Ian could have provided the benefits he'd promised. It wouldn't be a relationship, but it would be the nearest Rick could allow himself to have. Now he wasn't going to have the comfort of Ian's company ever again.

Sniffling, he wiped a shirtsleeve across his face to dry his eyes. Blotchy red was so not a good look for him. Crying over a man. He'd never done it and never thought he would. He'd have to make that another rule. No crying for any man.

As creaky and stiff as an old man, Rick levered himself to his feet.

He kicked off his shoes and dropped his keys in a bowl by the door. Then he walked, zombie-like, to his bedroom. He began peeling off his shirt when he caught sight of the clock. Was he seriously considering going to sleep at nine on a Saturday night? A flash of anger helped bury his sadness. What if Ian had been *trying* to make him jealous? The club frenzy hadn't even started yet, and he could go out and find himself a sweet twinkie like Ian had found. Show Ian two could play that game. A glance in the mirror dispelled that notion. *He* was the sweet twinkie. But a bear cub out on the town… that would be a great countermeasure to Leon. Assuming Rick ever saw Ian again, that was.

Tearing through his closet, he found the perfect outfit. One that said, "bring on the sex." Rick was determined go out and not return until he'd shared an orgasm with someone other than Ian. He'd already been weeks without having someone else bring him off. His right hand had never gotten such a workout. Tonight that changed. He was going to start a new roster. Fuck Ian for preventing him from building a new one.

In front of the mirror, Rick smoothed his hand down his sheer burgundy shirt. Along with the tight black pants, he looked great. Once he got to that club, he'd have a hot mouth around his dick inside of ten minutes; he'd bet money on it. If there was anyone here to bet with. Peering at his eyes, some of the blotchiness from his tears remained. He should probably put on some makeup.

Tears welled up again, sudden and unexpected, when he realized he'd managed to put on the exact same outfit he'd been wearing the night Ian had convinced him to try out this unorthodox friendship.

He couldn't decide between crying his eyes out or shouting out in anger. The warring emotions had almost sent him out to fuck some random stranger, and he felt like he'd been ripped apart inside. Then the tears burst their dam and streaked down his face, another rule broken, this one in record time. Fuck Ian. Rick threw himself across the bed, finally acknowledging he'd lost the desire to fuck anyone else, but didn't dare let himself have Ian.

He was losing his mind. Just like his mother had.

A FRANTIC knocking at Rick's front door made him raise his head from the damp pillows. It might be early for the clubs, but it was damned late for someone to knock on his door.

Then again, he'd sent Jon a brief text after he'd left the bar saying he wasn't feeling well and was going home. It wasn't completely out of the realm of possibility that Jon had come over to make sure he was okay.

The knocking paused for a moment; then the doorbell rang twice and then the knocking began again.

He wiped at his eyes, but there was no way he could hide the red remnants of tears. Although he wasn't eager to explain his foolishness, if he had to tell anyone, Jon would be his first choice. And since it didn't sound as though Jon was going away, he might as well get it over with.

He turned on the outside light and swung open the door.

"Jon, I...."

But it wasn't Jon. Ian stood outside, pale as milk, with a hesitant smile gracing those full and supremely talented lips.

"What are you doing here?" A surge of anger that Ian had ignored his wishes was quickly swamped by a wave of relief at seeing him again.

Which was the main reason he didn't slam the door in Ian's face, as he probably should have.

Ian's gaze took him in from head to toe, and the smile fell away as he paled even more. "Are you going out?"

"I...." Rick didn't know what to say. Despite having done everything in his power to avoid having a relationship, he sensed that he'd managed to hurt Ian deeply. The fact that he'd come home and gotten ready to go out right after had to seem like a knife in the back. Deliberately hurting Ian wasn't something he wanted to do, no matter how hurt or scared Ian made him.

"Please don't go out. I want to talk to you, get this sorted. I don't want to lose you. I don't want to be done. Please."

Redness rimmed Ian's eyes, a telltale sign he'd not fared any better than Rick the past hour. Knowing Ian cared so much warmed him as much as it terrified him. As foolish as it was, he couldn't bring himself to make the same break he'd made at the bar. If talking gave him the chance to keep a little bit of Ian, he'd take it. Anything more was out of the question, no matter what he wanted.

Heart beating furiously, he stepped back, letting Ian into his foyer.

Ian responded to the unspoken invitation and walked into his home, but he didn't bother looking around or making any comment on the interior.

"Were you going out?" Ian's voice cracked over the hurt he couldn't disguise.

Rick shrugged. "No. Not really. For a few minutes, it seemed like a good idea."

Cupping his face, Ian tilted his head, peering at him. Rick blinked, his eyes still swollen and sore. Ian brushed thumbs across the tender skin underneath his eyes.

"You'd have been going for all the wrong reasons." The tenderness in Ian's voice made him shiver. "Look at you. We're quite the pair, aren't we?"

With a tiny nod, Rick indicated his assent. He didn't trust himself to speak. Not yet.

"As gorgeous as you are in this shirt, we really do need to talk. Got someplace we can sit?"

A blush made his tear-swollen tissues throb. How could Ian still call him gorgeous? He looked like a train wreck. But Ian was right; they needed to talk.

"Sure." Crying had made his throat dry and his voice creaky. "Follow me."

Rick led them to the living room with its plush, comfortable sofa facing the TV. "Did you want something to drink?" He could use some liquid courage for this.

"Water, please."

Postponing their talk just a few more minutes, Rick got them each a glass of water. As much as he might yearn for alcohol to help him through this, he didn't need to be even more dehydrated than he was now.

When he returned to the living room, he considered sitting in the lone chair off to the right, but Ian patted the seat on the sofa beside him, and Rick gave in to the request.

Ian curled an arm around him, pulling him tight. The warmth of Ian's body seeped into him, a comfort he hadn't experienced since the last time he'd woken in Ian's bed. It was good, so good, but he didn't dare let himself get used to it.

They sat like that for several minutes, just touching. They sat there so long Rick wondered if Ian had fallen asleep, and he shifted to look up at him.

"I don't know where best to begin," Ian said, as though sensing Rick's question. "Leon's a friend. Nothing more, I promise. In fact, I haven't even slept with anyone else since I met you. I haven't wanted to."

There was no mistaking Ian's overwhelming sincerity.

"Me, neither." It wasn't stupid if they'd both denied themselves, right? The extra squeeze Ian gave him was assurance enough that he'd said the right thing for a change.

"I think there was more to tonight than Leon. I know my family makes you uncomfortable, but I don't know why. I know you're against relationships, but I don't know why. I think you want to be with me as much as I want to be with you, but something's holding you back. I'm hoping you'll trust me enough to tell me what's going on. If I know what the problem is, we've got a better chance of working it out together."

"Are you sure you're not a psychologist instead of an account manager?"

"That's *senior* account manager." Ian grinned at him and dropped a kiss on his temple. "And while there is certainly some psychology involved in keeping everyone happy and willing to accept compromise, I rather think it's nothing more than having picked up a few pointers from my sister here and there. Occasionally I do listen to them."

Ian's expression grew serious. "But you're stalling. Do you not trust me? No matter what else, we're still friends. Please tell me what you're so afraid of."

Rick's heart skipped a beat. He wanted to tell Ian. He'd never told anyone the whole story, not ever. Jon knew some of it, but when he'd met Jon, they'd both been so raw from their experiences, they'd bonded over that without ever getting the full details from each other.

"I'm afraid of me," he whispered. The confused tenderness in Ian's eyes gave him some courage, but he couldn't talk about it and worry about Ian's reaction to every word, so he tucked himself against Ian, facing the darkened television.

"My parents had a very volatile marriage. I realize now my mother must have been manifesting early symptoms of mental illness. Bipolar, maybe. They kept having affairs, then fighting with each other about them, then they'd get back together and things would be calm for a while before the whole cycle started again. I wasn't much more than an afterthought. An accident. They were too involved in their own drama to worry too much about the effect it had on me. But it wasn't so bad. Not until I was... fourteen. I already knew I was gay, and I didn't have much success hiding it at school. I got harassed a bit, not bashed, thankfully, but there wasn't anywhere... calm and safe. My parents weren't thrilled by my orientation, but they were so wrapped up in each other, they didn't much care one way or the other.

"One day, just a few days before the end of the school year, my dad came home and told my mother he was leaving. This time, the affair meant something, and he wasn't willing to give her up for the chaotic life he'd been living with my mother. She wasn't able to accept that, and she grabbed a knife from the kitchen and stabbed him seven times."

Ian gasped and held him closer. Until that moment, Rick had been expecting rejection. Disgust, maybe. It could still come—he wasn't finished yet—but he was thankful for Ian's presence.

The tips of Rick's fingers got cold and numb as he tried desperately not to remember the blood. His father's sightless eyes. He rubbed his hands against his thighs, hoping the friction would help.

Ian grabbed Rick's hands with his own free one. Compared to Rick's bloodless hands, Ian's hands were as fiery hot against his skin as the sun.

"Who... I mean... how...."

Rick knew what Ian wanted to know. "A neighbor heard the screaming and called the police. I got home from school to find my house surrounded by police cars and fire trucks and an ambulance. I got there just as they were taking my father out on a gurney. At first I'd thought maybe he'd had a heart attack or something. Until I got inside and saw all the blood."

He grabbed for his glass of water and took a sip. Even after all this time, the memory made him nauseous. He cleared his throat. No reason to talk about the ordeal of the trial and his lost year at school.

"My mother was eventually declared unfit to stand trial and was committed."

"And you were fourteen? What happened to you?"

Rick shrugged. "By that time I was fifteen. My only relative was my father's sister. She did her Christian duty and took me in, but she hated my mother for killing her brother. And she hated me for being my mother's son. I was allowed visits with my mother, which my aunt took me to, but my mother only wanted to know why my father wasn't coming to visit."

"You mean she didn't know she'd killed him? How is that possible?"

"I guess she blocked it. None of the doctors would tell me anything, and after she killed herself, I wasn't able to speak to find out the whys and wherefores."

"I'm so sorry, Rick. Wait... you weren't able to speak? You mean your aunt wouldn't let you ask?"

"No, I mean, I couldn't speak. The trauma, I guess. If it weren't for the counselor at school who was training to be a speech-language pathologist, I might never have shaken it."

His aunt had been just as happy he hadn't been able to ask questions or complain.

"So that's why you chose your profession?"

"Yeah. It probably wasn't entirely ethical for her to treat me while she was in training, but however much my aunt pretended, she didn't care enough to get me help or spend the money, and I was too frustrated and embarrassed to find help on my own. My friends all drifted away during the trial, and I had no one besides Miss Abernathy. And I was lucky for her help because as soon as I graduated high school, my aunt decided she'd done her duty by her gay nephew and tossed me out. Talking was a necessity to get a job. I moved to Toronto and started a brand-new life."

Probably it wasn't necessary to tell him that he still had occasional bouts of silence, usually triggered by women like Ian's mom, who tried to mother him.

"Needless to say, I haven't had the best role models for relationships nor do I have a lot of respect for families." Which was a nice, politic way of saying they scared the shit out of him.

"I… I don't know what to say. I had no idea."

Rick waited, expecting Ian to leave. God knows, he would. There was no way Ian had been expecting Rick to have such immense, boundless luggage. Any minute now, he'd realize he'd bitten off more than he was willing to chew and would leave. Even if he didn't, there was still one final nail to go in their relationship coffin. Until Ian took that final step to leave, he'd enjoy the comfort of Ian's arms. His fuck buddies weren't much into cuddling. Except for Oscar and that had always felt more like smothering than cuddling.

They sat in silence again, Rick's ear pressed against Ian's chest, listening to the steady, soothing thump of his heartbeat.

Ian shifted and Rick curled up on himself, prepared for yet another rejection as Ian left. It shocked him a little to find himself seated between Ian's legs, his back propped up against Ian's chest as Ian leaned back against the high armrest of his sofa.

Ian's warm hands rubbed down his arms, and for a moment, Rick expected Ian to make a move. Pleased beyond measure to find out he was wrong, he settled back against Ian, who wrapped his arms around Rick's chest.

"I am so sorry you had to go through that. I don't know if I would have survived, but you not only survived, you…. You're so strong. Funny, sweet, successful… I never would have guessed."

Strong? Successful? Ian had to be talking about someone else.

"Thank you for telling me. I definitely understand you better now and while it might take me some time to fully assimilate everything, there was one thing you said that confused me. You said you were afraid of *you*. What did that mean?"

Eyes burning, he blinked away the tears even as his limbs began to tremble. He'd set up his rules to avoid ever having to deal with this situation or even think about it, but he'd already given Ian so much, he might as well finish it. He couldn't have Ian hanging around under false pretenses anyway. That wasn't fair to either of them, not if Ian was after more than Rick could give.

"I'm my mother's son. What if I do the same thing? Mental illness can be hereditary. What if my jealousy tips over into a murderous rage? I can't take that chance."

Rick sat up. He couldn't do this. He couldn't jeopardize Ian like this. Not even if it meant his own happiness needed to be sacrificed.

"You should go now. We should make a clean break."

Standing, he stepped aside, facing away from the sofa, and wrapped his arms around himself. They weren't even a poor substitute for the strength of Ian's arms, but Ian's arms would be leaving and not coming back.

"No."

Rick turned around. "What do you mean, no?"

"Okay, I understand why you're afraid. But I'm not afraid. Not of you. I haven't seen anything that would lead me to believe you're dangerous. And I don't want to go. I think you're it for me. And I don't think being unfaithful will be an issue. I've fucked lots of other guys and not one has ever meant anything to me. I don't want to go back to that. I want to build a life with someone. Someone who gets me, someone who I enjoy spending time with, someone who makes me so damned horny I could come just from kissing him. I want that someone to be you, and I think maybe you want that too, which is why you told me all this. You trust me with your past, and I trust you not to hurt me. This will work, Rick. Please give us a chance."

This had to be a dream. No way would a guy like Ian sign up for this. "Are you sure? I can't… I'm not sure I trust myself. You'd be betting your life on the outcome."

Ian stepped close, and Rick fell into his arms like he'd always belonged there.

"I *am* willing to bet my life and as far as I'm concerned, it's a good bet. The best. But if you're worried, go talk to someone. There's no shame in getting help. Even if you've got the same condition your mother had—which I doubt—I'm sure there are medications available, and better ones than were available twenty years ago. We can get through this."

"Okay," he whispered.

Ian leaned back to stare into Rick's eyes. "Okay? Okay, what?"

He wanted this more than anything in his life and if it didn't work out, he didn't know what he'd do. "Okay, let's give this a chance."

Ian's smile was a beautiful sight, and it gave him hope that maybe, just maybe, this might all work out.

"You won't regret this."

But his fears weren't put to rest that easily. "Can we… can we not tell anyone? I've had such a hard stance against relationships, I don't want to have to explain about this unless I'm sure—we're sure—that this is working out."

"Anything you want, baby. We can keep this under our hats for a while. But you have to promise me you'll come to a family event as my date. It doesn't have to be right away, but I want my family to know how I feel about you."

"Okay. Yes, I can work on that." He didn't even feel the need to snark about being called *baby*. Normally he hated it, but for some reason, he didn't mind when Ian said it.

"And we're exclusive. It's just us."

Rick tilted his head. "I want that. I do. But what do either of us know about being faithful?"

"Has it been hard, not sleeping with other guys?"

He thought about that. "No, actually."

"Me neither."

"But how can we guarantee it will continue like that?" Probably his parents had assumed some degree of fidelity when they'd first gotten together, and that had gone completely down the shitter.

Ian shrugged. "We can't. All we can do is try." He paused for a moment. "How about this? If it gets too hard, we make sure we talk about it. I can promise that. We'll talk before it gets to the point of cheating."

Yeah, yeah, he could promise that. "That sounds good."

Feelings, promises, relationships, and broken rules. Rick should have been scared shitless. Instead, he just wanted to devour Ian.

"Now, my sweet boyfriend…."

A delicious shiver danced up his spine at Ian's words, his cock filling and pressing against his fly. He was someone's boyfriend. At thirty-five, he was a little old to feel as giddy as a teenager, but he couldn't quell his excitement.

"Yes?"

Ian pinched at his nipples, which had peaked when his cock hardened. "I think I need to express how very much I love this shirt on you. Where's your bedroom?"

A slight frown marred the moment. "Unless… is that too fast? Did you want to wait?"

If it was possible, he just got hornier. "No fucking way."

Ian's smile returned and he pulled Rick close, pressing their lips together.

Rick moaned and opened his lips under Ian's questing tongue. He'd never known what he'd been missing by not kissing guys—but then, maybe it was only Ian's lips that could make him feel this way.

He brought his hands up and held them against Ian's cheeks. The sensation of movement under his palms was surprisingly erotic, like the movement when a guy was sucking him off. But this was better. Sweeter and hotter and more delicious all at once. The faint trace of Ian's stubble rasped against his fingers, and he wanted to feel that against his belly, against the head of his cock, and against his face while Ian drove inside him.

But telling Ian where the bedroom was would mean losing the drugging pleasure of his kisses. Instead, he urged Ian backward, heading for the bed by guiding him with his body.

IAN had to be dreaming. Rick had agreed to give them a chance. Sure, he wanted to keep it quiet, but after all he'd been through, Ian couldn't blame him for that.

Now, Rick was kissing him like he never wanted to stop. Ian wasn't sure he wanted to stop either, but damn, he wanted another chance to explore Rick's naked body. He'd not fully appreciated what he'd had those first two times and he wasn't going to make that mistake again.

The back of his legs hit the bed. Finally.

He flipped them around and pushed Rick back on the bed. Their lips separated and Ian felt the loss like the loss of a limb.

Staring down at Rick, sprawled against the blue sheets, his cock pulsed in his jeans. His boyfriend—and he loved using that word—was so fucking sexy.

He stroked a finger down Rick's face, skimming over the collar of the shirt to those peaked nipples, so temptingly visible; the sheerness of the shirt added something delicious. It was all there for Ian to see, and yet, he still ached for naked skin. After giving those hardened tips a gentle rub, he moved his hand to trace the faint line of fuzzy hair that delineated the path from Rick's belly to groin. The edge of Rick's pants was low enough to show a faint hint of the trimmed bush barely constrained by the waistband. The temptation to slide his hands under that waistband and yank, freeing Rick's cock, was almost irresistible.

Rick might not mind if Ian pounced, ripping clothes and indulging in wild, animalistic sex. Ian might still succumb to that desire, but he wanted their first time as a couple to be something memorable—special. Perhaps that was pathetic and sappy, but he couldn't help it. His mom believed in romance with a capital R, and she raised all her kids to at least respect it, if not want it. Turns out, they all did, even though he'd never imagined that would be the case for him.

He tamped down his raging lust and straddled Rick. With arms braced on either side of Rick, he dropped his head and sipped gently at Rick's soft lips. Rick moaned and let him lead the way with tender kisses. A glint of gold stubble on Rick's jaw called to him, and he moved his lips over the slight roughness, nibbling at a strong jawline before brushing their cheeks together. This time, the low moan was his.

Moving on to the tender skin of Rick's neck, he mouthed and sucked gently, Rick writhing and panting below him.

"Harder," Rick demanded.

"It'll mark." Ian's cock, however, could see no downside to that happenstance.

"Good."

With a growl, Ian opened his mouth over Rick's neck and sucked. The long, low moan that tore from Rick's throat almost made him come in his pants. So fucking sexy.

Pulling back, he stared at the reddish mark, an unaccustomed sensation of pride filling him. That was his mark on his boyfriend and there was no denying the atavistic notion of "Mine!" ringing in his brain.

He couldn't wait any longer. He started on the buttons of Rick's shirt, unbuttoning them one by one and licking at the flesh revealed by the parted fabric.

Rick made an attempt to undress him, but Ian shifted downward and put Rick's hands back at his side. Instead of lying there and letting Ian do everything, though, Rick moved his fingers into Ian's hair and caressed his scalp. There was no pressure, no sense of Rick trying to direct him, only the vague impression that Rick just needed to touch back.

Ian placed a hand over Rick's belly and spread his fingers, easing the last of the burgundy fabric off Rick's torso. With Rick's golden skin bared to Ian's gaze, the pink flush of arousal that stained his chest and neck was readily visible.

He bent again to kiss the dark-blond treasure trail underneath Rick's navel. Resting his throat against the hot, hard bulge of Rick's trapped erection, he licked at Rick's lower belly. Fingers clenched in his hair at the extended teasing, tugging sharply each time Ian found a ticklish bit.

Finally the heat and musky scent of Rick's cock became irresistible. Ian was desperate to free his own cock and assumed Rick was in a similar state.

Running his tongue underneath the waistband of Rick's pants, he encountered the bare, moist head of Rick's cock. They moaned in tandem at the connection of tongue to cock. If Rick wasn't ready to explode for *him* right now, Ian might be a little pissed that he was going commando.

He sat up and wrenched Rick's pants open, reveling in the erection that sprang free.

"Please," Rick whispered.

"So, some total stranger rates going commando, do they?" Okay, maybe he was still a tiny bit pissed off.

Instead of looking abashed, as Ian had expected, Rick gave him a wicked smile. "I was going commando at Finn's."

Ian's mouth opened and he shuddered. If things had gone differently tonight, and if he'd known Rick was deliciously bare under his pants, he might very well have had Rick up against the wall of his parents' bar.

"Oh, God. I'm so glad I didn't know that."

Rick frowned. Ian replayed his words and realized that perhaps that they hadn't come out quite as complimentary as he'd intended.

"I only meant I wouldn't have been able to resist you. I would have wanted to put you face-first against the wall so I could push into you."

Rick squirmed a little, like he'd imagined the exact same scenario. Ian's fingers clutched restlessly against Rick's hips, enjoying how much his words made Rick squirm, how they coaxed tiny beads of fluid to the slit atop his dick.

"Greased you up if you'd brought a little slick." Rick's rosy skin flushed a little darker, and his eyes flickered to the bedside table where a pillow pack of lube resided, presumably the exact same one he'd carried in his pocket to the bar. Ian grinned at Rick's careful planning and grabbed the pack. He slid Rick's pants off and spread his legs wide then squeezed some lube on his fingers and matched words to action.

"But if there was no slick, I'd have to go down on my knees, spread your ass, and use my tongue to open you right up."

Nothing less than an agonized wail left Rick's lips and Ian grinned. Oh, yeah, he was going to enjoy trying *that* out later. At the moment, he was barely able to restrain himself from ripping Rick's pants off and plunging inside him. He didn't have the control left to drive Rick crazy with lust that way, although it seemed avoiding all touch of his cock was doing a pretty good job.

He wiped his fingers on his jeans, uncaring that they'd need washing, and dug around in his own pocket for a foil square that he placed on Rick's stomach.

"Then, I'd pull out my handy-dandy condom and roll it on my cock." Ian flicked open his jeans and yanked the fly apart. A black jock constrained his own hard cock, and he tucked the waistband under his balls, freeing his rampant erection. He opened the condom packet in record time and put it on. He positioned Rick's legs over his arms, raising and spreading them at the same time.

"Then I'd slide right in." Ian's last word was barely more than a grunt, the sensation of being squeezed in Rick's tight heat almost unbearably good. Rick squirmed, trying to get more of Ian inside or trying to get some contact on his dick—either way, it shredded the last of Ian's control.

He pulled back and thrust in hard, again and again. Rick grunted but met every thrust, sweat making their skin slippery.

"Touch me, dammit."

Ian still retained a tiny bit of control and grinned at Rick, deliberately ignoring his demand. Rick could have wrapped a hand around his own dick, but as with most things so far, they were on the same page. This one was all on Ian, and they both knew it.

He changed the angle of his thrusts and Rick bared his teeth. "Ian, dammit." Rick squeezed his internal muscles in frustration.

Suddenly, the precipice Ian had been skirting for the past few minutes appeared in front of him and he couldn't stop himself from barreling over. His hips jerked uncontrollably as he emptied himself into Rick, white noise in his ears as Rick's body wrung a mind-blowing orgasm from him.

Boneless, he slumped over Rick. When his mind cleared a few seconds later, Rick was trying to thrust himself against Ian's side, his whole body vibrating with his approaching orgasm. Ian shook his head and slid carefully out of Rick, who cursed him and pounded a fist against his shoulder.

"So fucking close, Ian."

Ian didn't bother replying, he just opened his mouth and sucked Rick's cock all the way in.

Rick keened and thrust, cock jerking and spilling salty cum down Ian's throat. He swallowed every drop, then kissed the mushroom tip before he moved to curl up beside Rick.

"Bastard," Rick muttered between harsh breaths.

"So you don't want to do that again?"

"Of course I do. Bastard."

Ian grinned against Rick's nape, reveling in the scent of sweaty, sated man. "So, when I said earlier I was glad I didn't know about the state of your underwear…."

He waited, and as he expected, Rick tensed in his arms.

"Well, if I'd known, tonight might have gone a little differently, and I might have been balls deep in your sweet little ass when my dad came out to look for me."

Rick held himself stiff, as though he wasn't sure how to respond, but then he started to laugh. Ian laughed along with him, and they shook the bed from the force of their mirth.

"Oh, man. He might be accepting of your sexuality, but I'm guessing he wouldn't want to actually see you fucking a guy."

Ian snorted. "Please. He wouldn't want to see any of his kids fucking anyone. Especially not outside where we could scare away potential customers or possibly need to get bailed out of jail. No matter whether you're a guy or a girl, I would have gotten a lecture on safe sex and respecting my partner."

Rick chuckled and turned to face him. "Maybe we ought to try it next time. Might be a thrill."

"Sure, sure. A thrill for you, maybe. You just want to see me get my ass handed to me by my dad."

"Maybe."

The lackadaisical shrug didn't fool Ian one bit. Rick would have loved to watch that. As much as he wanted to give Rick whatever he needed to be happy, he wasn't quite sure he could bring himself to get caught fucking by any of his family members.

A cooling sensation on his dick reminded him of the spent condom, and he levered himself out of bed.

"Bathroom?"

Rick stretched, catlike and sexy, before he pointed at the left-hand door.

When he returned, Rick hadn't moved, hadn't covered up. Ian might have been up for a second round, but there had been too much emotional turmoil and he was exhausted. He crawled into bed and tucked Rick against him like they'd been sleeping spooned together all their lives.

"No sneaking out on me this time, got it? We're together."

"Even if no one knows it?"

"Even if no one knows it. This relationship is for us, and we can make our own rules about how it should go."

"Okay, then, darling. I promise not to sneak out of my own house." Rick cuddled into his arms.

The sleepy contentment emanating from Rick reassured him that he wasn't at all upset to be falling asleep with a boyfriend. With his first boyfriend.

RICK shifted in the sheets, the sounds of Ian banging about in the bathroom unfamiliar and pleasing at the same time. The day stretched before them, with nothing to do but please themselves. A lazy day with his boyfriend. Rick had never imagined spending a day like this, mostly because he never expected to have a boyfriend. They'd woken late after the emotion-laden night, whereupon Ian had proceeded to fuck his brains out, again. Rick was nothing more than a limp noodle this morning. A limp noodle who felt surprisingly weightless. Between the orgasms, Ian's acceptance of his past, and assurance that he was willing to work with Rick's hang-ups, was a freedom and intense contentment.

Although he'd had other guys in his bed, he'd never allowed any of them to sleep there or stay the night. If guys stayed over, there was no easy escape, and there was an implied intimacy Rick had never been interested in fostering. Sleeping with Ian had been different than expected. Safe, comforting, and relaxing. And he wasn't going to give it up anytime soon.

Would Ian want to stay over on the weekends from now on? Rick wouldn't mind, and he loved his place. He'd be willing to stay at Ian's, but he couldn't honestly say he wouldn't bolt early in the morning if he were there. Leaving like that would likely make Ian furious, and Rick was starting to enjoy the relationship they'd started. For the good of their relationship, he'd have to convince Ian that sleepovers had to be on Rick's turf.

Ian came back from the bathroom, stark naked and warm from his shower. He slid into bed, breath minty and fresh, and Rick frowned.

"Darling, you brought a toothbrush? I'm not usually that easy." Because that was weird, wasn't it? How could Ian assume he wouldn't have slammed the door in his face or called the cops last night?

"Give me the benefit of the doubt, *darling*." Ian put a little mocking spin on his words. "I used your toothpaste and my finger. If you don't mind, though, I could keep a toothbrush here, maybe a razor."

It took him a moment to figure out how he felt about that. Surprisingly, it felt as right as letting Ian stay overnight. He had to commend Ian. Letting them become friends first had done wonders to make this all okay. Better than okay. Good, even.

"I think that would be okay."

Ian smiled, a sweet smile that made him look younger and not as jaded as he often did. Then, completely heedless of Rick's own lack of toothpaste use, Ian kissed him.

Rick pulled back before the kiss could develop into anything deeper. He had a date with the shower and a toothbrush before they had sex again.

His stomach growled as he got out of bed, and he paused for a moment. Ian laughed and grabbed him about the waist, kissing his empty belly.

"Go shower. I'll try to drum up some breakfast." Ian gave him another belly kiss before smacking him on the butt. "Go on."

Somewhat bemused, Rick found himself in the bathroom, preparing to hop in the shower. No one had ever made him breakfast before. Then again, that was probably reserved for guys who actually spent the whole night, which Rick had never done until now.

He showered with a grin. The whole boyfriend thing was shaping up to be a very good thing. He refused to give in to the deep-seated fear that this was nothing more than the calm before the storm. He'd been through enough stormy weather. Didn't he finally deserve a little sunshine in his life?

INSTEAD of the sweatpants he normally wore around the house, Rick pulled on a pair of simple black pajama bottoms. Sweatpants weren't part of the style he showed the world, and he was a little hesitant to let Ian in on yet another secret so soon, however minor.

Clean and refreshed, he wandered into the kitchen.

Ian stood at the stove, clad in only his jeans and given that Rick had kicked the man's jock out of the way just moments ago, there was nothing under that sexy, worn denim.

"Hey, big boy." Rick sidled up to Ian and stroked a hand up a very nice bicep and across a rather pleasant pectoral. Ian wasn't hugely muscular, but he was trim and fit and so fucking hot.

Ian grabbed his hand before it could explore farther south. "Hey now. None of that yet." He leaned over and kissed Rick to ease the sting of what sounded like rejection.

"Why not?"

"Because, I don't want you to starve to death. Food first, then...." Ian made an absolutely filthy, obscene gesture that Rick had no other way to interpret except as rimming. Blood rushed into his groin, and he wasn't entirely sure he could eat when he was shaking from pure, inhibited lust.

"Uh. Can't we skip breakfast?"

"Nope. Need to keep your blood sugar up, sweetheart. No passing out during sex." Ian stirred the eggs in the pan.

Rick was going to protest waiting another second when the scent of sautéed vegetables and spices hit his nose and his stomach growled again, louder than before.

"Fine. Fine, we can eat first, I suppose." It wouldn't be that much of a sacrifice. Not if those eggs tasted as good as they smelled.

Ian grinned. "Sit down before you waste away."

Like that would happen. He'd have to work out extra hard during the week to make up for missing his workout today.

"What did you want to do today?" Ian asked as he dished out eggs. "The farmer's market, the movies...."

The assumption they'd spend the day together would normally have him searching for excuses, but Rick only smiled back.

"I don't know. I... don't think I'm ready to go out somewhere." As much as he was enjoying the newness of this first relationship, he wasn't ready to share it with the world.

"What about just staying in? Watch some DVDs."

Yeah, he could do that. Simple, fun, and just enjoying each other's company in a way they hadn't—in a way Rick hadn't allowed them to before now with his rules.

"Sure. I have a ton of movies."

They ate in silence for a few minutes, Rick too damned hungry to do much more than compliment Ian and thank him for cooking.

Before he was finished, though, Ian put down his fork and stared at him thoughtfully.

"What?"

"Come with me to my brother's wedding? Meet my family?"

Rick's fingers shook badly enough that he, too, put his fork down.

"I don't know, darling."

"Please. It's a small start. You don't have to go as my *date* date. We can say you're just a friend. But I want everyone to at least know you're *my* friend too, not just Kurt's. I don't want to push you, but I hate not being able to tell people about you. I hate that Kurt gets to claim you as a friend and I don't. I want to tell people about how great you are and how much fun we have together. Someday, I want to tell everyone what you mean to me, and this is a baby step toward that day."

That mythical day far in the future seemed sunny and filled with rainbows, but Rick couldn't help but want that too. If he was going to be with Ian, he'd need to learn how to deal with family. And a wedding might be ideal. Everyone would be too busy to pay him much attention.

"Fine. Yes. We'll try it. But make sure you say friends only. I'm not ready to admit to more than that."

Ian gave him a wide, happy smile and started eating again. Strangely, Rick still had his own appetite, even after agreeing to attend a dreaded family event. He, too, picked up his fork to finish Ian's delicious eggs.

The second his plate was empty, Ian gathered the dishes and dropped them in the sink.

"Ready?"

"I guess. Did you want to pick out the first movie?"

Ian rolled his eyes. "We'll do that later. We've got a prior engagement."

The confusion lasted until Ian made his obscene rimming gesture and Rick was back where he'd been before breakfast—so horny he could barely stand it.

IAN couldn't stop smiling. The movie was some overly dramatic black-and-white mystery. Wasn't half-bad, actually, but certainly provided no reason for smiling. The man curled up next to him, faint breathy snores attesting to his exhaustion, was the reason.

Poor, sweet man. Ian had put all of his experience to the test after breakfast, and wore Rick out in the sexiest way possible. His jaw ached a bit, and Rick had been determined to follow through with their plan of lazing about and watching movies.

He'd spent weeks trying to get exactly where he was right now, and he wanted to shout to the world that he'd convinced Rick they could be good together. And they were.

Even more amazing was the fact that Rick had let him in. Now that he knew what Rick had gone through, he understood why Rick had been so gun-shy all those years. But gun-shy was no reason to be alone, and Ian was going to prove it to him.

All the angst Ian had had over hiding his sexuality all those years… well, it wasn't nothing. It had been emotionally damaging in its own way, but Rick coming through his ordeal as strong and self-sufficient as he was…. Ian admired his new boyfriend's fortitude more than ever. If he did nothing else, he was going to show Rick he could be trusted. Because he wanted the whole enchilada. He wanted everything with Rick, and more than ever, he believed they could have it.

Now if he could just convince Rick to attend one of his family functions—and not go running scared of his mom—Rick just might figure out families aren't so bad. After all, he'd spent his whole life with his, and they were pretty great.

He rubbed Rick's arm and tried to focus on the movie, but it was too late. He had no idea what was going on at this point, and he was more interested in Rick's warm body than he was in whodunit. What he really wanted to know was if he left to grab a suit for work in the morning, would Rick let him stay another night. By tonight, they both should have recovered enough to wear themselves out again.

Lips laid gentle kisses on his side and he glanced down.

"Hey there."

"Hey." Rick smiled up at him under a wild mess of blond hair. Stunning, stunning man.

"Nice nap?"

Slightly abashed, Rick nodded. "Sorry I missed part of the movie."

"Eh. You didn't really miss much."

"Well, now I'm even more sorry. You should have changed the movie."

Ian shrugged. "It wasn't terrible and I didn't want to wake you. Did I tell you what a great place you've got here?"

"No, but thanks."

The top floor of the house was maybe a little big for one person, but Rick had made it into a comfortable home. Making the ground floor into an office for his practice was a great plan, and he could barely believe Rick had managed all of this by himself.

"I bet the fireplace makes this room really cozy in the winter."

"It does."

"Just needs a piece of art over the mantle." The bare wooden boards screamed for a portrait or abstract or something. "Is there a fireplace down in your office as well?"

"Yes, but not where I take clients. I was very lucky to find a place that still had a fireplace at all, much less one on the second floor. Most of them get ripped out when the places are converted into apartments."

"This was an apartment?"

"Originally it was a pair of two-story dwellings, semidetached. Then the top floors of both sides of the building were converted, making four apartments. I was able to buy one side of the building first, and a few years later, the second. I only added a door between the two on the ground floor, but I took out the walls between the apartments up here and revamped the interior."

"Amazing. You've done a fantastic job." But he hadn't intended to get into an architectural discussion.

He took a breath. Aside from some pleasant reminiscing, he'd had a lot of time to think.

"Can I ask you a couple of questions?"

Rick's sleepy smile fell away as he straightened. Already, Ian mourned the loss of his warm armful.

"Yes, darling, I suppose you can."

Ian gritted his teeth. He was starting to hate those endearments, because he was coming to learn they were a protection mechanism Rick wore like a shield. Each time Rick trotted them out with him, he knew he needed to tread carefully. Not that he blamed Rick for being reticent. He threaded his fingers through Rick's.

"What happened after you left home? I mean, I know you've built up a great career for yourself. You've got a great place here. How did you do it? Don't get me wrong, I'm amazed, impressed, and completely in awe. I'm just curious."

Rick turned his head away. For a moment, he expected Rick to pull completely away from him, but instead Rick gripped his hand tighter.

"It wasn't as sordid as you're probably imagining. I got government loans to help with university and I supported myself by bartending at a strip club."

Ian blinked for a moment. He had a visceral tug at the pit of his stomach, imagining Rick up on stage, a cowboy hat on his head, ripping off a pair of tear-away chaps.

"Uh."

"Honestly. The owner tried to get me to strip a few times, but it wasn't something I was interested in. And I made enough money bartending."

"No, it wasn't that, I was just kinda… imagining you stripping."

Rick cut a glance at him and must have seen some of Ian's thoughts on his face. "Oh. I certainly learned a lot by observation. And I helped Jon out with a few of his routines."

"Jon?"

"Oh, yeah. That's how I met him, actually. He was stripping at the same club I got hired at as a bartender."

Ian nodded. He could see it. Jon was an attractive guy, although not as attractive as Rick.

"Have you got a cowboy hat, by any chance?"

"Mmm. You're a little perv, aren't you? I might be able to scare one up. If you're good." Rick's wicked smile stirred up his dick even more.

"Seriously, though." He tilted Rick's head toward him so he could look deeply in his eyes. "You know I wouldn't care if you'd been stripping, right? I'm so impressed with what you've accomplished."

"I don't like to talk about it, though. It's not exactly something that would do wonders for my career, you know. Even when it was just bartending. Just about everything from my younger days would cause complications for my career."

"They aren't complications for me."

Rick's wicked smile returned, along with suspiciously shiny eyes. Ian chose not to comment, mostly because Rick pounced and kissed him and Ian had better things to do than talk.

CHAPTER
Seven

IAN toweled off, wrapped the towel around his waist. Arms slid around him from behind, lips pressing against his spine.

He turned and kissed Rick. This was exactly what he'd been dreaming of as soon as he considered that he might be able to come out of the closet. He hadn't expected Rick to consent to a second night in a row, especially since he had to break the little bubble they were in to go home and grab a work suit. But the moment Rick had agreed, he'd taken off before Rick could change his mind, and returned in record time.

Then they'd spent another athletic night in bed and Ian had never been happier. It was too soon to think about moving in together, but this little taste of living together was enough—Ian was going to love it. It made a huge difference, having to maneuver around someone else to get ready in the morning, a little dance of companionship Ian enjoyed far more than the emptiness of getting ready alone.

Ian rubbed a finger over his chin. He could get away without shaving this morning. Good thing, too, because although the alarm had gone off plenty early enough for him to get ready for work, they'd, uh, lingered in bed for almost another hour.

"C'mon. I've got to get ready or I'm going to be late." He couldn't resist giving Rick another quick kiss.

"I know. Me too. I've got an early client showing up today."

Side by side, they pulled on their professional clothes.

Like a disguise, his super sexy club boy Rick became Richard Haviland, Toronto's soft-core porn version of Clark Kent. Über professional and sedate. Knowing what hid beneath that boring white golf shirt and beige chinos, knowing the sounds Rick made when he licked his ass, made the boring outfit unexpectedly appealing. A secret he shared with Rick, a secret that most of the rest of the world didn't know.

"Hey there, Richard Haviland. My sexy speech-language pathologist." Ian moved to push Rick up against the wall to see if he could muss him up a little, but Rick held out a hand.

"Oh my God, Ian. Is that what you wear to work?"

Ian peered down at the dark-green suit with black shirt and tie. He didn't see anything wrong with it—no stains, no wrinkles, and everything matched. "Sometimes, yeah, why?"

"I thought you worked for *Errant*."

"I do."

"But it's a celebrity gossip site. And paranormal whatever. I kind of expected you'd wear jeans. Or cargo pants or something. Rock band T-shirts."

Ian laughed. "You've described just about every one of my coworkers. But my department is responsible for bringing in the funds that support the site and pay the staff. There's no way I'd be able to bring in the kind of advertising revenue that I do if I didn't dress the part of your average successful businessman, at least on days where I have meetings with clients."

A dark, glittering gaze flickered over Ian's form, making his cock flex in response. "The suit is very, very sexy." Rick's voice dropped into a lower register, and Ian desperately wanted to ignore the time and throw the man back into bed, but he couldn't.

"Right back at ya, Richard Haviland."

Rick shook his head. "Don't be ridiculous. This isn't sexy."

Ian crept closer. "But I know what's underneath, and that makes it very, very sexy. I'm coming back tonight after work. And I'm going to muss up your plastic perfection. Strip you back down to your club bunny G-string, then fuck you until you explode." He'd noticed exactly what type of undergarments Rick had pulled on this morning and they sure as shit didn't match the outer shell.

"Make sure you bring the tie." Rick's chest lifted, his inhalations fast and heavy. He wrapped Ian's tie in a fist and pulled Ian close.

A tiny whimper escaped as he thought about everything they could do with the black silk strip tied at his throat. He advanced on Rick, gathering him close. He could get to work a little late.

A loud buzz interrupted his carnal intentions. "Ian, shit, that's my first appointment."

Ian's cock voiced its displeasure, but Ian forced himself to step away from Rick anyway. "Rain check, Mr. Haviland? After work tonight?"

"Definitely, Mr. O'Donnell." Rick smiled at him before scooting around him.

RICK whistled as he sorted through his files. His receptionist was on vacation this week, which meant he had a lot of extra work, but it also meant he didn't need to answer any uncomfortable, probing questions about why he was in such a good mood. He hadn't lied to Ian, though. He wasn't ready for anyone and everyone to know. A notion had taken hold of his brain that if anyone knew, his bright, shiny new relationship would blow up in his face.

After setting the files on Jenny's desk for her to put away when she returned, Rick wandered to the front of the house and grabbed the mail.

He flipped through the envelopes, but nothing leapt out as urgent. At the bottom of the pile was a plain manila envelope with no address. It must have been pushed through the mail slot by hand, but he had no idea what it might contain.

Curiosity riding him, he opened the fastener on the envelope's flap and pulled out a few sheets of printer paper. The color images took up almost the entirety of the 8 ½" x 11" inch sheets of paper, with a handwritten caption below that read "I see you" in red block letters.

It took a few minutes of staring at the printed images before he comprehended what he was seeing. Him and Ian, on the bed, fucking. Last night. Heart stuttering in his chest, he let the pages flutter to the floor while his mind rabbited around as he tried to decide what he needed to do.

No matter how he tried to come up with other options, the only thing that came to mind was calling Ian. They'd been a couple for less than forty-eight hours. Was this the sort of thing he could dump on his brand-new boyfriend? He had no fucking clue, but he damn well wanted Ian's brand of comfort.

He stared down at the images on the floor. He couldn't leave them there. With cold, trembling fingers, he squatted down and gathered up the sheets and tucked them back into the envelope.

After locking the front door, he sat at his receptionist's desk and quickly canceled the two sessions he was supposed to have later that afternoon. Then he pulled out his cell phone and called Ian.

"Rick?"

"Uh, hi, is this a bad time?"

"No, not at all. I just got out of a meeting. What's up?"

"Can you… can you…." How could Rick ask him this? He'd spent his whole life making his own way in the world. Aside from a few friends helping him, he'd done it all on his own. He should be able to handle this on his own, but in a very short period of time, he found himself needing Ian.

"Rick? Are you okay? What do you need?"

"Can you come home? I got something in the mail and… it's freaking me out a bit. Please."

"Of course, I'll be right there."

Ian disconnected and Rick couldn't hold back a sob of relief that he wasn't going to have to deal with this alone.

He shut off the lights in his office and unlocked the door so Ian would be able to get in without any effort on his part. Envelope clutched in a fist, Rick trudged upstairs and curled up on the sofa.

The minutes ticked by—he had no idea how long it would take Ian to get here from his office, or even if Ian had been able to leave right away.

After some indeterminate time, footsteps pounded up the stairs. Ian burst through the door. "What's wrong?"

Rick didn't move, just opened his hand, letting the envelope drift to the floor.

Rounding the sofa, Ian scooped up the envelope.

"What the fuck is this?"

"I don't know. I mean, I know. It's pictures of us. Kissing. Fucking. Naked. From last night."

He didn't know what was going on, but these pictures could ruin his career. Ruin it. He worked with a number of kids. Their parents had never cared about his orientation, but being gay was a hell of lot different than naked pictures. Naked pictures of him fucking, for God's sake.

"Where did these come from?"

Rick shrugged. "I don't know. I didn't even realize anyone was watching."

Ian shuddered. "Exhibitionism is one thing, but this is something entirely different. Who do you think could have done this? That Oscar guy?"

"Honestly, I don't know. He certainly cared more than I ever realized, but he never seemed the obsessive type."

"I think we should call Kurt."

A flare of panic chased away some of the depressive lethargy the pictures had brought. "No. No, we can't. No one needs to know."

If Kurt knew, everyone would know. The photos had already cast a pall over what had been one of the happiest days he'd ever had. The last thing he needed was gossip about him and Ian spreading through their group of friends and Ian's family.

"Rick, please reconsider. This could be dangerous."

"I'm sure it's nothing. Just a mistake or something. I'll talk to Oscar."

"I don't know. This is… kind of stalkerish. Even if we don't call Kurt, having a police report on file might be smart. Especially given the other things that have happened to you lately. They might be connected."

What? No way was Oscar a stalker. No way. "No. I'm sure it's just a misunderstanding." He just had to make Oscar delete all copies of these pictures. He couldn't afford for these pictures to make it out in public or on the Internet. He'd have to change his fucking name again, and he'd really grown to like Rick Haviland.

Ian sat down beside him. "Okay, but please don't meet him in private. I'd like to be there with you if I can. I still think a police report would be wise."

"Oscar was a good guy. He doesn't deserve a police record if this is just a simple mistake."

"It couldn't be anyone else, could it?"

The thought that anyone he'd slept with could do that to him made him sick. He didn't object to sex photos, although given his profession, he'd never trusted anyone enough to take any. He didn't even object to a little controlled voyeurism, but there was something sordid about these photos that made him feel violated. Their resemblance to blackmail photos, like the ones in that movie last night, made him wonder if there was more to come. He'd spent years assessing men for his roster, to ensure he could trust them enough. Oscar wasn't the first time he'd misjudged a guy's likelihood to want more from him, but other than a few ugly words thrown around, he'd never experienced any real negative consequences.

"No. I don't think so. I can't think of anyone who would do such a thing." A sudden thought struck him. "This wouldn't be about you, would it?"

Dark red suffused the skin of Ian's face. "Uh. No. I can't imagine it would be."

A tiny bit of mirth battled with his depression. "Oh, right. How would they even find you, *Steve*, darling?" He scrubbed the drawl from his tone. "I am sorry I called you at work. It wasn't exactly an emergency, even though it freaked me out. Do you need to get back?"

"Don't be ridiculous. I've got plenty of flexibility in my schedule, so no, I don't need to get back." Ian grabbed his hand and hauled him up into a tight hug. "I'm really, really glad you called me."

Clinging to the warmth he'd been craving since opening that envelope, Rick couldn't do anything but nod. He might be a flamboyant gay man, but this woke emotions far too similar to his pre-eighteen life. Being the center of attention in this manner, without his choice or consent, was not welcome. The overtones of malevolent jealousy were also far too reminiscent of the violent dissolution of his parents' marriage and the end of his childhood.

"Maybe you should come and stay with me for a few days."

"No. I'll be fine. I'll talk to Oscar and get this sorted out." Rick had spent a lot of time and money making his place into the perfect venue for his home and office, and he wasn't willing to give it up. He liked his home and he liked having Ian in it. He was, however, glad he'd gotten the basement window fixed.

"Then let me stay here tonight at least."

Rick wasn't sure he'd mind if Ian never left, but a leap that big made his heart pound. Especially because there'd be no hiding it from anyone. He wasn't ready for that. Not any time soon. "Tonight. Okay." One more night, then they'd have to discuss how often this would happen in the future.

"Promise me you'll call me—or Kurt—if you notice anything unusual, okay?"

That he could promise. He was poised on the cusp of a life he'd never dreamed he could have: a career that fulfilled him, good friends who accepted his idiosyncrasies, and a boyfriend who... maybe didn't love him but definitely cared for him. He wasn't going to let anyone take it away from him.

ADJUSTING the tie at his throat, Ian strode off the elevator, only a few minutes late despite having come into the office from Rick's place. His own condo was a stone's throw from the office building, but Ian was certain he could get used to the commute from Rick's. Not that it was out in the suburbs or anything. Rick's house was still inside the confines of what Ian considered downtown Toronto, and it only took an extra twenty minutes or so to get to the office. Ian hoped to be spending enough time at Rick's that the longer commute would be a regular thing.

He hadn't been a bit surprised Rick had refused to stay at his condo, even for a few nights. Under the best of circumstances, Rick was going to feel more comfortable on his own turf, and having a stalker snapping pics of them could hardly be called the best of circumstances.

As he walked down the hall to his office, he briefly considered calling Kurt and getting his advice. Rick seemed convinced—after his initial upset—that the compromising photos were a minor thing and the whole issue could be cleared up easily.

Ian wasn't so sure. Stalking was one of those crimes that was rarely so cut-and-dried—his brother had said so more than once after investigating homicides of stalking victims. The problem was that Rick's trust was so fragile, if Ian made the wrong move he could shatter it into a million pieces and never be able to put it back to rights. He'd come so close to losing everything over a simple misunderstanding, but neither was he willing to lose Rick to an obsessed ex. Especially one that had already demonstrated some serious anger-management issues. For now, though, he'd wait and see.

Lost in his own thoughts, he almost stumbled over Leon.

"Hey, man, how are you doing? Everything turn out okay?"

Ian frowned, trying to turn his brain away from Rick's stalker. He wasn't quite sure what Leon was referring to. "Okay? Yeah, sure, I guess."

"Your mom said you had a friend that needed some help Saturday night?"

Oh holy fuck. "Oh, man, yeah, sorry. Didn't get much sleep last night. I'm really sorry for bailing on you."

Leon gave him a big smile. "It's all good. I had people to talk to, and Parker offered to introduce me to a few of his friends from school."

That made sense. Leon was surprisingly easy to talk to, but Parker was much closer to him in age than Ian was. Parker's friends would probably be more interested in doing things Leon was interested in doing.

"I'm glad."

"So everything turned out okay for your friend?"

Ian was very conscious of the immense trust Rick had placed in him. He wasn't about to violate Rick's confidence, and especially not with Leon. Rick would never forgive him. "Mostly. There are still a few issues going on, but so far, everything's under control."

"Good, good. Did you want to have lunch together today?"

"Absolutely. My treat, okay?" It was the least he could do for bailing on the guy and leaving him with the whole O'Donnell clan. And given that Leon was just recently out of school and hadn't lived in Toronto for very long, he probably didn't have a lot of extra bucks anyway.

"Thanks." Leon smiled again. "I'll meet you at your office at noon?"

Ian nodded and clapped him on the shoulder.

RICK tapped a finger against the envelope he'd laid on the table. He didn't want to order, because odds were good he wasn't staying. When Oscar was working, there was always a possibility he'd have to deal with an emergency and would cancel last-minute, but Rick hadn't wanted to wait until Oscar's next day off to get this dealt with. Even if Oscar did show up and didn't have a satisfactory answer about those pictures, Rick wouldn't be staying. Also, this particular sandwich shop wasn't great, but it was next to the hospital, so it was convenient for Oscar.

His phone beeped and he pulled it out.

But the text wasn't Oscar canceling, it was Ian.

Let me know how it goes. I might be a little late tonight—want me to bring dinner with me?

Rick smiled a little and touched the screen. Somehow, he'd found a keeper who made him warm and gooey inside, who he didn't mind seeing every day, who he missed when he was alone. Ian had sort of snuck into his life and heart. This was how it was supposed to be.

Thai or Italian would be great :)

A flash of blue fabric as someone slid into the seat across from him had him tucking his phone in a back pocket and looking up.

"Oscar." The blue scrubs didn't quite fall into his uniform fetish, but he did approve. But he thought he might be developing a suit fetish, especially when Ian wore them.

"Rick." Oscar seemed to have trouble looking at him.

How did one bring this up?

"I'm so sorry."

Oh. Maybe he didn't have to bring it up at all. The relief that Oscar had broached the issue was still overshadowed by the disappointment that Oscar had been responsible for these photos. He didn't like knowing he'd misjudged Oscar so badly. He still didn't quite know how to respond.

"I was drunk and I saw you with that guy, and well." Oscar sighed. "You were very up-front and clear when we met. We had some great times, and just because I wanted you to change your mind doesn't mean I had any right to get upset when you didn't. Then I saw you with that guy and I could tell you liked him. A lot. And I got mad. I'm really sorry."

Rick frowned. Did people take voyeuristic photos and deliver them in manila envelopes as a spur-of-the-moment drunken mistake?

"Um, well."

"And grabbing you—that was completely out of line. I should have contacted you earlier and apologized. I could lose my residency over shit like that, and I really appreciate you not making a big thing about it."

This reasonable, logical man was the one he'd originally judged and found acceptable for his roster. But he was apologizing for grabbing him, which meant Oscar was talking about the night at Lettie's, not photos from the weekend or even the petty vandalism.

He pulled out the sheets. "What about these?"

Oscar looked at the first one and his eyebrows just about flew up into his hairline.

"Okay, so you really like this guy. Why are you showing me this?"

"You didn't take these?" Rick realized he'd rather be disappointed with Oscar than to have some nameless, faceless guy out there spying on him.

"No, of course not. Why would you even think that?" Oscar shoved the sheets back at him.

"I… I do like this guy. These arrived yesterday at my house, and after that blowup at Lettie's, I thought… well, I didn't really believe you were that sort of person, but you were the only one who'd gotten so emotional when we stopped seeing each other."

Oscar gave a rueful laugh. "I guess we didn't really know each other that well. My job is what I've wanted more than anything in this world."

Rick nodded. That had been one of the reasons he'd thought Oscar would have been happy with their arrangement.

"When I saw you at Lettie's, I'd just come off a thirty-six-hour shift, I hadn't eaten in twelve hours, and stupidly downed two beers before the food came. It was a momentary lapse, which I recognize was so incredibly stupid. There's no way I would have followed it up by stalking you and taking pictures, for God's sake."

No, there was no way Oscar would have jeopardized his career like that. Rick hadn't been wrong, not at all, about Oscar's character and the truth was evident in every word.

"I'm sorry for thinking that about you."

Oscar patted his hand. "I'm sorry I gave you reason to think that about me. I just hope you'll be happy with this guy. If you're not, call me."

Rick nodded, but there was only one keeper he was interested in. If he couldn't make things work, he wasn't going to be looking to replace what he'd discovered with Ian.

Oscar stood. "Be careful, though. Whoever took those pictures could be dangerous."

He couldn't think about that now, even if Oscar agreed with Ian. Stuffing the pictures back in the envelope, he was ready to leave too. He was going to find some fucking cheesecake for lunch. Maybe if he got fat, the damned creep would leave him—and Ian—alone.

He'd let Ian soothe him tonight; maybe he'd even give Ian a couple of pointers on stripping. After he made sure all the curtains were closed, of course.

IAN walked into the wine bar and spotted his coworkers. He didn't want to be here, but Avery was a great coworker and a lot of fun. She was one of the editors who'd been on board since almost the beginning of *Errant*, starting as a freelancer. It was his efforts to bring in the advertising dollars that guaranteed her a full-time position, one of the few nonfreelance editing positions at *Errant*, and they'd bonded three years ago when she'd gotten the job. She'd never forgive him if he missed her birthday happy hour.

Still, he'd been meaning to check out this place. Rick had been drinking wine mostly, and although Ian often drank beer, if the atmosphere was good, he'd bring Rick.

Today, though, he'd grab a few munchies and a quick drink or two before leaving. For the first time in ever, he was eager to get home. Get home, grab a change of clothes, and then head to Rick's. Somehow Rick had unbent enough to let him stay over—four whole nights in a row. It could be the stalker thing, but Rick didn't seem overly concerned. Actually, this birthday thing was great timing. He didn't really want to be in Rick's face so much that Rick regretted the step forward in their relationship.

But Rick had invited him to come over after Avery's party, and he wasn't going to pass that up.

"Ian! You finally made it!" Avery raised a wine glass and gave him a one-armed hug. When she let him go, she swayed a bit but didn't move far away.

"Happy birthday, Avery."

Someone grabbed a handful of ass and he jumped. Leon slid around him, a wide smile on his face.

Leon looked a little unusual wearing his customary tight T-shirt and cargo pants while holding a large, bulbous wine glass filled with deep purple liquid. Judging by the ass grab and the unfocused look in his eyes, the glass in his hand wasn't his first. It might not even be his second.

"Ian! I thought maybe you weren't coming."

"Leon, I hadn't realized you were going to be here."

"Yeah, Avery and I have become close. And not just because our desks are close."

Leon and Avery made funny faces at each other and fell against Ian, laughing like crazy.

"How much wine have you guys had? I thought I was only about an hour late."

An exaggerated shrug had Leon's wine splashing out of the enormous bowl of his glass, barely missing Ian's white shirt. Wasn't a dress shirt today, but that didn't mean he wanted to have it irreparably stained.

"This stuff is awesome! And it's buy-one-get-one-half-off. A bargain!" Leon took a huge sip, and the dark wine left a tiny stain at the corner of his mouth, reminiscent of a Kool-Aid mustache.

Ian shook his head. "Just go easy on it. Getting drunk on red wine can be pretty rough."

Dylan had stolen half a case of red wine from Finn's when they were teenagers. Neither he nor Kurt had enjoyed the taste enough to get more than slightly buzzed, but Dylan had loved it. For a few hours. After puking purple fucking everywhere and dealing with a hangover like Ian had never seen since that day, Dylan hadn't touched another drop of red wine.

"Puh-lease. I can handle my liquor." Leon rubbed up against him like a puppy.

Avery's attention moved away from the two of them—only natural since she was the birthday girl—and Ian flagged down a waitress. Even in a wine bar, he knew he could get a beer. It would be more fun to test out a variety of different wines with Rick, and he wanted to save that experience for another night with him.

"Leon, I'm really glad you're making friends and fitting in. I like working with you, and I'm glad you're happy."

"Thanks, Ian. It's a great place to work. And I like working with you too."

He'd had a little bit of guilt for not inviting Leon to more events, but his friendship with Leon started just as his relationship with Rick had heated up. Even though Rick wanted their relationship to remain quiet for now, he was certain Leon would understand if he knew. Being forgiven for friendship absenteeism during the early stages of a new relationship was pretty standard. Leon could do worse than cultivate a friendship with Avery. She was a lot of fun to hang out with, especially after she'd realized Ian wasn't attracted.

Avery called for Leon, who squeezed his ass again before leaving. Ian chuckled. He was certain Leon would be embarrassed by that in the morning.

CHAPTER
Eight

"HEY, Ian, you got a minute?"

Ian looked up from his computer. "Sure, Leon. What's up?"

Leon clutched a tablet to his chest. The kid's entire wardrobe consisted of T-shirts, which may have been a fashion choice or it may have had to do with them being all he could afford, although Ian remembered a time when T-shirts were all he and his brothers would wear too. Then again, Leon was an attractive, well-built guy. The tight T-shirts might be an integral part of the mating plumage of the twentysomething gay geek. The pallor and dark circles under his eyes, though, wasn't plumage so much as a billboard advertising too much wine and quite possibly a long night hanging over a porcelain bowl.

"Can you give me your expert opinion on these pages? This is the first time I'm doing a whole layout, and I'd like some input before I hand them over to Avery."

"Of course." Ian extended his hand for the tablet.

Looked like they were doing another of those old "where are they now" stories. Every couple of months or so, the editors scared up one of these nonsense stories for a slow Friday. Called them the Friday Lost Ones. Usually, it didn't even matter if the story had any legs. The editors would massage the damn things to bring in the clicks and the advertisers. Ian didn't much care about the stories appearing on the site, one way or the other, but these stories were always a little depressing. Some rising starlet was either homeless or a drug addict, or some average person who had a brush with notoriety was tarred with the brush of evil. And if a case couldn't be made for a murderer, then the editors would try to convince the readers that evidence existed these poor schmoes were aliens or vampires or werewolves. Ridiculous. Most of the people featured didn't even have the wherewithal to fight back, although the site was excellent at stopping short of actual libel.

The sensationalism was incredible, and Ian often worried how many readers took the stories as truth.

Leon had chosen an eye-catching font for the headline. Not the clichéd letters dripping blood, but the harsh slashes put one in mind of graffiti made by gouging letters into wood with a knife.

"Like Mother, Like Son?"

Ian didn't think much of the title, but there was only so much real estate in a headline. Ignoring the rest of the copy, since Leon didn't have anything to do with writing it, Ian took in the aesthetics of font, whitespace, placement of images and ads.

"Er, can I leave this with you for a bit? Come back and get it later?"

Lifting his gaze, he took in Leon's now-greenish pallor.

"Of course."

Leon ran from Ian's office. He considered for a moment following to make sure he was okay, but Leon was a big boy who'd managed to drag himself into work, despite the copious quantity of wine he'd consumed the previous night. Leon would be fine—eventually.

When he bent his head back to Leon's layout, a picture of a blond teenager caught his eye. The guy looked a lot like Rick. Weird.

Then the headline twigged something in his memory. Surely they hadn't….

In a flash, Ian stood, shut his office door, and sat back down behind his desk to read.

Like Mother, Like Son?

Twenty-one years ago, Maria Svenson stabbed her cheating husband to death, shattering the peace of a sleepy Northern Ontario town….

The story continued, spelling out Rick's story in the most sensational way possible. Each detail was like another ice pick to his heart, but the one that shook him most was the name of the son Maria left behind. Sandor Svenson, whose real identity, along with some other "shocking news," would be revealed next week. Were Sandor and Rick the same guy? All signs pointed to yes, but why hadn't Rick mentioned that he wasn't Rick?

He was gutted. Completely gutted. And he had no idea what to do about it. Between the details and the photo, Ian had to assume his boyfriend, Rick Haviland, was none other than Sandor Svenson. He was torn between running to Avery's office, demanding to read next week's installment, tracking down the freelance shithead writer responsible for this travesty and beating him up, or calling Stephanie, his future sister-in-law, and having her threaten to destroy *Errant* with a lawsuit.

But he hadn't seen anything that hadn't been technically the truth. Even though the implication was that Rick had stripped and possibly whored on the side to make ends meet, the truth was Rick had worked at a strip club. And while the story had been cleverly crafted to imply Rick had done far more than bartend, there were no actionable statements. Hell, even if there were photos from Rick's strip club days, which Avery might be holding back for next week's conclusion, they could be of Jon. The two of them looked similar enough that a bad photo from fifteen years ago could easily be misattributed. Dammit.

The name change upset the shit out of him. Well, not the name change itself, but the fact that Rick hadn't told him. After knowing the whole story, he wasn't surprised Rick had done it, but he'd like Rick to explain why he'd left that little detail out. Worse than that, though, was how the public was going to interpret this story. Whichever of Avery's pet writers had dug this up, he'd managed to put the worst possible spin on each of Rick's actions, and Ian wanted to erase every last byte of data in *Errant*'s computers.

God. The story made Rick out to be some sort of demented deviant who might pose a danger to the kids he helped. Whatever fears Rick had about inheriting his mother's instability, he wasn't dangerous. There was no doubt in his mind about that. But this story would kill him. He might even blame Ian. And Ian didn't know how to stop the story from going live.

"AVERY, dammit, you can't publish this." Ian banged into Avery's office; she winced at his arrival and clutched at her temples.

"O'Donnell, what the fuck? Stop fucking shouting." He'd never seen anyone put so much venom into a whisper, but Avery managed.

"This story." He brandished Leon's tablet in front of Avery, and she swallowed heavily as she tried to focus on his bobbing hand.

"What's wrong? It's a standard Friday Lost Ones story."

"You have to pull it."

"No, I don't. It's a great story. You know the policy on stories. People get pissed about our stories. As long as the chief editor approves, nothing gets pulled. This one pushes the libel line, but never crosses."

"But I know this guy."

Avery laughed, but cut herself off midcackle and closed her eyes. She was still for so long, Ian almost threw the tablet against the wall to wake her up.

She opened her eyes. "What are you still doing here?"

"Avery, for fuck's sake. Pull this story."

"No. It's a done deal."

"I know this guy, Avery. Please. This will kill him."

"Oh, I know you know this guy. It's going to make the big reveal next week even juicier."

"What?"

A churning started in Ian's stomach like he'd been on the bender the night before, not cut himself off after two beers and gone home to virtuously fuck his boyfriend's brains out.

"I always knew you'd look fine completely naked." Avery's leer was ruined by another wince. "You should have told me you were gay. I would have stopped hitting on you. Or I would have offered a threesome with another guy...."

"Holy...." He sank into a nearby chair, tablet slipping from nerveless fingers, the metallic crunch barely even making a blip on his consciousness. Okay, so, he was going to get outed online in the most graphic way possible. His mother would undoubtedly be disappointed, although he didn't think his family bothered with the site. Most of them were too practical to be interested in the scandalmongering.

"Avery, please. We're friends. How could you send some photographer to Rick's house to get compromising pictures?"

"Don't be ridiculous. They came from an anonymous source."

That fucking stalker. Ian was going to kill him. Or sic his family on the little weasel. Rick may not be convinced it was Oscar, but Ian was.

After this, Rick would have no choice but to call the cops and find out for sure.

"Don't do this, Avery. Pull the story."

She shrugged, and suddenly he saw the heart of a shark that beat within the breast of a ruthless editor. "This is business. You should know that better than anyone. This is a great story."

"No, it isn't. It's not like he murdered anyone. All he ever did was try to rebuild his life and you're going to take it away from him."

"Policy. Sutton approved it. No pulling stories. It would destroy our journalistic integrity. Now get the hell out of my office before I barf all over you."

Since that wasn't out of the realm of possibility, Ian scooped up the tablet and left.

Journalistic integrity. How the hell had Avery been able to apply those words to the product they produced and not laugh herself silly?

He stumbled back to his office and shut the door behind him. The only problem was Avery was right. Hector, the owner of *Errant*, was adamant about not pulling stories, because more than one celebrity's PR person had offered them money to remove stories and had laid down the law years ago—if his Editor in Chief, Randall Sutton, approved, the stories were a go. Even the threat of lawsuits didn't move him. They'd yet to have a lawsuit that they'd lost. *Errant*'s lawyers were a slippery bunch.

Ian had to tell Rick about the story, but how? Rick would be devastated. He was devastated too. Of course, he didn't have the second part of the story, no real guarantee the big reveal would say Sandor was Rick, but the stories were so similar, he didn't have any doubt. And yet, Rick hadn't bothered to tell him Rick wasn't his real name.

What did that say about their brand-new relationship? What about the breakthrough Ian had thought he'd had? He had no idea where he stood, and he had no idea what Rick was going to do.

IAN paced Rick's living room instead of sitting on the couch beside Rick. He was too agitated to sit. They were supposed to be having their rescheduled movie night, since Dylan's rehearsal dinner fell on a Thursday night, but before Ian left work, he'd called Rick to ask if they could watch movies at the house instead. He didn't expect there would be any movie watching, but neither had he wanted to utter those fateful words "we have to talk."

"What's wrong?"

Oh, God. The words slipped out before he could stop them. "We have to talk."

Rick froze like a statue. Yeah, relationship or not, those words held a lot of power.

"*Errant* is doing a story about you. Part one will post Friday, and part two will post a week from Friday. And the stalker sent them those pictures."

Ian had seen a movie once where an archeologist found some ancient scroll and the minute he touched it, it crumbled into dust, destroying his life's work. Watching Rick fall apart at Ian's words was far too reminiscent of that scene.

Then rage coalesced all those motes of dust into a rampaging animal.

Rick let out a wordless howl and swept a lamp off the end table. He cleared papers and coasters and glasses off the coffee table with a second sweep of his arm before he collapsed back on the sofa and sobbed.

Ian leapt over the broken glass and ceramics to sit next to Rick and hold him close.

"Hey, hey. It will be okay, I promise."

"You can't promise that." He'd never heard Rick sound so defeated; he just hoped that was because Rick's mouth was muffled by his shirt.

"I can. We can talk to Dylan's fiancée. She's a lawyer."

Ian swallowed heavily. This was where he expected Rick would throw him out. "I don't know if there's any way to pull the story. Stephanie's good, but I don't think we'll have enough time to get her involved, especially with the wedding, and there's not a really great track record for anyone getting stories pulled. But we can talk to her. There's got to be a way around this, or a way to protect you, even if the story runs. And if there's not… we'll weather it together, I promise."

"I don't want to tell anyone else. I just want to forget."

"Shh, shh, I know." Ian rocked a little, wondering if he was helping at all.

"I'm going to have to change my name again, move away."

Panic washed through him. He couldn't let that happen.

"No, no, you don't have to do that. This will all blow over in time. No one takes those stories seriously." Shitloads of people read them, but they'd need their heads examined if they took those words as gospel. He had to believe people read *Errant* in the true spirit of the site: entertainment.

Rick lifted tearstained eyes. "Are you sure?"

"I am. Positive. Last Friday was an article about how to tell if your lover was an alien. Come on, now. Even if there are a few clients who read *Errant*, even fewer will likely believe that, at least not without giving you the opportunity to rebut. So you think about talking to Stephanie, or another lawyer if that will make you more comfortable."

Rick took a deep breath and swiped his hands across his eyes. "I like what I do, Ian. I don't want to give it up."

"You don't have to, I promise." Somehow, Ian would make that promise come true.

"I suppose you're right. Not all of my clients will read or believe that story, and if I lose a few clients, well, I'm sure I won't lose my longtime regulars."

"See, now, that's the way to look at it. And you may even gain a few clients. The notoriety seekers."

Rick made a face. "Ew. Really? Well, I may not be able to be choosy."

Ian took a deep breath. If Rick wasn't going to go to a lawyer right now, there wasn't much point in speculating how the story would affect his business. Not until they knew for sure if it was going to have any effect at all.

"WHY didn't you tell me about the name change? That's a huge, huge part of the story that you just… omitted. A part that you can't convince me you forgot." It wasn't precisely a change of subject, but it was part of the puzzle that concerned Ian, especially since they were supposed to be a couple.

"No, I didn't forget, not exactly. I'm Rick Haviland. That's who I am. Sandor Svenson went through a lot of shit, but when I became Rick, I fought to leave Sandor behind. As Rick, I put myself through school, I supported myself, I started a practice, I bought a house, I made friends. Sandor had been shunned by family and friends because his mother was a crazy murderer. I'm not Sandor. I haven't been Sandor in over fifteen years and I'm fucking glad of it."

"I don't even understand how anyone found out. I thought changing your name would have prevented anyone from learning who you are."

Rick shrugged. "It's not like I was in witness protection or that I was trying to erase my identity. Anyone can go in and change their name, and if someone's determined enough, they can find the records of my name change. I just didn't want to carry the stain of the Svenson tragedy for the rest of my life. Moving to a new city and changing my name seemed like the best way to start fresh."

"So, where did Rick Haviland come from? What made you decide on that?"

"My favorite movie as a kid was *Spaceballs....*"

"*Spaceballs.*" Ian paused and thought about that for a moment. "Wait. You named yourself after the guy who played Dark Helmet? Seriously?"

Rick chuckled, and Ian thought he'd just about faint with relief. He hated Rick being unhappy.

"Yeah, I thought he was funny. I called myself Richard because I liked the idea of having both a long name and a short. There's not any good ways to shorten Sandor."

"Dark Helmet. You really are a geek like the others. No wonder you fit in so well with those guys! What about Haviland?"

"Honestly, I hadn't really decided on a last name until I got off the subway at the government office where I was going to fill out the paperwork. There was a newspaper box with some article about a de Havilland aircraft. I took off the prefix and changed the spelling. I thought it sounded pretty grand."

"Well, you're definitely Rick to me."

Ian had somehow dodged a fucking bullet because Rick could have blamed him for at least part of this mess. They still had a mountain of stress generated by this story, but they'd muddle through somehow, as long as they were together.

RICK sat on the edge of the bed watching Ian put on a suit before he went to the rehearsal dinner. Ian had stayed at his place every night this week, and he wasn't sure how he felt about it. No, he knew how he felt about it. He liked it too damned much. Was this how it was in the early days for his parents? Wanting to spend all their time together? Would he ever think Ian in a suit wasn't so sizzling hot all he could imagine was stripping him out of it?

He wasn't particularly thrilled that the rehearsal dinner was on a Thursday, making them miss their movie night. Ian had said something about it being a more reasonable price on a Thursday instead of the Friday before, but that didn't make Rick any happier.

Every minute he was away from Ian was a minute he spent missing the man. That wasn't normal, was it? Was his mother's obsessive, jealous mental illness finally taking root in his own brain?

He also feared becoming a burden. He was so fucking scared about the fallout from this news story. At times he waffled between thinking it wouldn't matter and deciding if he'd started over as a new person once, he could do it again. The biggest stumbling block to starting all over was that he wouldn't be able to take Ian with him.

Still, Ian had been so incredibly supportive, trying to get his employer to cut the story, staying with him, reassuring him that no one took *Errant*'s stories seriously anyway. Before this latest roadblock, he'd seriously been considering going to Dylan's wedding as Ian's date. Maybe erase the secret label from their relationship. With all the familial eyes on the happy couple, his presence as Ian's date might go largely unnoticed. The only other friends of his who'd be there would be Kurt and Davy. Neither of them was likely to give him shit about dating Ian, although Kurt might tease Ian.

But with this story supposed to go live the day before the wedding, all he was picturing was a church full of disapproving women in hats, whispering behind their gloved hands before staring at him like his favorite pastime was kicking puppies. He had visions of Ian's mom pointing at him, escorting her grandchildren out of his presence, and standing up in the middle of the ceremony to have him cast out of the church. In all of those scenarios, he was alone. Painfully alone. Even as

Ian's date, there would be so many things he'd have to do alone. Sit in the church while Ian stood up with his brother. Mingle with the guests while Ian was in the receiving line. Have to tell folks who he was and how he knew the bridal couple while Ian was posing for the photographer. Hell, he might not even be able to eat dinner with his date, if Ian's brother decided to have one of those enormous head table thingies like he'd seen in the movies.

The strain of having to endure all those whispers and stares and not know if it was due to people not realizing Ian was gay or due to that fucking story about his mother would be untenable.

He probably owed Ian attendance as his date. God knew, Ian had put up with tons of Rick's shit and all he'd really asked for was to be able to tell his family the truth. For whatever maggoty reason, Ian wanted everyone to know about them. But Rick couldn't handle it. Not yet.

"I can't do it."

Looking up from putting the finishing touches on his tie, Ian met his gaze in the mirror.

"Can't do what?"

"I can't go to the wedding."

Ian's face sagged in shock and he turned around. "Of course you can. You said you'd come."

"Ian, it's just too much all at once. You know I don't do the family thing. This is a lot of family and a lot of pressure."

"They're going to love you. It will be fine. We're just going as friends."

"Please. How can it be fine? They're all going to assume we're fucking and by Saturday, they're all going to know my secret."

Heedless of the sharp creases in his pants, Ian knelt on the floor in front of him and rubbed his knees. "Okay, first, we are… fucking, so that really shouldn't bother you, even though I'll lie myself blue in the face. And I promise, they won't have time to even read that story, they'll be so busy with wedding preparation."

Rick opened his mouth but Ian held up a hand to forestall him.

"Besides, even if they do read it, they won't care. I know my family."

"But I don't."

A tiny hint of exasperation crept into Ian's tone, and he rocked back on his heels. "Because you won't meet them." Ian stood and started pacing. "My family is a huge part of my life. I can't cut them out; I won't cut them out, because they are not the enemy here."

"Oh, and I am?" Almost like a disinterested observer, Rick could see himself fucking this up more and more, but he couldn't stop himself. Not when the fear and exasperation were squeezing out logical thought and any other feelings.

"No, of course not. But I want—"

"What about what I want? Why doesn't that seem to matter here?"

"Of course it matters, but—"

"But nothing. You've been pushing and pushing at me ever since we met. I haven't been able to catch a breath, and here you are, sleeping over, leaving toothbrushes, wanting me to meet your family, ignoring the fact that I don't want that. It's too much, too soon."

All the expression left Ian's face. "And when will you want that? When will it not be too much or too soon?"

"I don't know. I probably won't know until it happens, if it ever does."

"You can't wait for perfection to start living. Life is never *just right*, Goldilocks. But you just let me know when everything's perfect for you."

"If I waited for perfection, I'd never leave the house, darling." His breezy response wasn't quite appropriate for a serious discussion, but Ian had blown this all out of proportion.

Ian's nostrils flared. "Don't fucking call me *darling*. I'm not one of your retinue of boy toys."

Ouch. That one got him right in the stomach. An unexpected blow to his psyche.

Ian marched into the bathroom. Rick didn't bother to follow him until he heard Ian walking down the hall, away from the bedroom.

"Ian? Dar…." He stopped himself just in time from saying "darling," although he really didn't know why Ian had suddenly taken offense to the word. He used it all the time.

His front door slammed and Rick ran. "Ian?" He threw open the door and dashed out, but the roar of Ian's car as it skidded away told him he was too late.

He blinked. Ian was usually so calm and collected. What was so great about family that Ian wanted to force it on him? What was it that got him so emotional and angry? It shouldn't have been a surprise that Rick didn't want to go, but he didn't understand why it was so important to Ian.

Once they'd both calmed down, maybe he could get Ian to see his side of things. This might be as much relationship as he could ever handle.

But he didn't like the way Ian had left. He didn't like the unsettled feeling, knowing Ian was angry with him. Despite what happened with his parents, he wasn't at all afraid for his safety, but he'd grown accustomed to Ian's calm, understanding company, and to endure such an abrupt switch left him with a cold ball of regret in the pit of his stomach.

Without any inclination to watch a movie or read or make dinner—all the things he'd originally planned to do while Ian was at the rehearsal dinner—he didn't know what to do.

Returning to the bedroom, he gathered up the clothes Ian had shed before getting ready, and he folded them up and piled them on the chair he'd gotten used to thinking of as Ian's.

Maybe Jon wanted some company this evening. No matter what, he couldn't stay in. The house was too empty and quiet. Even if he just went to a club and danced, that would kill the time until Ian returned.

Rick wandered into the bathroom to brush his hair and teeth.

The sight of a single toothbrush in the holder, all alone, was like another, harder punch to the gut. The cold ball of regret expanded steadily outward, engulfing him, chilling him.

The knowledge that Ian wasn't coming back home sent him sliding to the floor. Besides the limping, stuttering broken beat of his heart, the only other thing he could feel was the tears pouring like lava down his face.

CHAPTER
Nine

IT WAS a good thing Dylan had asked Mike, their oldest brother, to be his best man, because he was the only one paying attention at the rehearsal. Both he and Kurt were admonished several times to pay attention and step here or walk there. Ian was too sunk in his own misery to even ask what had Kurt so distracted, and he was just as glad Kurt hadn't asked him, either. Because he didn't want to lie to his baby brother—again—but he couldn't talk about Rick. Not when thinking about the guy made him want to pound the ever-loving shit out of something.

His mother would never, ever forgive him if he ended up tussling with one of his brothers the night before Dylan's wedding, but he was so unsettled, annoyed, and hurt, he was worried that if anyone gave him too much shit about his distraction, he wasn't going to be able to keep his aggression in check.

He couldn't fucking believe Rick had bailed on him. Could not. Rick was worried about the impending story in *Errant*, and Ian could certainly understand that. Which didn't change the fact that Rick didn't trust him. Somehow, he made it more or less through the portion at the church and found his way to the restaurant where the rehearsal dinner was to be held, but he had virtually no memory of doing so.

His dad stood and clapped his hands to get everyone's attention. "Deirdre's got something to say, so listen up." From behind her chair, he pulled out three large frames and placed them on the table in front of them. From this angle, he couldn't see what was framed, aside from it appearing to be three photos.

His mom rose to her feet. "I've always been blessed with family. My children have always loved each other and gotten along with each other… eventually."

The assembled family from both Dylan's and Stephanie's sides laughed dutifully.

"But my three baby boys, Dylan, Ian, and Kurt, have always been especially close. Dylan's the first of the three to get married and when my Sean and I were trying to come up with a little gift for him, like the ones we got for his four older siblings, there was only one thing that came to mind. For those of you who maybe don't know...." His mom nodded at Stephanie's parents and her two sisters and smiled.

"We've lived in the same farmhouse in the suburbs since we moved to Toronto. We raised all of our children there, and out in the backyard was a huge fallen tree that Sean made into a log bench. Now, most times, my three little hellions ran around, screaming like banshees, over and around that bench. They never sat still unless they were passed out. Unless one of them was upset about something."

Ian was suddenly aware of the curious scrutiny of a number of people in the room. Judging from the slight frowns on Kurt and Dylan's faces, they didn't know where his mom's speech was going any more than he did.

"When one of them was upset, the other two would take him out back to the bench and they'd sit him down in the middle and talk it out. I didn't always know what prompted those little powwows, but I always knew my boys would come back happy and content. And so did my Sean, who did his best to make sure nature didn't reclaim that log bench. Thinking about that tree gave me the perfect gift idea, a reminder of family. But I also realized such a reminder was also a gift for my other two baby boys, and so there's one of these for each of them."

His mom lifted one of the frames and flipped it around.

All three pictures were taken of them from behind as they sat on the tree in his parents' backyard. The top had been taken when they were around eight. Kurt, with his reddish head, sat in the middle. The second photo was during their early teens. Dylan's sandy-blond hair had the featured spot in the center. The final photo... well, that had been taken the day Ian came out to his family, with his distinctive almost-black hair in between his two brothers. Without his mother drawing it to their attention, he might never have realized how many times he and his brothers had helped each other through rough times.

Ian sniffed. He wished Rick could have had a taste of what it was like, having that support all his life. Then he might have understood Ian's position, might have accepted that Ian's family was an integral part of him… before it was too late, before Ian had taken the final step he'd taken tonight.

There were a few more toasts before dinner was served. If Ian was pressed, he could have said there was meat and vegetables, but it had all tasted like so much cardboard.

ONCE dinner was over, the group moved and mingled through the room. Dylan left the side of his bride-to-be to round up Ian and Kurt.

Dylan peered into Kurt's face. "You're okay. I don't know why you're so distracted. Probably some weird sex thing." Dylan made a mock disgusted face that made Kurt laugh.

"Davy is pretty good at the sex thing."

Dylan clutched his chest like he'd been mortally wounded. "Jeez, don't frigging tell me about that. I don't want to know anything about my brothers' sex lives. But, the point is, you're distracted but not unhappy. This is my fucking wedding. I'm leaving on my honeymoon in exactly fifty-six hours, and until then, you're mine, so get with the program and think about your crazy monkey sex on your own time, got it, squirt?"

Kurt laughed again. "Got it."

"And you." Dylan poked a finger in Ian's face. "If I could take you back to the log bench in the units' backyard, and sit you in the middle, I'd find out exactly what rabid squirrel crawled up your butt."

Kurt swiveled his head and peered at him. "Shit. You're right. Ian, dammit. What the hell is wrong?"

"I don't want to talk about it."

Although, if there was a giant log he could sit on between his brothers, yeah, he might.

"Mom told me you were bringing a date. Is that what's wrong?"

"Kurt, man, shut up. I don't want to talk about it." Because now he wasn't going to have a date, and he shouldn't be so miserable. Dylan was right; this was his weekend. He should be able to leave his own personal drama out of the weekend. Problem was, he'd just broken up with a guy he… fuck. The guy he wanted to be his like Kurt had Davy. But he couldn't be happy if he couldn't tell his family. He'd spent too long living that secretive life, and he knew how much it sucked.

His mom wandered by, interrupting their "brotherly" discussion.

"Ian, honey. You bringing your cute boy to the wedding?"

"No, Mom. I don't have a cute boy." The interrogations were never ending. Didn't this qualify for cruel and unusual punishment?

"Okay, honey." She patted his cheek.

God. He couldn't listen to that question any more tonight. It would even be worse at the wedding, him having to tell everyone that his friend bailed and he had to attend his brother's wedding stag. The only one in the entire family who didn't have anyone. A loser who couldn't even keep a secret boyfriend.

"Excuse me, I have to go to the washroom."

He escaped his loving family and the crowded restaurant for a few moments of peace and pulled out his phone to call Leon.

"Hey man, I know this is short notice, but are you busy Saturday? My friend Rick was supposed to come to my brother's wedding, and he can't now. You want to come keep a guy in a tux company?"

"Ian, of course I'd love to come. Um… I don't have to wear a tux, do I?"

Ian let out an unwilling chuckle. "No, of course not." But remembering Leon's normal work clothes and the few comments he'd made about financial difficulties, he realized Leon might not even have a suit. "Do you have a suit?"

Silence greeted his question. "Never mind. I've got one you can borrow."

He took a deep breath before going back inside to endure, as best he could.

FUCK this. Over the span of the entire night, every goddamn sib and their spouse had asked him who he was bringing to the wedding and he didn't want to tell them Leon. He'd stupidly lost the man he was falling for… had fallen for… with his own stupid words. Might as well make this week one to remember. Ian strode out behind the building. He didn't want his family overhearing this.

Pulling up his contact list, his finger hovered over Hector's name. Not everyone had the big boss's private number, and Ian had never used it before. If that damned fucking story hadn't forced his hand, he'd still have Rick. He'd been so close, with Rick having agreed to come with him to the wedding. Once Rick saw his family was okay with him, they'd have been able to tell people they were a couple and then they could eventually find what his brother—what his whole family—had found.

He stabbed a finger at his phone, and in a few seconds, he'd been connected with Hector's private line.

"Ian? What can I do for you?"

The calm, reasonable tone of Hector's voice, the voice of someone who wasn't seeing their life unravel around them, only made him angrier.

"I quit."

"What? Ian, are you drunk? You're my best account manager. Have you had a better offer somewhere? Don't do anything rash. We can talk about this in the morning. I'll clear my schedule."

"I'm not drunk, Hector. But I refuse to stay somewhere that will not only destroy the livelihood of a hardworking man, but will stoop to using an employee's private life to help."

"What are you talking about?"

The panic in his boss's voice was certainly gratifying, but Ian was under no illusions. The big boss had definite visions of how *Errant* should be run, and it didn't matter if he cleared his schedule for the next year. He would never do what Ian was about to ask, which meant Ian had no choice.

"The Sandor Svenson story. If that goes live, I'm gone." Wow. Two ultimatums in one day. He was on a fucking *roll*.

"I don't even know what that is."

"It's a Friday Lost Ones story. And it will not only end a good man's career, but it's going to out me to the world, and not by my choice."

He bit off the words that he was also going to sue for defamation of character. He'd seen a number of people try that and fail, but he still intended to talk to Stephanie and find out what the options were. Obviously a lawsuit wasn't going to happen in time to prevent damage to

Rick's practice, but maybe there was a chance the lawsuit could help ease the pain.

"You know what's a good story? The story of how Sandor made his way in the world with everything against him, how he overcame some significant odds to make himself not only a functioning member of society, but also growing up to be a good man. That's a fucking good story, not this sordid tale, dripping in falsified muck."

There was no turning back now, but with each word he spoke, Ian got angrier. How had he not realized he worked at such a despicable place?

"I'll be in next week to get my stuff." He sure as shit wasn't going in tomorrow, especially since he'd already booked it off to help with wedding preparations. Ian cut the connection and then turned off his phone. That way he could ignore any callbacks from Hector and also ignore the fact that he wasn't getting any phone calls from Rick.

He broke up with his boyfriend, he lost his job, was going to have his naked ass plastered all over the Internet, was going to have to put on a happy face while yet another sibling pledged life and soul to another person, and would have to keep smiling until he shoved Dylan on that plane to Hawaii. He went back inside to find a beer or four.

Worst week ever.

THE minutes alone in his house ticked by, each one longer than the last. Even if they hadn't fought, Ian wouldn't be back, because of the wedding. But Rick was finding out there was a significant and painful difference between Ian at work or running errands and Ian not ever coming back.

Instead of going out Thursday night, he'd spent a fair portion of the night curled in a ball on the bathroom floor, and the rest of the night staring sleeplessly at his ceiling in bed. He'd tried to call Ian a few times, but it only went to voice mail. Which may or may not have been Ian screening. Rick hadn't bothered leaving a message; he didn't know what to say.

Screening or not, their fight had been far more monumental than he'd understood at the time, and he didn't know what to do to fix it. Funny thing was, he had this overwhelming urge to ask Ian what he would suggest. Not that Ian had any more experience with romantic relationships than he did, but Ian did have a lot of relationships with people he loved. Ian probably knew what Rick had to do to fix this, but he wasn't around for Rick to ask.

The only thing he had the energy to do during the day was call his appointments and cancel. Nothing more than a logical preemptive strike. Even if he had the energy for clients, they'd be canceling in droves as soon as *Errant* published that fucking story.

He hadn't even turned on his computer to search for the damned thing. Just lay around like a dead fish waiting to go bad. Not one person called his cell, but more importantly, Ian hadn't called either.

Now it was Saturday. Somewhere, Ian was dressing in a tux, preparing to socialize with his big, boisterous family. Drink some, dance some… maybe even meet someone. His soul withered a little inside as he imagined someone else admiring how gorgeous and strong Ian would look in a tux, and when he imagined Ian admiring back, he wanted to throw up.

Which left him with only one option.

AT LETTIE'S, Rick made sure he got a table out of view from the one he'd shared with Ian. It wasn't difficult. It was a little too early for the downtown preclubbing or pretheater dinner rush.

Jon didn't make him wait long, and with a breathless rush, he slid into the seat across.

"Rick, sweetie, seems like it's been ages since we've done this. I've been crazy busy with the club and I guess you've been busy too."

His jaw tightened painfully. He had been busy, but not the way Jon thought. "Yes, well, that's sort of the reason I wanted to meet with you. Can we order first, before I get into it?"

With his stomach twisted up, he didn't think he could eat, but a glass of wine would go down really well. He'd much rather have a margarita, but he wasn't willing to risk upsetting his stomach any further. He ordered a bottle for them to share, knowing Jon would drink just about anything.

With a half-empty restaurant, but a full staff on hand anticipating the later dinner rush, they got their food and drinks in record time.

Despite the mouthwatering aroma, Rick pushed his plate away. His throat was so tight he'd never be able to swallow solid food. Instead, he sipped at the sweetish Chardonnay and wondered where he should begin.

Jon took a bite, then put his fork down and peered across the table. "What the hell is going on? You look like hell."

"Thank you, darling. Way to make a girl self-conscious." Rick blinked. Sarcasm wasn't setting the appropriate atmosphere. "I'm sorry. I shouldn't have said that."

Jon frowned. "Why not? That was classic Rick, exactly as I expected. But now you're really worrying me."

Rick pulled in a deep breath and let it out slowly. There was no stalling, though. His oldest and best friend wouldn't allow it. In fact, if it hadn't been for his new investment in Anaconda, Jon would have sussed out Rick's secret liaison well before this.

"I've been seeing Ian."

"Ian? Ian who…. Wait. Ian O'Donnell? Kurt's brother that you slept with twice and then… what?"

"He wanted to become friends, so we started hanging out."

"And yet you never mentioned him once? We never ended up out with the two of you together? That doesn't sound like a friendship, that sounds like an affair. Why the hell would he want you to hide a friendship?"

Rick raked his fingers through his hair. "He didn't want to hide it. I did."

"Why? I mean, I know you've never had or wanted a boyfriend, but if you started seeing Ian, why would you keep it a secret?"

He pressed a fist to his stomach and told Jon everything. Absolutely everything. The things from his childhood, his name change, all the things he'd only ever told one person—Ian.

When he was done, their food was cold and their wine was nothing more than drops at the bottom of their glasses.

"Jesus Christ on a pogo stick. Rick, why the hell didn't you ever tell me?"

Rick bit his lip and shrugged. Although this second telling had been easier than the first, the addendum of his fight with Ian had him feeling unaccountably weepy.

"Okay, okay. It was a big thing. You were probably worried I'd hate you or not want to be your friend or something. I get that. But you know this changes nothing between us, right? You're still the first friend I made after my parents kicked me out. My first roommate. You've always been there for me, and I'm always there for you. Always. Got it?"

Sniffing, Rick lost the battle to restrain the tears that had threatened while he spoke.

"Oh, hey, Rick. You and me, we're all good. And we're going to make you and Ian good."

Jon slipped out of his seat and joined Rick on his bench and curled an arm around him. Burying his face in Jon's neck, he let himself sob. At the back of his mind, he wondered if anyone recognized him and was this very minute appending footage of his breakdown to his *Errant* story. So far, his notoriety had been far more low-key than he'd expected.

When he'd cried himself out, Jon handed him a napkin. He wiped his face and blew his nose while Jon returned to his seat. At some point during his meltdown, the wait staff had brought them lattes. He wasn't sure if that was Jon's doing or if they figured he was one of those people who got weepy and emotional when they drank and were trying to sober him up. Either way, the hot, steamy beverage was welcome.

"I know you. The real you, whether you call yourself Sandor or Rick." Jon stared at him, forcing him to keep his burning tear-swollen eyes directed up. "You've spent your whole life engaged in battle. Every time someone suggested you couldn't do something, you went and proved them wrong. Every time you were afraid you'd fail, you found some deep well of determination and persevered. Which is why you own that great house and why you've got a thriving practice. Why aren't you turning that determination to your personal life? I know you want Ian or you'd have never started dating him. I know you care for him, maybe even love him, because otherwise you'd move on to the next ready cock without a single regret, like you've done your whole life. You need to go fight for him, even if that means fighting yourself and your fears."

"Well, that sounds good, but what if he doesn't want me?"

Jon rolled his eyes. "Honey, you should have had a boyfriend or two before this. Everything you've told me were actions taken by a man trying to get you to commit. He was doing whatever he could to make you comfortable with it. You just pushed him too far and pissed him off."

"What if he cheats on me? What if I'm too much like my mother and hurt him?"

"There are no guarantees in this life, but how do you feel about having sex with only Ian and nobody else?"

Rick thought about it for a moment. It had been surprisingly easy to let other guys go, and the thought of trying new things with a man he could trust was like being given a fantasy he'd never dared to dream about.

"Good. Happy."

"Okay, then. Why do you suppose it will be different for him?"

Good point. If he was willing to be faithful, then there was no reason to assume Ian wasn't.

But Jon wasn't finished. "And let's just say it was. Think about it. Pretend you've been living with him for years. You've got a dog together, a house, a life."

It sounded so good. More things he hadn't known he wanted.

"And one day you come home and find out he's cheated on you. Or he's leaving you for another man. How do you feel?"

The opposite of his fantasy, it was painful to consider, but for Jon, he did. "Hurt. Sad. Angry."

"And what would you do?"

"Kick him out, probably. Keep the dog."

Jon picked up a steak knife from the table and brandished it at him. "No burning desire to stab him in the gut with a knife?"

Rick gasped and reared back. "No!"

"I rest my case. I'm not saying you shouldn't go talk to someone who might be able to help you work through this, deal with your fears. Ian was right about that. But if the worst should happen, you'll get through it, and go on, with me at your side. Got it?"

He smiled, feeling hopeful for the first time since Ian walked out of his house. "So what do I do? And All-Knowing-One, why can't I call him darling anymore?"

Jon wiggled his fingers like an oracle at a street fair. "First of all, *darling*, you call simply everyone *darling*. Or honey or sweetie or big boy. It probably represents intimacy to him, intimacy that you share with everyone, making them all… common. If you want to call him something that's not his name, find him something unique. He wants to know he's special to you."

The heavens didn't break open with golden light or erupt in song, but Jon's interpretation was a revelation, all right. Rick thought he might have just the ticket. It had been threatening to pop out of his mouth for days, and it was an endearment he'd never used with anyone before. "And how do I fix this when he won't answer my calls?"

"Well, that's simple. Go see him. Now."

"Now? He's at his brother's wedding!"

"No sense in letting this fester. They should be finishing dinner up right about now. Speeches while you drive, then nothing but dancing. He'll be more likely to listen to you because he won't want to cause a scene in front of his family."

A reason to be thankful for family. Who knew? But he was going to have to get over his hang-ups about family. Ian was right. Asking him to give up six siblings and two loving parents because they made his boyfriend nervous was ridiculous, and he had no right or even grounds to expect it. Especially if he was going to fight to live the dream of a happy, adult, partnered couple.

ATOP his perch on the dais at the wedding party's table, Ian stared down at the "parents, spouses, and dates" tables arrayed in front of them. Leon looked good, although Ian's suit was a bit too big. He seemed to be getting along just fine with his family. Considering Ian had barely had time to say more than hello, make brief introductions, then thrust a suit at Leon for him to change into, Ian was glad Leon didn't seem uncomfortable. His family—the ones who weren't part of the wedding party—were good people and they wouldn't have left Leon on his own, but a tiny lick of resentment curdled his belly, because it should have been Rick sitting there, getting to know his family. If Rick had only had the guts to overcome that stupid story....

The only good thing about that fucking story was that at least Ian wasn't commemorating Dylan's wedding day with naked pics of him boffing his ex-boyfriend posted on one of the most popular gossip sites in Canada. Nope, he got to save that little gem for next week's entertainment.

Leon would probably get a kick out of it. Younger guys didn't seem to have the same issues with privacy he did. Perhaps it was a result of spending the majority of his adult life in the closet, but he suspected it was more of a generational thing. The Internet wasn't a part of his life growing up, and he was in awe of its power to destroy lives in a way that younger people weren't.

None of them ever seemed concerned about what they posted or who might see it or how it could affect chances for employment or even the mental health of those whose pictures were posted without consent. It was a completely different mindset, and one that he hadn't even realized applied to his job until now. How many other people's lives had been uprooted or destroyed by one of *Errant*'s sensationalist stories? Made him sick to think about, even worse because he *hadn't* thought about it until it affected him personally.

Then there was the dread of explaining his online nakedness to his parents. Yep, this had to be the worst week ever. He glanced over at his brother who was wiggling his fingers at Davy like a giddy kid with his first love. Bastard.

But no matter how personally demoralizing this week was, it wasn't the worst. The worst had been when Kurt had been shot and they weren't sure if he was going to pull through. This week ran a close second, though.

The waiter gave him an odd look when he gathered the plates and found Ian's still mostly full. He hadn't eaten a full meal since before the rehearsal and wasn't about to start tonight.

When the speeches started, Ian sat back, pretending to listen, letting the actions of the crowd dictate whether he should laugh or clap. Not having to give a speech was one tiny saving grace.

The full Roman Catholic ceremony had taken forever. The drive to Casa Loma had been even longer, an accident causing a vicious snarl of traffic on the Gardiner. The picture taking itself had been interminable, and dinner had dragged on and on. He wanted nothing more than to curl up in his cold, lonely bed and wonder when he'd have the energy to look for a new job.

He stayed in his seat as the bride and groom had their obligatory parental dances. After that, he'd expected the DJ to play something a little more energizing to get the room on its feet after being stuffed to the gills with a hearty eleven-course meal. It was only four courses, but pretending to eat those four courses made it seem like there were eleven. The DJ surprised him, though, and went slow again. His mother made a beeline for his seat and he groaned under his breath.

"C'mon, boyo, you've avoided me long enough today."

Why couldn't she be a typical mother of the groom and only worry about what was going on with Dylan, for God's sake?

"Hey Mom." Ian led her out onto the dance floor. "Lovely ceremony, wasn't it? Stephanie was beautiful."

"Oh, you aren't going to get out of this that easily, my son. That boy, Leon. He seems a nice enough boy, but he's not that adorable skittish blond, and his name isn't Rick. What's got you looking like one of your brothers just punched you below the belt? Because that little Leon is pleased as punch to be your date and I haven't seen you go near him once."

Just like that, his throat closed up and his eyes started burning. But the time when tears could be explained away by the joy of the day had long passed.

"Leon's my date, Mom. Not Rick." Never Rick. "Rick is just Kurt and Davy's friend. That's all." And he'd have to remember that.

"Oh, you little fibber. We talked about this at Erin's birthday party. I saw you looking at him, and if there's one thing I know about the O'Donnell men, it's when they've found the one."

"I didn't know Rick was the one that early."

His mother smirked and his cheeks heated when he realized he'd admitted he thought Rick was the one. Damn his mother for being such an over-the-top romantic.

"Oh, honey. Your head might not have known, but your heart and stones knew."

"Mother!" He could not believe his mother had referenced his balls twice at his brother's reception.

"You should have brought Rick. Getting him accustomed to us is the only way he'll settle. Like all the boyfriends and girlfriends had to."

"We broke up. I think."

It had felt pretty damn final when he'd stormed out of Rick's place, but he really hadn't wanted it to be. As Rick accused him, though, maybe he'd been guilty of not taking Rick's wants and needs into account.

"Then you need to fix it."

"How? If he wants what I'm offering, shouldn't he tell me?"

His mother shook her head sadly. "Honey, I could see from a mile off that man was like an abused dog. He wants so much to make someone happy, but he's scared and he doesn't know a bit how to make it happen."

"I don't know either. I've never had a relationship before."

"Really? No relationships? Not with brothers or sisters or parents? You know how to fix arguments and hurt feelings with loved ones. He doesn't. Fix it."

Ian wondered if Kurt or Davy had told her about some of Rick's hang-ups because otherwise how could she know? Then again, he'd often joked she was psychic—when it came to her kids, at least.

"I will, Mom."

"And you're going to have to apologize for bringing Leon here."

"I will?"

"Yes. You know in your heart it should have been Rick here, and you shouldn't have tried to substitute."

She was right, and it was the reason he hadn't been able to even talk to Leon all night. His family was going to make assumptions about the man he brought with him, and they were all the wrong ones. He should have come alone.

The song ended, and she patted him on the face before whirling back into the throng of wedding attendees. A fresh group of people flooded the dance floor as the tempo picked up and Ian set about trying to find Leon.

THE music changed back to a slow song just as he managed to find Leon at the edge of the dance floor.

"There you are, I've been looking for you." Leon's eyes were bright and his smile wide.

"Leon." What was he supposed to say? He needed to take him home because he wasn't Rick? The damage had already been done, and it's not like this was a date. They were friends and he might as well try to enjoy himself. Even if he had his mother's permission—which he wasn't quite sure he did—Dylan would murder him if he left early and Kurt would help.

Of course, he'd seen Kurt and Davy sneak off to the enclosed garden off the conservatory about ten minutes ago. There wasn't much doubt about why they'd snuck off, either. Assholes.

"Did you want to dance?" Leon wrapped his hands around Ian's neck and stared up at him. The simple touch paralyzed him for a moment. Then Leon kissed him and his perception of the world altered. Leon was interested in more than just friendship or even a fuck. There was only one reason to kiss a man in front of his family, and it wasn't to request a blow job in the bathroom.

He pushed away. Oh fuck, fuck, fuck. "Leon, man, we can't do that."

"Why not?" Leon pushed back, trying to wrap his arms around Ian again. This time, Ian grabbed Leon by the shoulder and steered him to an empty table near the door.

"Sit down."

"I don't understand."

"Leon, man, I'm really sorry. I didn't know… you were interested in me like that. I'm in love with someone else."

He'd tried so hard not to say, not to think it until Rick was ready to hear it. Now he just blurted it out to some nearly random guy. His mom was right. Rick was the one and he'd need to do whatever he had to fix it.

Leon's face crumpled and tears welled in his eyes.

Kurt and Davy approached the table, giving Ian some breathing room from Leon's sudden and unwelcome emotional attachment.

"Hey, did you invite Rick?"

Ian frowned. Where had that question come from? "Why?"

"We thought we saw him leaving just as we came back in from the garden, but he was too far away and moving too fast. We didn't invite him, and Dylan doesn't know him well enough to have him here, so we thought you might know why he was here."

His heartbeat raced as adrenaline pushed through his veins. There was only one reason Rick would have come looking for him at the wedding, and there was one big fat reason why Rick would have left before talking to him.

"Leon, I have to go after him. Kurt and Davy will make sure you get home safely."

"But, but I can do everything in those pictures. I can make you happy."

No.

Hell, no.

Leon did not just say that.

"What pictures?" Kurt sounded like he was interrogating them.

Ian flapped a hand at Kurt, and amazingly he shut up.

"Avery let you see those pictures?" A terrible suspicion teased the edges of his consciousness, confirmed by the fiery blush that flared on his thin cheeks.

"I took them," he whispered.

"Why? Why would you do that? And what about the other vandalism?"

Leon squirmed in his chair, the too-big suit contributing to his incredibly youthful appearance. "I followed him home. The night I saw you together at Anaconda. I was so mad. I wasn't going to do anything, but then I saw the dead squirrel. After that, it seemed like I saw the two of you together everywhere, and you never, ever looked at me like you looked at him. Finally, when you invited me to that party, I thought you were coming to your senses, but you left with him. Again. I followed you and took those pictures. I don't understand what he's got that I don't. We have tons of stuff in common and we work at the same place and, I'm positive I'm more flexible than he is, and, and...."

He paused to sniffle, and Ian barely restrained himself from shaking the kid.

"So you gave them to Avery?"

"Not exactly."

"You know my brother here is a cop, right? A lot of what you did was illegal. I want some answers or I'm going to have him arrest you. Tell me everything."

He ignored Kurt's frantic eye wobbles, not caring that he might be lying through his teeth and Kurt might not be able to do a damn thing to this kid.

"I was so mad. So I went to Avery to find out if she could help me find something that would... change your mind about him. Between the two of us, we found out about the name change, and the rest was easy."

"Name change?" This time, Ian paid no attention to Davy's question. Inconsequential until he knew what was going on.

"And she decided it would make a great Friday Lost Ones story." Getting a choice story like that, just dropped in her lap… no way was Avery going to pass that up.

"Yes. I maybe shouldn't have told her about the pictures of you and Rick."

Ian almost let his head thud down on the table.

"Right, now I need some answers." Kurt put on his angry cop voice, which didn't intimidate Ian in the slightest, but he was willing to listen, because he really was hoping to convince Kurt to arrest Leon, maybe give him a taste of police brutality on the way.

Kurt pulled out a chair for himself and Davy, and the pair of them sat. Ian wondered how long they could stay here before a friend or family member wandered over.

"There are pictures of you and Rick?" An auburn brow rose up. "The same Rick that tore ass out of here a few minutes ago? Is that what's had you all twisted up?"

Ian took a deep breath. "Look, Rick and I have been seeing each other."

"You have?" Davy's shock was apparent. "In secret?"

"It's what he wanted." And most of the cat was out of the bag, thanks to Leon, so he didn't think there was any harm in telling at least part of the story.

"Yeah. Pretty much since the day we met at your painting party."

This time, both Kurt's and Davy's eyes rounded.

"He didn't want to tell anyone. He's got a fierce aversion to romantic relationships and families, mothers in particular, and well, you know Mom. She freaked him out at your housewarming." But that didn't get them any closer to the point. "Anyway, we'd just gotten to the point where he accepted that we were an exclusive couple and he'd agreed to come to the wedding with me, even though we weren't going to tell anyone we'd been seeing each other."

"Can I go, please?" Leon spoke up plaintively.

Kurt shot him one of his most evil glares. "You sit until I've heard this. I might still be arresting your ass."

Leon subsided, a nervous sweat breaking out on his face.

"Go on." Kurt turned his gaze back on Ian.

"First it was a bit of vandalism. Flat tires, stuff in the mailbox. I wanted Rick to report it, but he figured it was some kids and they'd eventually stop. But then Rick found a set of photos. Well, photos printed on paper, of the two of us. Explicit photos. We thought it might have been the guy Rick had been fucking before me. He got a little belligerent when Rick broke it off."

"You're telling me you got photos that could have come from a stalker or blackmailer and you never called me?"

Okay, now he was a little intimidated by Kurt's angry cop voice.

"I told Rick we should call the cops, but he didn't want to. Probably because he didn't want to explain the name change thing."

"I definitely want to know about the name change." Surprisingly, Davy was a lot more forceful than Ian would have guessed.

"I can't be the one to tell you, but you can read about most of it on *Errant*. He was featured on the Friday Lost Ones story this week. Part two, next Friday, will also include our sex pictures."

"No, he wasn't." Davy shook his head.

"Yeah, he was. Check out the Sandor Svenson story."

"There was no Sandor Svenson story."

Ian stared at Davy. "Don't tell me you read *Errant*?"

A cute blush colored the tips of Davy's ears and the tops of his cheekbones. "Guilty pleasure. And according to last week's quiz, Kurt might actually be a werewolf."

Kurt twisted his head to flick an incredulous gaze over Davy before turning his attention back to Leon.

Huh. There really was no accounting for taste. "You must have missed it. I saw the layout that he put together." Ian jabbed a thumb in Leon's direction.

"I'm telling you, there was nothing about Rick. Or this Sandor person." Davy started tapping at his phone.

Ian pulled out his phone too, and turned it on. Prominent were the number of voice mails he had. None from Rick although he had missed several calls. Hector had called three times as well, and sent a text.

Curiosity getting the better of him, he checked the text.

Story pulled with apologies. Your job is here if you wish, but I understand if your resignation stands.

Ian took a deep, cleansing breath. That was more consideration than he'd expected from Hector and *Errant*. But he couldn't compromise his integrity any further to work at that place.

"They pulled the story."

"But, but…," Leon sputtered. "I thought after the story ran, you wouldn't want him anymore."

"Leon, that story could utterly destroy a man's life, his career."

"What story?" Davy pounded a fist on the table. Kurt did not look any more patient.

"Guys, it's not really my story to tell. But all I can say is that Rick is an amazing, strong man. And Leon, even if Rick leaves me after the mess you made, I won't be having you pick up where he left off. In fact, after tonight, I very much doubt we'll ever see each other again."

"But what about work?"

"I quit." His simple statement drew three sharp inhalations, but only Leon tried to protest. "I'm going to go find Rick, try to make things right."

Dylan might kill him, but he couldn't drag this out any longer.

"But, Ian, I didn't mean for this to happen, wait…." Leon stood up, but Kurt pushed him firmly back in the seat.

"No, you sit. We're going to have a long talk about privacy and stalking. Assuming you don't want to have a similar discussion at the police station."

The last Ian saw of Leon, he sat like a scared boy getting chastised by his father. The very least of what he deserved, considering he was plenty old enough to understand there were consequences to his actions. At least he could rest easy knowing it was a young man who hadn't fully thought out what the end results of his decisions were, and not some dangerous stalker after Rick.

CHAPTER
Ten

RICK parked in the driveway and stared up at his house. He loved his house, but he hadn't been able to return to it last night after seeing Ian kissing that… that… hot twentysomething kid. Had Ian even waited an hour before seeking solace in that guy's bed? Seeing Leon in one of Ian's suits had been the final twist of the sword in his back. His house held too many memories of Ian that he'd headed straight for Jon's place, who luckily hadn't gone out for the night.

But then, as Jon had so aptly put it, his own actions had hardly been above reproach and if he let his fear drive away a man he cared about… a man he loved, well, he only had himself to blame. If there was any salvaging this relationship, he was going to have to suck it up and talk to Ian.

Jon had stayed with him as long as he could before he had to go and check things out at Anaconda, leaving Rick to toss and turn in Jon's guest bed all night. The only good thing about this shit-fest of a night was that Jon had spoken the truth. Losing Ian had hurt and made him cry like nothing else since his parents had died, but he never had even a momentary thought about physically hurting or killing Ian. One less thing to stress about.

What he needed was a shower, a charger for his phone, and something to eat that wasn't ice cream. That bastard Ian was going to destroy his waistline, especially if he wasn't going to be around to sex it all off.

He swung his legs out of the car and stretched, his lower back protesting how fucking soft Jon's guest bed was. The early morning sun only illuminated how fucking depressed he was, and he trudged toward his front door, planning to spend the day hiding in his own guest room, where Ian hadn't even set foot. Maybe he could get enough rest that he could find the courage to chase down Ian at his place and throw out that Leon kid.

Almost at his door, he didn't notice the lump on his porch bench until it moved and he jumped, squealing like a girl.

"Rick?" Ian's eyes were red-rimmed and bleary.

"Ian? What are you doing here?" Had he truly been there all night? The déjà vu was uncanny, although he was far happier to see Ian than Oscar.

"Waiting for you."

They both spoke softly, as though afraid the other would spook.

"Um, I spent the night at Jon's. I, uh, went to the wedding, and uh…."

"I know. I know what you saw, and believe me it wasn't what it looked like. I tried to call you." Ian waved his phone gently.

"I forgot my charger." He took a deep breath. It was now or never, and he pushed his fear back again, plunging headfirst into what he desired most. "Want to come in?"

"Please."

Rick led them inside, and they sat at the kitchen table.

"I'm so sorry for everything." Ian spoke before he could, even though Rick thought he should be apologizing.

Then Ian proceeded to tell him a nearly unbelievable tale about that harmless-looking kid Leon.

"I don't really think he was being truly malicious about it. I just think he was being selfish. If I were young and impulsive, I might have done the same to try and keep you." Rick gave him a tremulous smile, unsure if Ian was truly here for reconciliation or only for closure.

"Really?" Ian stood and pulled him to his feet. "I was such an ass. I shouldn't have left like I did. I know it was only for… a few hours all together, but I missed you so much."

"I'm sorry too. I shouldn't have let my fears ruin what we had together."

"It's not ruined, and it's not past tense. Unless that's what you want." Ian's serious blue eyes stared into his own.

"No. That's not what I want."

Ian cradled his face with both hands and brought their faces together, Ian's lips as necessary to his happiness as air was to his continued existence. The kiss was soft and warm, Ian's tongue gently slipping between their lips to coax open their mouths.

An alarm rang out, and Rick pulled back.

"What's that?"

"Oh, I set my alarm in case I fell asleep out there. I've got to get ready for the 'morning after' breakfast with the family." Ian grimaced. "I could skip it."

Rick had to man up. Ian came with family, like he came with the baggage of a 1920s socialite on a transatlantic cruise.

"No. I don't want you to skip it. Maybe there's room for one more?"

Judging from the enormous smile and tight hug, it had been just the right thing to say. The butterflies of dread in his stomach were nothing to the doldrums of despair that tore at him when he thought he'd lost Ian.

"Really, you'll go with me?" The wattage of his smile dimmed. "We'd have to go now. Which means no make-up sex."

"Don't think you're getting out of that...." Rick sucked in another breath. Time to go for the gold. Darling was out. "Love."

Ian's lips trembled and he clutched at Rick's waist. "I... I love you."

Rick had never been so happy yet so close to crying in his entire life. "I love you too."

"Dammit. Now I really want to skip that breakfast."

Laughing and sobbing at the same time, Rick kissed Ian. "It's okay. You can make it up to me later, love."

"Can I get ready here? I've probably got something suitable to wear upstairs."

"Share a shower?"

"Weren't you the one who just said we were going to the breakfast?"

Rick rolled his eyes. "Fine. Go on, I'll see if I can scare up some coffee."

"Oh my God, coffee. I love you even more."

Rick laughed, his very soul lightened by Ian's presence.

IAN in a dress shirt and khakis was almost as sexy as Ian in a suit. But then, Rick found Ian hot all the damned time.

"Will you drive with me? I'd like to go together."

Another rule crumbled into dust. It was going to be a relief not to adhere to those rules anymore. "Of course."

As Rick got into the car, a large frame wrapped in brown paper caught his eye. Mostly because it took up the entire backseat. "What's that?"

"Oh, shit. We need to stop by my condo first and drop that off. Mom said I was going to have to haul some stuff back from the hotel where the bridal party got ready, so I'll need the backseat free."

"Oh, I see why you wanted me to come with. I'm the muscle." Rick flexed his biceps and was amazed by the heat in Ian's eyes rather than laughter. "Seriously, though, what is it?"

Ian proceeded to tell him an incredibly touching story about a family that would never treat anyone like a castoff, and for the first time in decades, true hope for the future bloomed in his chest. He could do the family thing with a family like the O'Donnells.

"I want to see it."

"Sure, when we get it upstairs, I'll unwrap it. We'll have a few minutes' grace before we're totally and irredeemably late."

Upstairs in Ian's condo, Rick ripped off the paper and propped it against a wall so he could take a good look at it. The picture was even sweeter than he imagined. "This one here, with you in the middle. That's recent." Ian had said the one in the middle was the brother with the weighty problem, but he hadn't bothered to mention what any of the problems were. Rick hadn't realized the images spanned such a large number of years.

"It is. Mom took it the day I came out to the family."

Rick brushed his fingers over it, hoping Ian would never again have reason to be the brother in the middle.

"Where are you going to hang it?" There didn't seem to be a perfect place to hang it in Ian's condo.

Ian shrugged. "Don't know if I will. Since I don't have a job, I might not be able to keep the condo, anyway."

"You don't have a job? They didn't fire you over that story, did they?" Ian had said he'd gotten them to retract the story, but he'd given no more specifics than that.

"No, I quit. I can't work there anymore. Not once I realized how devastating those stories could be, and how much they skew the perspective in them."

"But we'll probably both be out of work. That's not good."

"How so?"

Rick shrugged. "The story's out there. We've probably only postponed the inevitable. Without jobs, we'll both be homeless." He smiled to let Ian know he was teasing. He'd thought long and hard about it and while it would hurt his practice in the short term, he was damn good at what he did and he'd be able to tough it out.

Ian winked at him. "We'll have to move in with my parents to keep from being homeless."

"Don't be silly." He lightly punched Ian on the shoulder. "My place is paid off. You can move in with me."

Tension filled the room and they froze as they realized what Rick had said.

"Not yet, though, eh?" Ian's voice trembled just a bit.

"No, not yet." Rick touched the edge of the picture frame. "This would look perfect over the fireplace at my house."

"But you said you're not ready." Ian's desire for that to change, as well as his love, was there for Rick to read in his eyes.

"I'm not." He gulped. "But consider this a promise that I will be, one day soon."

"Thank you." Ian gathered him close and gave him another sweet kiss. "I love you."

"Me too."

Ian cleared his throat. "All kidding aside, I think we'll talk to Stephanie to see what legal options you've got, but I'd be surprised if this story issue cropped up again. It was only Avery's spin and Leon's desire to dig up dirt on you that manipulated the story from being one of personal growth and strength. Which it is. And I'm an account manager. I can work just about anywhere that sells advertising. We'll be fine. And when we're ready, we can talk about moving in together."

With Ian's reasonable nature and Rick's comfort level at having Ian around all the time, Rick suspected he'd be ready sooner rather than later. He was tired of being afraid of life. He wanted to live it, with Ian.

RICK stared at the room the hotel restaurant had set up for the morning-after breakfast. Ian's family… and the bride's, he supposed, looked like a small army.

"Hey, it's okay," Ian whispered. "We can still tell them you're just a friend."

"No." Rick shook his head. "No. We're not just friends."

Trying to calm his rampant pulse, he threaded his fingers through Ian's. With a smile and a comforting squeeze, Ian led him into the room.

"Ian, honey, you made it." Deirdre O'Donnell leapt up to greet her son and Rick had to steel himself to stand still. "Hello, Rick, I'm so glad you could make it. And you're going to start calling me Deidre, right? Or Mum."

Like her son's, Deirdre's eyes were so very expressive. She was truly glad he was there, but Rick wasn't ready to call her Mom. "Thank you, Deirdre."

Rick let out a deep breath, more relieved than he could probably express to anyone that he'd been able to speak without impediment.

She quickly introduced Rick to everyone, taking the initiative of telling everyone he was Ian's boyfriend. He wasn't sure if she just knew or if Ian had told her, but he didn't object. Kurt and Davy gave him encouraging smiles, but they weren't surprised either.

After they'd all been served, Deirdre turned what Rick could only term as a look of motherly disapproval on her two youngest sons.

"I'll expect you both for Sunday dinner with the family. Bring Rick and Davy."

"Mom, don't freak Rick out. This is all new." Ian had let Rick's hand go so they could eat, but at his mother's words, he slipped a hand under the table to rest on Rick's leg.

"I'll do my best, but I only have two kids left to marry off." Deirdre raised her brows, giving him and Davy expectant looks.

Kurt and Ian both went red, and Rick laughed, genuinely if a little breathlessly. He placed his hand over Ian's and squeezed. "If it's all the same to you, can we start with Sunday dinner?"

KC BURN has been writing for as long as she can remember and is a sucker for happy endings (of all kinds). After moving from Toronto to Florida for her husband to take a dream job, she discovered a love of gay romance and fulfilled a dream of her own—getting published. After a few years of editing web content by day and neglecting her supportive, understanding hubby and needy cat at night to write stories about men loving men, she was uprooted yet again and now resides in California. Writing is always fun and rewarding, but writing about her guys is the most fun she's had in a long time, and she hopes you'll enjoy them as much as she does.

Visit KC at her website: http://kcburn.com/
on Twitter: https://twitter.com/authorkcburn
or on Facebook: https://www.facebook.com/kcburn

Toronto
Tales

COVER UP

KC Burn

http://www.dreamspinnerpress.com